Everyman, I will go with thee,
and be thy guide

THE EVERYMAN
LIBRARY

The Everyman Library was founded by J.M. Dent in 1906. He chose the name Everyman because he wanted to make available the best books ever written in every field to the greatest number of people at the cheapest possible price. He began with Boswell's 'Life of Johnson'; his one-thousandth title was Aristotle's 'Metaphysics', by which time sales exceeded forty million.

Today Everyman paperbacks remain true to J.M. Dent's aims and high standards, with a wide range of titles at affordable prices in editions which address the needs of today's readers. Each new text is reset to give a clear, elegant page and to incorporate the latest thinking and scholarship. Each book carries the pilgrim logo, the character in 'Everyman', a medieval morality play, a proud link between Everyman past and present.

The Chariot of Wisdom

Subramania Bharati (1882–1921) was a Tamil journalist, translator, writer, poet, visionary social reformer and passionate independence activist. Popularly known as Mahakavi Bharati (great poet Bharati), he was a pioneer of modern Tamil poetry and is considered one of Tamil's greatest literary figures. His prolific output covered a wide range of topics, including nationalism, democracy, religion, the emancipation of women, child marriage, the caste system, nature and the environment, love and romance, philosophy and spiritualism and the Tamil language. During the colonial period, his pro-independence journalistic writings and patriotic songs led to him being marked by the authorities. In 1908, he moved to Puducherry, where he lived in exile until 1918. On his return to India, he was arrested and imprisoned. Bharati died in poverty in 1921 from injuries sustained from a temple elephant in Chennai. In recognition of his exceptional contribution to Indian culture, the Government of India conferred him the title of Indian 'National Poet', and Bharathiar University, a state university established in Coimbatore in 1982, was named after him.

Gregory James is a graduate of the Universities of Edinburgh, Reading, and Exeter. He followed a career in language education in England, Germany, India, Iran, and China (Hong Kong), where he now lives in retirement. His publications include *Colporuḷ: A History of Tamil Dictionaries* (Chennai, 2000), and translations into English of works by Erode Tamilanban: *Poems of Questions* (Chennai, 2018), and *Glow-worm Woods* (Chennai, 2019), the former with Loraine Bock, also into Spanish, *Poemas de Preguntas* (Chennai, 2019). In 2020, Professor James was presented with the Veeramamunivar Award of the Government of Tamil Nadu.

Mission Statement

This is an initiative of the Tamil Nadu Textbook and Educational Services Corporation (TNTB & ESC) under the aegis of one of the announcements for the year 2023–24, by Honourable Minister for School Education Thiru. Anbil Mahesh Poyyamozhi to identify and translate nationalized works by Tamil writers into English that they might enhance the reach of Tamil antiquity, tradition and contemporaneity and enrich World literature.

Members, Academic Advising Committee (Translation)

1. Dr R. Balakrishnan, IAS, Researcher and Writer
2. Thiru. S. Ramakrishnan, Writer
3. Thiru. S. Madasamy, Educationist

Project Execution Team

1. Thiru. Dindigul I. Leoni, Chairperson, TNTB & ESC
2. Tmt. R. Gajalakshmi, IAS, Managing Director, TNTB & ESC
3. Dr S. Kannappan, Member Secretary, TNTB & ESC
4. Thiru. R. Dhayalan, Financial Advisor, TNTB & ESC
5. Dr T. S. Saravanan, Joint Director (Translations), TNTB & ESC
6. Thiru. P. A. Arumugam, Deputy Director (Publications), TNTB & ESC
7. Dr P. Saravanan, Assistant Director (Publications), TNTB & ESC
8. Thiru. M. Appanasamy, Consultant, TNTB & ESC
9. Tmt. Mini Krishnan, Co-ordinating Editor, TNTB & ESC

The Chariot of Wisdom

SUBRAMANIA BHARATI

Translated and with an introduction by

GREGORY JAMES

EVERYMAN

hachette INDIA

TAMILNADU TEXTBOOK AND EDUCATIONAL SERVICES CORPORATION
LEARN THOROUGHLY

First published in India in 2023 by Hachette India
(Registered name: Hachette Book Publishing India Pvt. Ltd)
An Hachette UK company
www.hachetteindia.com

1

The Tamil text conforms to the first 1910 printing, amended to take account of the 1978 Tamil spelling reform.

Subsequent edition/reprint specifications may be subject to change, including but not limited to title, subtitle, cover or inside finishes, paper, text colour and/or colour sections.

ISBN 978-93-93701-84-8 (Paperback)
ISBN 978-93-5731-168-7 (Limited edition hardback)

Hachette Book Publishing India Pvt. Ltd
4th/5th Floors, Corporate Centre,
Plot No. 94, Sector 44, Gurugram 122003, India

Typeset in Calluna and Adobe Tamil
By Anfarnd Infotech

Printed and bound in India
by Manipal Technologies Limited

MIX
Paper from responsible sources
FSC™ C043100

Contents

Major Milestones in Bharati's Life

1882, 11 Dec	Born in Ettayapuram, Tinnevelly (Tirunelveli) district, Tamil Nadu
1893	Accorded the title of 'Bharati'
1894–1897	Attends Hindu College High School, Tirunelveli
1897, 15 June	Marries Chellamma (aged 7)
1898	Death of father, Chinnaswami Iyer
1898–1901	Higher education in Benares (Varanasi), while living with his uncle and aunt
1902–1904	Appointed court poet at Ettayapuram
1904, Aug	Tamil teacher at Sethupathi High School, Madurai
1904, Nov	Joins *Swadesamitran* (சுதேசமித்திரன் *Cutēcamittiraṉ*) as sub-editor
1905	Partition of Bengal; attends Indian National Congress meeting in Varanasi, presided over by Gopal Krishna Gokhale
1906	Meets Sister Nivedita, who was to become a major influence; later dedicates his nationalistic poems to her, his 'guru'; attends Indian National Congress session in Calcutta (Kolkata), presided over by Dadabhai Naoroji, where demands for Swaraj and the boycott of British goods are raised
1907	Attends Indian National Congress meeting in Surat with V.O. Chidambaram Pillai and Mandayam Srinivasachariar; meets freedom fighters Bal Gangadhar Tilak, Sri Aurobindo

Ghosh, Lala Lajpat Rai; Dr Rash Behari Ghosh nominated President of Indian National Congress, leading to the party splitting between Extremists, led by Tilak, and Moderates; Bharati, an Extremist, is greatly impressed by Tilak who later features in his poems. Edits English weekly Bala-Bharata, or *Young India*; also associated with nationalist newspapers *India* (இந்தியா Intiyā), *Vijaya* (விஜயா *Vijayā*), *Karmayōgi* (கர்மயோகி *Karmayōki*) and *Sūryōdayam* (சூரியோதயம் *Cūriyōtayam*)

1908 Brings out a pamphlet of his experience at the Surat Congress entitled, எங்கள் காங்கிரஸ் யாத்திரை *Eṅkaḷ Kāṅkiras yāttirai* (Our Congress Tour); publishes his first book of poems, சுவதேச கீதங்கள் *Cuvatēca kītaṅkaḷ* (*Songs of Freedom*), dedicated to Sister Nivedita

1908, Sep M. Srinivasa Iyengar, de jure editor of *India*, arrested by the British, and imprisoned for five years, while Bharati, the de facto editor, escapes to the French territory of Pondicherry (Puducherry), on the advice of friends

1908, 20 Oct Resumes publication of *India* from Puducherry, with a circulation of over 4,000 copies; Bharati calls for political freedom and denounces the British for their injustice to the people of India

1909 Publishes second volume of poetry, ஜென்ம பூமி *Jeṉma pūmi* (Birthplace), again dedicated to Sister Nivedita

1910, April	Sri Aurobindo goes to Puducherry seeking political asylum; he and Bharati spend many hours discussing a wide range of subjects
1910, March	British Government bans India in British India; journal ceases publication for want of funds
1912	Writes major works – கண்ணன் பாட்டு *Kaṇṇaṉ pāṭṭu* ('The Krishna Songs'), குயில் பாட்டு *Kuyil pāṭṭu* ('The Cuckoo's Song'), பாஞ்சாலி சபதம் *Pāñcāli capatam* (*Panchali's Pledge*), and a Tamil translation of the Bhagavad Gita
1917	A collection of poems under the title நாட்டுப் பாட்டு *Nāṭṭup pāṭṭu* (*Songs of Our Nation*) is released
1918, 20 Nov	Courts arrest at Cuddalore (Kadalur); imprisoned for about a month
1919	Lives in Kadayam (his wife's home village, in Tirunelveli district); meets Mahatma Gandhi in Madras (Chennai)
1920, Nov	Returns to Chennai and rejoins *Swadesamitran* as sub-editor; continues to seek funds to publish his books, but without success
1921, July	Attacked by Triplicane Parathasarathy temple elephant; saved by his friend Kuvalai Kannan, but sustains heavy injuries
1921, 11 Sep	Dies in Chennai at the age of 39

Introduction

Chinnaswami Subramania Bharati (சின்னசுவாமி சுப்பிரமணிய பாரதி *Ciṉṉacuvāmi Cuppiramaṇiya Pārati*) (1882–1921) is a cultural and literary icon in Tamil Nadu, where his prose, poetry and patriotic songs are held in the highest esteem. He was born in Ettayapuram in Tuticorin (Thoothukudi) District, at the time part of Tinnevelly (Tirunelveli) District, to Chinnaswami Iyer and Lakshmi Ammal. His father was an employee of the local rajah. Bharati, an epithet of Saraswati, the Hindu goddess of Knowledge and Music, was an honorific title conferred upon him in 1893 – at the age of eleven – by the rajah, in recognition of his exceptional proficiency in poetry. Popularly known in Tamil Nadu as Mahakavi (great poet) Bharatiyar, he is, however, not widely appreciated beyond India, and even in much of India itself, despite being an innovative *littérateur*, pioneering journalist, dynamic social reformer and independence campaigner, and now a National Poet. Although there is a considerable body of research literature in Tamil on his life and work, an in-depth English-language study of his *oeuvre* is lacking.

During Bharatiyar's lifetime, over one-fifth of the world's land mass, comprising a quarter of its population, would be directed from London, the capital of the British Empire. Any stirrings of separatism were generally regarded as localized nuisances by an establishment that ruled as if by divine right. Nonetheless,

> the awareness of other cultures which came with British and European colonization... raised the level of anxieties about the empire and threatened the Western sense of cultural pre-eminence. [K]nowledge of other myths and religions and cultures was... a challenge to the classical and biblical traditions and deepened the doubt of freethinkers who were already critical of the Christian hegemony.[1]

Despite its repression of opposition, Britain's global supremacy was beginning to wane. Rudyard Kipling's 'all our pomp of yesterday / Is one with Nineveh and Tyre'[2] in echo of 'Ozymandias', Percy Bysshe Shelley's powerful metaphor for the impermanence of imperial dominion,[3] had already presaged the inexorable putrefaction of British jingoistic might.

In the early twentieth century, Bharatiyar was a leading Tamil journalist and activist in the Indian independence struggle, 'the voice of the newly awakened national consciousness'.[4] Indeed, one of his lexical contributions to the Tamil language was the calque from English, புரட்சி *puraṭ ci* 'revolution' < புரள் *puraḷ* 'to roll over, to be overturned'. Aspects of his vision of a free, democratic, non-sectarian India are woven into his dream-fantasy, ஞானரதம் *Ñāṉaratam* (*The Chariot of Wisdom*). This story was written in 1908/1909, at the height of the Swadeshi movement, a self-sufficiency campaign formed in 1905 with the aim of breaking the imperial monopoly over essential goods. Bharatiyar had attended the session of the Indian National Congress held in December 1906 in Kolkata, at which resolutions concerning Swadeshi and self-government were passed:

> This Congress accords its most cordial support to the *Swadeshi* movement and calls upon the people of the country to labor for its success by making earnest and sustained efforts to promote the growth of indigenous industries and to stimulate the production of indigenous articles by giving them preference over imported commodities even at some sacrifice.
>
> This Congress is of the opinion that the system of Government obtaining in the self-governing British Colonies should be extended to India.[5]

The view that attacking the Empire on the economic front was a key contingency to its rapid decline is a point made in *Ñāṉaratam*. In 1908, Bharatiyar had begun to serialize his story in the Tamil nationalist weekly, இந்தியா/ *India*, which he had edited since early 1907.[6] The magazine was considered subversive by the British authorities, and when M. Srinivasa Iyengar, *India*'s de jure editor, was arrested,[7] Bharatiyar himself, faced with imminent detention for his feisty writings and cartoons, escaped to the French littoral enclave of Pondicherry (now a district in the Indian union territory of Puducherry). France was a rival colonial power to Britain, no less exploitative but happy to offer a haven to anti-British irredentists.

From Pondicherry, Bharatiyar continued to edit and publish *India*, as well as a political daily, விஜயா *Vijayā* (victory) – both periodicals were soon proscribed in British India, and eventually had to cease production because of lack of revenue.[8] He resumed writing *Ñāṉaratam*, but only for two further instalments, with a promise that his story would be completed, and published as a book. In January 1910, all the parts that had already appeared were assembled and printed as a single work, in five chapters, but nothing more materialized.

Ñāṉaratam is written as a *visio*, or dream vision, a genre in which authors typically portray themselves as falling asleep and encountering in a dream a series of emblematic characters or symbolic events often in an idealized world, with a veneer of authenticity and an ambiance imbued with the colours and sounds of Nature.[9] Within this tradition, *Ñāṉaratam* is presented as a first-person reverie; the narrator is ostensibly Bharatiyar himself.

The story opens in an ocean-front tenement flat in Triplicane, a coastal neighbourhood of Madras (Chennai). As the morning breeze from the Bay of Bengal wafts in over his balcony, the narrator yearns to take a trap-ride along the Marina.[10] But realizing that such a diversion is beyond his means, in the half-light he languidly trances himself instead into a daydream[11] to board the Chariot of Wisdom, an illusory vehicle that could apparently usher him away from the stresses of his daily life. Thus begins an allegorical journey through different Worlds.

Bharatiyar's initial objective is the World of Tranquillity, where he discovers that he can abandon his worries and sorrows, but only at the expense of his joys and desires, and thus his mind:

> There exists a Hindu notion that the mind is the vehicle of desire. You mount your mind or wish-car and reach your destination, that is to say, the object of your desire. From this arises a part equation between *manas* (mind) and *kāma* (desire), so that either of them... may be mounted and ridden to the goal. And, vice versa, *manas*, which is primarily merely the vehicle of desire, turns almost into a synonym of *kāma*.[12]

As he cannot commit to such a Faustian bargain, he leaves in disillusion, and continues on to the carefree World of the Gandharvas, celestial nature-spirits renowned for their proficiency in music and dance. This happy World is eventually also a disappointment to him, since he is unable to evade the comparison of what he deems the afflictions of the 'land of sorrow', India, which he sees as a decrepit, subjugated state over which the denizens of the plundering colonizer lorded with impunity[13] – poverty, famine, and subjection having bespoiled the populace of a glorious ancient civilization. While Bharatiyar looks to a renaissance of Indian grandeur, he rejects what he perceives as the hypocrisy of its oppressively conservative zeitgeist, in contrast to the Gandharvas' realm of splendid hedonism, where he is overawed by new sensual pleasures:

> As soon as I reached the World of the Gandharvas, I felt euphoric in a way quite new to me. There was delightful music in the air... that seemed like a continuous shower of melody pouring into my soul.

A common feature of *visio* compositions is the inclusion of a local guide to accompany the narrator around the dreamland and lead him or her to an understanding of the novel milieu. In the World of the Gandharvas, Bharatiyar's chaperone is Parvatakumari, a young lady who shares with him her knowledge and experience of her home domain.

> 'I'm quite moved by this sweet sound. Where's it coming from?' [he asks her]...
>
> 'This dulcet music's in the nature of the moon's rays,' she replie[s]. 'It's clearly audible in this World, but not to the ears of you earthlings. Even on Earth, though, the ears of gifted poets can perceive this music.'[14]

Inspired by the Keatsian concept of Beauty as Truth, Bharatiyar is nonetheless disconcerted by the Gandharvas' plastic lives, their seeming unwillingness, or inability, to innovate or to develop their society, and their lack of spirituality. Parvatakumari understands his dilemma:

> You're not to be blamed for being dissatisfied with our life. Because however pitiable human birth may be, it's superior to ours in one important respect. That is, that human nature's perfectly designed for spiritual quest. To be dissatisfied with anything's a protective quality of human nature, and also an indication of its rare excellence. Man perceives an ephemerality in material things and becomes dissatisfied with them.

Bharatiyar is, on the other hand, impressed by the achievements of Western civilization. Like Keats, and Shelley, he had great admiration for the glory of ancient Greece. He observes, for example, that its sculptors had reached eminent heights in realization and interpretation.

> In the World of the Gandharvas, the statues, except those of gods, showed off its sculptors' skill in workmanship and did not reflect their inner quest. In that respect, in the Earthly World, the sculptures of Greece are greatly renowned. Their carvers envisaged perfect beauty and represented it in stone through their inner vision, even though what they actually saw were the defective human forms.

However, he is critical of the West's application of its accomplishments to the pursuit of violent ends.

During his tour of the World of the Gandharvas, including visiting a festival to Manmata, the god of Love, Bharatiyar becomes enamoured of his 'ideal', Parvatakumari, perforce platonically. Despite this mystical experience, however, he grows restless for novel emprises; mere pleasure had become unsatisfying.

> Kumari had become my soulmate. I felt an elation that I had never before had, even in my dreams, and became completely freed from fatigue and disease, depression and melancholy. However, my Mind remained unfulfilled. Something seemed to be missing. In the course of time, even what the World of the Gandharvas offered, although still exceptional, wore off.

The chapter ends somewhat abruptly, and 'the following day' Bharatiyar finds himself in the World of Truth. But here again, he does not find contentment. He realizes that his own shortcomings vex his quest for Truth, and that such a pursuit constitutes unanticipated challenges, which have to be confronted by sustained effort.

> Even as I've crossed into this World in search of Truth, vile Sloth comes along to frustrate it.... The entire cosmos functions only by virtue of relentless labour. The darkness of sloth is the forerunner of destruction; indolence leads to ruin.

He is advised by a disembodied voice to go to the World of Dharma, to help him understand the full measure of the nature of the undertaking.[15]

Then, once again suddenly, he is awake in the familiar surroundings of his Triplicane flat. This leads to a light-hearted, semi-autobiographical interlude, in which he recounts some of his experiences of the grind of ordinary life, beset with everyday personal conflicts, health issues, and financial worries, as well as something of his political activities.[16] He characterizes the real world as unethical, manipulated by deceit and hypocrisy, and controlled by an obsession with money.

Despair gives way to optimism, however, at his final destination, the World of Dharma, where fulfilment is found in an ideal, hierarchically structured society, in which people are differentiated in terms of their innate qualities and abilities, and accept their moral and social responsibilities (Tamil, தர்மம் *tarmam*; Sanskrit, धर्म *dharma*) according to their standing in the societal framework. Bharatiyar acknowledges that in every society there are distinctions of status, but he opines that only in India had this code metamorphosed into the caste system. In real life, although born into an orthodox brahmin family, he eschewed his own caste identity: 'Bharati was the poet devotee par excellence, his putative Brahmanness set aside in favor of the passionate poetry he produced.'[17] He long fought against caste in Hindu society. In பாப்பாப் பாட்டு *Pāppāp pāṭṭu*

('Songfor a Child'), for example, which appeared in the February 1915 issue of his short-lived Tamil monthly, ஞானபானு *Ñāṉapāṉu* ('The Bright Sun of Wisdom'), he was to write of a merit-based social order:

சாதிகள் இல்லையடி பாப்பா! –குலத்
cātikaḷ illaiyaṭi pāppā! – kulat
தாழ்ச்சி உயர்ச்சி சொல்லல் பாவம்;
tāḻcci uyarcci collal pāvam;
நீதி, உயர்ந்த மதி, கல்வி; – அன்பு
nīti, uyarnta mati, kalvi; – aṉpu
நிறை உடையவர்கள் மேலோர்.
niṟai uṭaiyavarkaḷ mēlōr.

There's no such thing as caste, my child! – A crime
it is, a birth as low or high to deem;
In justice, wisdom, learning, love sublime,
the pure and fine are those who rank supreme.

This is an echo of stanza 2 in நல்வழி *Nalvaḻi* ('The Right Path') by the thirteenth-century AD Chola court poetess, Avvaiyar, who wrote didactic works explaining to youngsters the basic wisdom governing daily life:

சாதி இரண்டொழிய வேறில்லை சாற்றுங்கால்
cāti iraṇṭoḻiya vēṟillai cāṟṟuṅkāl
நீதி வழுவா நெறிமுறையின் – மேதினியில்
nīti vaḻuvā neṟimuṟaiyiṉ – mētiṉiyil

இட்டார் பெரியார் இடாதார் இழிகுலத்தார்
iṭṭār periyār iṭātār iḻikulattār
பட்டாங்கில் உள்ள படி *paṭṭāṅkil uḷḷa paṭi*

On earth, just two caste kinds are there,
Through rules of justice nature bound –
The high are those who give and share,
The low are ones as churls renowned.

In the World of Dharma, Bhartiyar presents his arguments through brief dialogues with 'wise men'. However, he still hankers after his forlorn attachment to Parvatakumari, and, once jolted out of his dream, he is awakened to the chastening realization that he has not succeeded in overcoming the control of his mind. The desires from which he had sought liberation for his self-actualization have not left him, and he recognizes reluctantly that his illusory ideal has been hijacked by natural human yearning, which he was unable to sublimate.[18]

To travel among and within the worlds, soaring through the air seemingly at the speed of light, Bharatiyar uses a chariot (except in the World of the Gandharvas, where he sprouts angelic wings like the Gandharvas and flies around independently with Parvatakumari). The nature of his chariot is somewhat obscure, and few details of it are given.

The choice of the chariot imagery was, however, purposeful. One is reminded of Surya (Tamil சூரியன்

Cūriyaṉ, Sanskrit सूर्य *Sūrya*), the Hindu god and personification of the Sun, often depicted riding in a chariot drawn by seven horses across the sky, dispelling darkness. *Surya* is linguistically cognate with *Helios*, the ancient Greek god and personification of the Sun, who every morning drove his four-horse chariot across the sky, dispersing the darkness of the night.

> Both in the Homeric epics and in the Vedic hymns the chariot is sometimes envisaged as a means of communication between the world of men and the world of gods; likewise, in both literary traditions chariot imagery is employed as a metaphor of the poetic word granting the poet access to other planes of consciousness.[19]

In Vedic literature, the chariot was an artefact imbued with religious significance and symbolic values.[20] For example, in the chariot image in the Katha Upanishad (कठ उपनिषद् *Kaṭha Upaniṣad*) ([?]c. tenth–fifth century BC[21]), the self, or soul (ஆன்மா *āṉmā*, आत्मन् *ātman*) is allegorically postulated as the rider, whose charioteer is the intellect, which controls the mind (மனம் *maṉam*, मनस् *manas*[22]), the reins, to direct the senses, the horses, to travel appropriately on the perceived road ahead. That is to say, people should use their intellect to control their minds, and restrain their senses, as well as not lose sight of their destination.

> Know the *ātman* as the lord of the chariot, the body as only the chariot,

> know also intelligence as the driver; know the minds as the reins.
>
> The senses, they say, are the horses; the objects which they perceive, the way.[23]

And in the Brihadaranyaka Upanishad (बृहदारण्यक उपनिषद् *Bṛhadāraṇyaka Upaniṣad*) (*c.* seventh/sixth century BC) 4.3.10, we meet a description of an oneiric chariot ride, where everything is a figment of the mind:

> There are no (real) chariots in that state, no horses, no roads, but he himself sets forth (creates) chariots, horses, and roads.[24]

The Vishnu Smirti (विष्णुस्मृति *Viṣṇu Smṛti*) – which modern scholarship places between AD 700 and 1000,[25] composed as a dialogue between Vishnu, the God of Preservation, and Prithvi (पृथ्वी *Pṛthvī*), Mother Earth – conflates the mind as the charioteer and the reins, but also has the senses as the horses:

> The man who rides (as it were) in a chariot drawn by his five senses and directed by his mind (as the charioteer), who keeps it on the path of the virtuous, can never be overcome by his enemies (lust, wrath, and greed), unless the horses (unrestrained by the charioteer) run away with the chariot.[26]

In addition to these and other Vedic sources[27] that may have provided inspiration for *Ñāṉaratam*, among Bharatiyar's chronologically more immediate influences were certainly the writings of Percy B. Shelley, 'whose spirit of rebellion against the tyranny of established institutions, his revolutionary ardour, his championship of women and above all his idealism greatly appealed to the imagination of the Tamil poet'.[28]

In his verse drama *Hellas* (ll. 197–206), Shelley describes the immortal soul travelling through mortal life as on a chariot:

> Worlds on worlds are rolling ever
> From creation to decay,
> Like the bubbles on a river,
> Sparkling, bursting, borne away.
> But they are still immortal
> Who, through birth's orient portal,
> And death's dark chasm hurrying to and fro,
> Clothe their unceasing flight
> In the brief dust and light
> Gathered around their chariots as they go...

And in *The Triumph of Life* (1822),[29] Shelley recounts a vision of a procession of 'life' in which a chariot is led by winged horses guided by a blindfolded 'Janus-visaged shadow'. In this poem, Shelley's challenge of the servile acceptance of authority, and his desire for people to achieve their highest potential and greatest happiness, is inspired by the Enlightenment philosophy of optimism regarding human nature but censure of human institutions, embodied in the work of the Genevan philosopher Jean-Jacques Rousseau, who advocated individual civil and political liberty, and religious tolerance in the form of a personal and emotional response toward God rather than adherence to dogma.[30]

In 1902, Bharatiyar had formed a literary circle in his birthplace, Ettayapuram, the Shelleyan Guild (ஷெல்லியன் கில்டு *Ṣelliyaṉ kilṭu*), and one of his early noms de plume was Shelleydasan (ஷெல்லிதாசன் *Ṣellitācaṉ*) 'devotee of Shelley'.[31] A major influence for *Ñāṉaratam* would have been *Queen Mab*, a utopian allegory telling of the eponymous miniature fairy queen referred to in William Shakespeare's *Romeo and Juliet*, who, in a chariot the size of 'an emptie Hasel nut … gallops night by night, throgh louers brains and then they dreame of loue'.[32] Shelley's Queen Mab, a 'supernatural figure, who seems to know all about mankind',[33] descends to where a young girl, Ianthe, is sleeping, isolates her soul from her body and conveys it to the edge of infinity. She shows Ianthe's spirit visions of the world, characterized by misrule, corruption, venality and misery, leading the spirit to ask (VI.12–16):

> It is a wild and miserable world!
> Thorny, and full of care,
> Which every fiend can make his prey at will,
> O Fairy! in the lapse of years,
> Is there no hope in store?

Queen Mab replies (VI.29–32):

> Yes! crime and misery are in yonder earth,
> Falsehood, mistake, and lust;

> But the eternal world
> Contains at once the evil and the cure.

Thus, a vision of a future golden age when the human condition will be enhanced and the utopian 'sunlit uplands' will arise. *Queen Mab* has been said to be an expression of duality of matter and spirit, body and soul – Ianthe's soul leaves the body, to see the world as it is, and as it could be: 'Body belongs to earth; soul transcends it.'[34]

Shelley had been greatly motivated by British philosopher, William Godwin, a rebellious ambassador of rationalism, egalitarianism, and anti-authoritarianism. Godwin's major treatise, *An Enquiry Concerning Political Justice, and its Influence on General Virtue and Happiness* (London, 1793), was the first modern work to expound philosophical anarchism, in which he advocated the abolition of government, and the establishment of small, autonomous communities. Shelley espoused his philosophy of communalism and extreme rationalism, and fiercely rejected institutionalized religion. Similarly, Bharatiyar was severely critical of the social conditions of his time and he evinced a passion for social justice, which stirred the empathy of his compatriots. His early political extremism and social radicalism were tempered by increasing spirituality:

> He was an ardent admirer of Hinduism and he never denounced any revealed religion. ... in his songs and essays he made it clear that all religions are the same in nature and he never held one superior to another.

> Further he declared that faith in God was a great virtue and faithlessness an illusion.[35]

In *Ñāṉaratam,* for example, he has Parvatakumari offer a syncretic declaration, echoing John 14:2: 'In my Father's house are many mansions':

> God is what your mind makes Him. Whichever form you worship God in, God manifests in that form to you and grants you His grace. What is God after all? God is perfection. God is the mind's ideal. God is truth. God is beauty.

'Every heart,' says Shelley in *Queen Mab* (V.147), 'contains perfection's germ'; and in a letter to his friend and fellow British poet, Leigh Hunt, he writes of 'the God of my own heart'.[36] As British columnist and author, Ann Wroe opines in 'Good self, bad self' (2008), 'The imagery is closer to the Hindu *Upanishads* – which he had never encountered – than anything we know he read.' With change and counterchange, some of the influences on Bharatiyar can thus be seen to be woven into the fabric of *Ñāṉaratam*, where the chariot led the poet on a psychological journey, through a dream that began in mental confusion, and ended with an unfulfilled vision of constancy and harmony. It is less of a story, more of an allegorical manifesto. Nevertheless, the unfinished narrative is a rich text, which warrants close reading.

Gregory James

Ōm

Dedicated to

Srimati Nivedita Devi[37]

Preface

Tradition dictates that if you write a book, you have to write a preface to it. No matter what one does in the world, the spirit of 'tradition' prevails and stands foremost. But I have no intention of boring the reader by unduly extending this. I would just like to say one thing here. That is, that I was not alone in writing this book. The Supreme Soul, who directs everything, took this benighted individual and mounted him in the Chariot of Wisdom. This is one of the many curiosities. [**] Therefore, I am not responsible for any shortcomings here.[38]

One further snippet. I wish to express publicly my thanks and respect to my friend, Mahesh Kumar Sharma,[39] who wrote me words of great encouragement when this work was published in the magazine.[40] Many times has he well demonstrated to the people of Tamil Nadu his erudition, his insightfulness, and his refined taste. So I don't want to elaborate on these. However, I do feel sad that the people of Tamil Nadu have not sufficiently supported or safeguarded scholars such as him, to prevent their minds getting involved in other, mundane, undertakings. I have taken this opportunity to speak out openly about this. Vande Mataram![41]

Pondicherry, 28 January 1910[42] C. Subramania Bharati

Prologue

Morning twilight.[43] Veeraraghava Mudali Street, Triplicane.[44]

I was slumbering on a couch on the terrace of an ocean-facing house. A pleasant breeze was continuously wafting in from all directions, through the windows, and the frames of the outer door. How can I describe the freshness and the pleasure that the breeze and the dawn light brought me! I thought to myself, 'How nice it'd be to go for a bathe right now, jump into a sleek pony trap, head south along the foreshore to Adyar,[45] reading Kalidasa's *Shakuntala*[46] or an Upanishad on the way, and then return home!'

But then I remembered, I didn't have a pony trap.

'Oh dear,' I thought, 'without great wealth, you can't enjoy even the basic pleasures of life, let alone the more dignified ones.'

My Mind chided me. 'Don't be silly! The Good Lord has bestowed on every human being a divine chariot called

Wisdom, capable of guiding you in any direction, and letting you see every sight you may desire. Without taking advantage of this chariot, why would you want a shabby wooden cart that could at any moment topple and injure you?' There and then, I ordered my attendant, Volition, to prepare the Chariot of Wisdom.

The chariot arrived, and I jumped in. But my Chariot of Wisdom was not as dynamic as those of others, nor was it fit for use with ease over long distances. It was a tad lame, even. But what could I do? After all, ought we not to make the best of whatever we have? So, I hopped into the chariot. The things I saw, and the feelings of wonder they evoked in me, are described here in this book.

I

The World of Tranquillity

(A lightsome land)

Turning to my Chariot of Wisdom, I ordered, 'Take me right now to a carefree land, if such a place exists anywhere.' To think that all the time, I had had this chariot in my possession but had not known how to keep myself free of worries and anguish! For so long had I let my Mind writhe in pain like a worm on a fish-hook, without knowing of any means of relief. My heart takes fright at thinking of what the worries of this world wreak. Shall I recount the venomous power they harbour? They blight the beauty and the appeal as well as the youthfulness of one's countenance. They dull the glint in one's eyes; and the sheen of one's complexion dims. These baleful worries bring furrows to the brow and wrinkles to the cheeks. The throat emits a hoarse, grating sound in place of the sweetness of the voice. The chest and the shoulders lose their vigour. The blood-flow rate turns sluggish, like that of a polluted stream. The energy withers from the legs. The body gets gnawed away from within by those poisonous creatures known as worries. But the body is not their only victim. In addition, they mar the intellect. They boost forgetfulness: one fails to remember all sorts of important things at the right moment.

All one's studies pass into desuetude, like rain in a desert. Learning loses its sheen, to remain ever clouded. Thought knocks up. Even the most terrible disease-carrying micro-organisms discussed by medical experts do not have the potency of these minute, venomous little insects called worries. But I'll stop there.

'Chariot of Wisdom, take me now to a world free from all cares,' I ordered.

Just then, my Mind came up, and blocked the chariot.

'That world isn't such a happy place, you know,' it said. 'Is freedom from care alone enough? Rather, shouldn't you be thinking of somewhere where you can manage to enjoy a little happiness? It seems to me that anywhere with no worries at all wouldn't be a joyful place. And – and – I dunno, I can't say why, but I've no wish to go there.'

I chided my Mind angrily, 'Agh, sad mind! I'd sympathized with you for your incessant pains and sufferings, and had intended taking you to a world of peace just for a while, and then returning. Should you really be objecting?'

My Mind persisted in its sulking and maintained its resistance. I have a great love for that femme fatale, my Mind. I can't elaborate here on how this infatuation for her arose. That is a secret. But as the days went by, my passion for the enchantress intensified to the extent that I almost forgot the dualistic thought that my Mind and I were distinct.[47] My wish to have a glimpse of the World of Tranquillity was only because I could not bear to see this Mind's afflictions. Now that she had turned hostile to that idea for no reason, I was glutted with a combination of astonishment, pity and anger. In so many ways did I strive to bring my Mind around, but she closed her eyes and stood her ground with blind, foolish obstinacy.

I didn't know what to do. Then I said firmly, 'Mind, in this matter, I'm not going to listen to you. I'm doing this for your own good. Chariot of Wisdom, set off now.'

The next moment, we arrived in the land of Tranquillity.

The chariot came to a halt at the gate of a towering castle wall. I had seen the castle from a distance, and thought that its gates would open as soon as my Chariot of Wisdom approached. But to my surprise, they did not. Was this world so hallowed that even a Chariot of Wisdom would not be able to make it inside, I wondered. As for my Mind, it began to quiver a thousand times more than it had done earlier. So much so that it was completely dumbstruck.

Outside the castle gate, there stood a guard holding an unsheathed sword that glowed the colour of flame, and seemed as if it could level even the Himalayas with a single swoop. On it was written 'Discrimination' in dazzling letters.

'Who goes there? State your purpose!' said the sentry.

Saluting him, I said, 'I've come to visit the World of Tranquillity.'

Hearing that, he let out a hearty laugh.

'Sir, what makes you laugh?' I asked.

He gave no answer, but continued laughing.

With every passing moment, my poor Mind's fright increased. I, too, was quite surprised. So, with an angry look, I asked the sentry, 'Well, can I go inside or can't I? Just tell me. Why all this laughter?'

At this, the sentry muttered to himself sotto voce (but within my earshot), 'You and Tranquillity are far apart.' Then, in a louder voice, 'Don't get angry, young man! You said you intended to visit this World of Tranquillity, and then go away again, assuming it to be some sort of theatre. That's why I laughed. In fact, folk who come to this World usually don't leave it.'

'All right! So please, tell me, can we go inside or can't we?'

'By all means you can come in,' said the sentry. 'This is a maternal home for all mortals. I've no authority to prevent any mortal from entering. But the pretender called Mind that has accompanied you doesn't have the right to cross into this fortress of Detachment. If it did come in, it'd be utterly consumed, like a rag doll in a furnace.'

Only now did I realize why my Mind had begun to tremble at the very mention of the World of Tranquillity, why it had begged me not to go there, and why it had stood bewildered and terrified at the castle gate like a tyrant king standing before the god of Dharma. After this, the desire to enter that world left me. No longer had I any interest in enjoyments, which would come at the expense of the extinction of my Mind by which I was so captivated.

'What do you want me to do now?' I asked the sentry.

'Human,' he replied, 'Tranquillity abides only after the death of the mind. For as long as the mind is in being, any idea that your worries will be over is futile. The mind is the mother that never ceases to beget the demons of care. You still have a love for that dissembler. Once you attain the state of perfection, you can come here alone. For now, you should leave.'

All of a sudden, the castle, the sentry and everything disappeared. For a split second, all went dark. Then I awoke. I was back in Veeraraghava Mudali Street once again, and on the very same terrace of that house, lying alone on the couch, relishing the sweet sea breeze.

'Fine, what's past is past,' I thought to myself. 'I'm not blessed with Tranquillity at this moment. But that's no great problem. Wouldn't killing off my guileless Mind and seeking pleasure just for myself be an act of ingratitude? Whilst I'd thought only about the worries and afflictions of my Mind, I hadn't considered the great benefits that'd come to me through it. My worldly life has been achieved through this

Mind. It can even be called the Supreme Being. Besides, who else is there who could be seen as a life companion apart from me for my Mind, and my Mind for me? Would it be right for me to betray it, no matter what heaps of worries that might entail? I wouldn't wish for the World of Tranquillity, however exceptional it may be, if it meant living alone, with my Mind dead. Look at the people of the world praising those who clamour for Tranquillity, calling them "ones with God" and "great sages"! It seems to me that they're all nothing but fools and traitors.'

Having understood the train of my thought, my Mind heaved a sigh of relief at this consolation, and its shudders of fright abated. I, too, was filled with happiness. I gave a kiss to my Mind, my allurer.

2

The World of the Gandharvas

(A world of pleasure)

The next day, I asked my Mind, 'Where shall we head for now?'

'How about the world abounding in pleasures and free of worries?'

'Good idea,' I said, happily commending my Mind.

I climbed into the Chariot of Wisdom as before, and arrived at the World of the Gandharvas.

I write as truthfully as I can of the sights I saw and the joys I experienced there. I am not to be blamed if there are those who consider some of these pleasures inimical to the mores respected nowadays by the people of our country. It really makes me laugh when I hear such pontifications of the abject people living in today's India as, 'This pleasure's immoral' or 'That act's improper'. Even though they are of the lineage of great sages and celestial nymphs, the present-day people of this country are inferior to all the uncivilized peoples of the world. Even the folk who roam around naked like beasts in forests and on islands, with shells and rings dangling from piercings in their ears and lips and noses, and tattoos all over their bodies, have freedom. Our people have lost that great good fortune.

Education has declined in our country. Just ask ninety per cent of people to write the element அ, and all they will do is draw an elephant,[48] or at least its trunk. Our scriptures are altogether hackneyed. The brahmins, who had been the custodians of the repositories of the wisdom of this country, meaninglessly croak out a few quite irrelevant mantras, like channel frogs, with no understanding whatever of their fundamental true wisdom. It's no secret that the brahmins, the descendants of great sages, have taken up the profession of cookery,[49] making a wretched living by serving vile, ignorant people for money, and spend their time in countless other even more degrading activities. Our country's arts have been forgotten. Our vigour has gone. Virtues such as strength, happiness, and prosperity have all vanished. In our nation, its servile people, dispirited in mind and enervated in body, with emaciated stomachs and sunken eyes, eke out their lives most pitiably.

I appeal to the friends who read this book kindly to bear with my folly of writing a few lines about this land of sorrow, India, whilst I am on the subject of the pleasure world of the Gandharvas. I suspect that some people of our country, where dharma itself has become sorcery, might consider the things that I am going to write of the World of the Gandharvas are unworthy of being written about. The foregoing observations are intended respectfully to inform readers that the slavish people of our country command no right to exercise any authority of ostentatious dharma. I'll stop here.

As soon as I reached the World of the Gandharvas, I felt euphoric in a way quite new to me. There was delightful music in the air, resonating like the hum of golden-throated female bees. No, that is not an apt simile. But I know of no appropriate comparison by which to describe this sound that seemed like a continuous shower of melody pouring into my soul.

I thought to myself, 'What kind of sound is this? Where's it coming from?' My Mind was unable to make out what it was. And my eyes – they were enraptured. The tenements, mansions, temples, gopurams,[50] theatres – every building radiated a cool, pleasant, golden glow like the rays of the moon. In these, and in other things there as well, such as the soil, the rocks and the beach, I saw that glow, blended with many variations in colour.

Have you ever sat on the sands of a beach on a rainless evening and seen displayed the wonderful range of the myriad delicate colours under the rays of the setting sun, shining over the soft clouds and the visible spaces of sky in between? Living in this land of servitude, you have probably not often had the chance to experience the thrill of seeing the splendours of Mother Nature. But, would you not have seen, at least once, that spectacle of colours I have mentioned? If you have, I can say a little of the nature of the World of the Gandharvas, for you to understand it.

There, was the finest range of liquid colours but ones that had the added allure of the rays of the moon.

Before I could savour the delights of the radiance and the music even for a moment, a young Gandharva lass appeared before me and took me by the hand, saying, 'Come, young human, let me show you all the wonders of our World.'

I felt as though I would fall in a faint, overcome at her shapely beauty. Still, I managed to steady my thoughts and said, 'Before we move on from here, I have a question for you.'

'Ask me,' she said, her words seeming like a human voice rising from a golden veena.[51]

'I'm quite moved by this sweet sound. Where's it coming from?' I asked.

'Look up,' she replied.

I saw the moon enthroned among the stars studding the azure sky.

'Look at the rays of the moon,' she said.

'The rays of the moon? What've the rays of the moon got to do with this beautiful music?' I asked.

'This dulcet music is in the nature of the moon's rays,' she replied. 'It's clearly audible in this World, but not to the ears of you earthlings. Even on Earth, though, the ears of gifted poets can perceive this music.'

I was amazed to hear this. I walked along with her.

'Go on, fly,' she said.

I laughed in astonishment.

'Are you telling me to fly?' I asked.

I saw that she had a pair of milk-white wings on her, fashioned from clouds. Shall I venture to describe briefly this young lass, who at first sight had stunned me with her shapeliness? Let me try.

A face that radiated moonlight. On her head, a floral coronet, just over two inches[52] high. Two dark eyes resembling fountains of wine into which had lurched the bee called Life, having lost its wings. And teeth seemingly not for eating with but for being eaten. A heavenly figure unmarred by the white wings. A petal. With hands that by touch could spark currents of rapture through one's body. When people speak of women of the Earth, they describe them as having the gracefulness of the Gandharvas. How can I describe her form and grace? It is a divine form, a divine grace.

Coyly, she said, 'For one of the Earth, you have good insight,' adding, 'don't just stand there lost in your thoughts, fly.'

'What's your name?' I asked her.

'That's rich! When I say one thing, you talk about something else. Why do you want to know my name?'

'Come on, tell me.'

'Parvatakumari,[53] but I'm usually known just as Kumari.'

'Right. May I call you by your name?'

'Of course.'

'So how can I fly, Parvatakumari?' I asked her. 'Do I have wings like yours?'

'Did you see that I had wings when I came here?' she said.

'I was so taken by your face that I didn't pay attention to any wings. I saw them only when you started mentioning flying.'

'Let's leave flattery for later. Tell me, did you see the wings at the beginning?'

'No.'

'In this World, the moment you think of wanting to fly, these white wings sprout. So, decide that you want to fly.'

'All right.'

'Now, look at your form in my eyes.'

In that moonlight, shining as bright as day, I gazed into her lovely eyes. I was amazed to see that my reflection appeared as a Gandharva form. Truly, this was the vision of myself that I had seen in my dreams... disease-free;

unwrinkled; with nothing of earthly nature – simply comeliness! And I, too, suddenly had two wings on me. I was delighted to see how much I had changed, and straightaway I looked at her face. She understood what was going on in my mind from the expression of my eyes.

'Oh, that was a mistake to tell you to look into my eyes,' she said.

'Why?' I asked her, with a laugh.

'Up to now you've looked on yourself as someone with a human form, and treated me as someone with a Gandharva form. Now you take me for your match.'

'Oh, you loveable form! Even if I were to turn into a god, I'd not stop marvelling at you. So wouldn't you be happy if I considered you my match?'

'I would.'

Our eyes met. *When eyes with eyes commingle, What do words avail?*[54]

'Fly,' she said.

Perhaps inspired by the love newly aroused in my heart, or by the aid of the wings, or by following her flight naturally, as does a needle the pull of a magnet, I flew along with her. But I did not feel that I was flying with the help of wings, because flight seemed so effortless and natural to me.

'Where are you going? To your mansion?' I asked.

'Contrived distinctions such as "your house" and "my house" don't exist here. This is a world of freedom.

Indistinction[55] can be thought of as a state in the absolute enjoyment[56] of life, in the same way as it is in mature wisdom. Here, all the mansions belong to everyone. All can live wherever they wish. Now, I'm taking you to the seashore, to the Fragrant Mansion.'

'You utter such lofty words as "distinction" and "indistinction". Where did you study Vedanta philosophy?'

'The understanding of non-duality occurs quite naturally to those who have a clear realization of the state of enjoyment,' she replied. 'Talk by folk who haven't come to know enjoyment is false. In your human world there's a profusion of such bogus wisdom. For us, transcendental cognition is easy. Likewise direct cognition. The World of Tranquillity is very close to our World. Do you know that Vishnu the god of Enjoyment, and Shiva the lord of Yogic Meditation, are one and the same? But let's put this aside. Now's not the time to talk about spiritual wisdom. Look around down there.'

Keeping at a height of two palm trees,[57] we flew over such marvels of the Gandharva city as its mansions, music halls and recreation centres. Flying gave me not a little pleasure. Among all Earth's creatures, the birds should be considered the ones that enjoy themselves the most. Swimming in flowing water is fun for a while but swimming across the heavens is a pleasure always. And then, when we find a travelling companion like Parvatakumari, we can keep flying throughout life.

The Europeans are a race that idealizes the Gandharva pleasures of life. They make sky-chariots and fly them. But because of the feature of witlessness prominent in their nature, they do not know how to develop this innovation in ways for pleasure. Even before their flying machines have been perfected, they have started asking, 'Couldn't future wars take place in the air?' and have begun to put forward a number of ideas on this. But war using aerial chariots has become commonplace now.[58] Because all their thinking is about war and killing, they put themselves out of contention to harness this innovation.

That aside, I have mentioned that at the beginning of my visit to this land of nature spirits,[59] I was racked with bewilderment and wonder. These sensations gradually gave way to an abiding feeling of pure joy. I attained clarity of mind. As I was flying in the air, everything below gleamed at me vividly in the same way as things appear before the eyes of one who wakes up in the morning, splashes his face and stands by the ocean. A thousand chapters would not be enough for me to expound on all the sights I saw then. I mention just a few of them here.

The Ball Game

On a dais, some Gandharva children were playing with balls made of roses. One of the boys said, 'Rasika, you keep skewing the ball on purpose so that it flies straight at my face, and not towards the bat. I'm not playing with you any more.'

The other children fell about laughing when they heard this, and, chattering away, they carried on romping about among themselves, dashing around, dancing, singing, laughing – but one boy sat apart, leaning on a rose-coloured marble seat and watching the game with his eyes half-closed.

I turned to Parvatakumari and asked, 'Over there, who's that boy sitting by himself?'

'That's my younger brother, Chittaranjan. He's favoured by our clan deity, Manmata,[60] but even though he's still a boy he shows no interest in playing with other children and just spends his time writing poetry and in romantic daydreaming.[61] He's in divine love with Rasika, the girl who threw the rose-ball at Kritaraman. It seems he's writing some form of poem right now. I'll call him up here. Would you be interested in hearing the poem?'

I was taken aback. 'Oh yes, I'm really fond of poetry,' I said.

Parvatakumari waved her hand in the boy's direction. He immediately spread his cloud-wings and in the twinkling of an eye, came up into the air where we were.

Parvatakumari hugged and kissed him. Next, gesturing towards me, she said, 'This gentleman's come to visit our world. He's our guest.'

'Welcome,' said the youngster, approaching me, his palms joined in greeting.

I responded in turn with an embrace, and an affectionate peck on his forehead.[62] Then, with a sidelong glance at Parvatakumari, I reminded her of the poem. 'Ranjan, recite that poem you were composing in your mind,' she said to her brother. 'He'd like to hear it.'

The boy was somewhat embarrassed.

'Don't be shy, lad. Just say it,' I said to him.

Then he recited a poem on Kritaraman's annoyance with Rasika for having thrown the ball at him, full of sweet words in the Gandharva language, that sounded like the Prakrit tongues[63] of our terrestrial world.

Need I say that the voice of Parvatakumari's brother itself was mellifluous? I cite the poem in translation here in my poor diction in our language – just like making a drawing of the sun. I translate anyway:

Like one cursing at a benevolent cloud
That struck him on the head with hailstones
While stands there another silent in the crowd
Scorched by lightning to his very bones,
Raman chides the sweet pretty petite jeune fille
Whose flower-ball softly struck his head
While remaining heedless to the agony
Of passion her piercing eyes o'erspread.

(The meaning of this is that just like someone struck on the head by hailstones and becoming angry and shouting abuse at the clouds, while another, burned by a bolt of lightning, remains silent, Raman rebukes Rasika for having thrown a rose-ball at him, but is oblivious to the pain in my soul from the intensity of the ardent glances she cast around.)

(Author's note: Right at the start, I indicated that my Chariot of Wisdom was in need of repair. In its wheel and linchpin, called Practice and Clarity, there were some longstanding defects. The forelegs of the horse, Zeal, were a touch lame. The driver, Resolve, was sick. On top of all this, the chariot suffered yet another plight. A massive effort was under way on Earth to transform the desert-like region called 'the condition of the Indian people' into a city with rivers, streams, and refreshing gardens. Many good people, with huge, sturdy chariots, toiled ceaselessly day and night. Our own crippled vehicle, in an excess of desire, went there, but kept tiring after doing only a modicum of work. So, our hero and the Gandharva maiden were left alone for two weeks in the World of the Gandharvas. Now, I am directing it there again.)*

---

*This note was written with regard to the brief delay which occurred when this story was first published in instalments by the magazine.

The Manmata Festival

After a while, Chittaranjan bade us farewell and left. We continued our flight. All along the way, with the soft music of the moon's rays playing around us, we had the wonderful spectacle of Gandharva men and women, young and old, in every mansion, passing their time in a thousand leisurely ways. On Earth, I had not, even in my wildest imaginings,* seen so many means of enjoyment.

A little farther on, Parvatakumari pointed towards something, and said, 'Look there!'

'Oh, what's so special there?' I asked.

Then I spotted a very large mansion, with, it seemed, over fifty thousand people in it – a vast gathering. But there, there was no jostling, falling on one another, pushing, trampling, scowling, or heavy sweating in the heat, as in such crowds in the human world. Even as the Gandharvas moved around constantly, they allowed enough space for others, they put no one else to the least inconvenience, and they wore smiles on their faces. Where there was no room to move aside when women were coming from the opposite direction, they would immediately spread their

---

**Piratipai* – Visualizing the movements of the mind as done by people like gifted poets. [Bharatiyar's footnote expands on his use here of the term பிரதிபை *piratipai,* < Skt प्रतिभा *pratibhā*, defined in the *Tamil Lexicon* as 'intellectual alertness in acquiring new knowledge by experiment or research'.]

wings and flit up, and drop down again after the women had passed. I was quite amazed to see such a large crowd behaving so good-naturedly. They would hug and kiss one another, sometimes give a greeting very respectfully with palms joined, and laugh and chat around together. What love, what decorum! There is no way I can describe it.

'Parvatakumari, what's going on over there?' I asked.

'D'you see the pavilion there in the mansion grounds?'

'Yes.'

'What's that on the parrot *vahana*[64]?'

'An idol of Manmata.'

'This is his festival,' said Parvatakumari.

I was immediately riveted by the sight of the Manmata idol.

'Kumari, who carved the idol?' I asked.

'Our native sculptors,' she replied.

At once the present state of decline and ruination of the trade of idol-making in India came to mind.

'Oh goodness, even whilst I'm in the World of the Gandharvas, I can't get my troubled country out of my head,' I said bluntly.

'Do you see that even though physically you've briefly changed into a Gandharva, the characteristics you were born with haven't changed,' said Kumari.

'True. Do you have many such idols in your World?' I asked.

'Tomorrow I'll take you to the art gallery near the Waterfall of Immortality,' she said. 'You'll be able to see them all there.'

All the time I was talking to Kumari, my eyes remained fixed on the Manmata idol down below.

'Despite their considerable talent in carving, it's a wonder your native sculptors don't know that Manmata shouldn't be captured in an image,' I said.

'Fine, that is!' she responded. 'You come from the human world, and now you've started finding fault with Gandharva workmanship. We've no other statue of comparable excellence in our country. Look at it closely. But however closely you keep looking at it, you won't understand the true nature of this sculpture unless you're told about it. It's not made of clay or marble, but of a subtle, ethereal element gleaned through mental perception. This is the true form of Manmata, born of the mind. We call the artisan who made it the second Brahma.[65] The Manmata created by Brahma is a living entity. Although this sculpture doesn't have physical life, it has artistic life.'

I have become tired of repeating, 'I was amazed', 'I was amazed', as I write about these things. The Gandharva country is indeed a wonderland.

'How is it that there's no sculpture of Rati beside the one of Manmata?' I asked.

'That's a secret of the World of the Gandharvas,' she said, 'which is not for you to be told.'

'You're forgetting that at this moment I'm a Gandharva too.'

'In that case, you'll understand it yourself if you apply your mind. Leave it. Come on, let's go down for a bit to see everything more clearly. It'd be better to go there and see things, rather than carry on talking about them from up here,' she said.

We landed, and saw all the wonders of the holy festival. On one side, they were performing ritual worship before the idol of Manmata; on the other, there were vivid portrayals in statues and pictures telling the story of the incineration of Manmata up to the stage of his resuscitation.

I also saw representations of spring. In fact, it was spring in the World of the Gandharvas at that time, and the festival was being held for that. Hence, Mother Nature came to the aid of the Gandharva sculptors in their wonderful work.

From koels singing, trees in bloom, a pond, and frolicking deer, to pollen being brought by bees and the wind – all these vernal representations looked even more lifelike than the real thing. There, on a quartz platform in a large hall built of cedar wood, was an idol of Lord Shiva, manifested in a motionless state, like a ripple-free ocean, controlling his determinative faculty[66] and directing the vision of his three eyes through the tip of his nose.* In front of him, like a lovely angel emaciated by supplicatory austerities, was goddess Parvati standing in penance mode, chanting litanies in worship. Behind her was an idol of Manmata flexing his sugarcane bow, setting the floral arrow, and standing as if on guard.

On another side was displayed a depiction of the incineration of Manmata. The sight of the picture showing Shiva turning back and standing with flames of fury surging on his face in the manner of the goddess of Truth in burning wrath,[67] and the flood of anger flowing down from the 'wisdom' eye in his forehead and incinerating the form of Manmata, sent shivers down my spine. My hand was interlocked with Parvatakumari's, but I snatched it away from hers.

'You're scared of a picture!' she said with a loud laugh.

I could not bring myself to check that it was no more than a picture. Even though the image of Rati was not to

---

*Panakavi. Translation by Swaminatha Iyer. [Bharatiyar's source has not been identified, but his reference is to the seventh-century AD Sanskrit writer Bāṇabhaṭṭa (बाणभट्ट) – in Tamil பாணகவி *Pāṇakavi*, that is, 'Poet Bāṇa' – in whose prose-poem *Kādambarī* (कादम्बरी) an idol of Shiva is described as being in 'a crystal shrine resting on four pillars' (*The Kādambarī of Bāṇa*, tr. C. Mary Ridding [London, 1896, §257]).]

be seen near Manmata in the temple precincts, she was represented here as wailing in grief near his burning body. It is impossible for me to describe the sorrow and despair visible on her face, indeed over her entire body. How creative that Gandharva artist's stylus was, as against my poor pen – there is indeed no comparison!

On yet another side, there was Shiva in the wedded state with his lustrous consort Parvati. With Rati coming in and standing with palms joined in supplicatory greeting, and Shiva smiling and extending his grace to her, Manmata redux was rising alive from the ashes, bowing his head toward Shiva and Parvati, and, with his hands, shooting his amorous arrows at them both. Parvati was coming to hold the deity in an embrace.

Such were the scenes in the Manmata temple, and the Gandharvas were venerating each of these pictures in several different ways. And there were some women playing the yazh.[68] On another side young men and women were moving two by two around in a circle, performing a variety of dances.

The Bird Dance

In one direction, a young man and a young woman were standing gazing at each other as if in a trance. There were many more scenes as well.

On yet another side, a bird dance was being performed, where they whirled one another around in a thousand and one styles, and danced without missing a beat in the music – no mean wonder indeed. One of these dances was very graceful. There was a young woman in the middle. At some two yards[69] from her, two young men were pirouetting around her, up and down like a cartwheel revolving around its hub. When one man was above, the other would be below, beneath his feet. There were two beautiful women at her sides, keeping the same distance, and turning around her like a millstone rotating around a spindle. When one woman came to face her right hand, the other would be facing her left. Now, as they all gyrated, in each cycle they would meet up twice, wouldn't they? The kiss-like sounds they smacked with their lips at these points would strike the metre of the music which the girl standing in the middle played on her flute. A thousand such simultaneous manoeuvres makes for quite a circle! After ten minutes or so,[70] another style would take its place.

'It's getting late,' said Parvatakumari. 'Let's head off to the beach.'

I really had no mind to leave the festival, but who would think of gainsaying Parvatakumari?

The Beach

We flew along, and arrived at the seashore. As we were coming closer, a sweet, mild, evocative aroma of such delight penetrated our very being. I then realized that we were nearing the Fragrant Mansion, which Kumari had mentioned. Even before I began to ask, 'How did this mansion come by such a sweet perfume?' she sensed what I was thinking and said, 'This mansion's built of musk-infused stone and celestial sandalwood. And in the park around it, there are varieties of flowering plants with scents unknown to your world.'

While we were speaking, we landed on the podium at the top of the Fragrant Mansion. I saw that many couples, like us, were already there, enjoying the prospect of the sea. We went to relax quietly on the two seats in a corner. These were stuffed with some cotton, kapok-like material and covered with white silk. As I reclined, I felt the kind of inner solace one draws when lying in one's mother's lap.

Before us was the sea. The moon's rays had invested the waves with a glow of vitality, the ships looked like hills adorned with white flowers, and in the distance, pleasure boats floated like swans. Overhead, the moon and the silvery clouds, some of which appeared like unfurled nets, others like rolling waves. There was yet one like strewn flowers, and others which seemed like reflections mirrored in the sky of the boats drifting below. And the stars – diamonds splintered across the celestial ocean! Such delectable scatterings! In the great pond of the firmament, innumerable flowers, from which the tiny bee called Mind could drink its illuminating honey; and sparks of fire given off when so-called Direction struck so-called Divine Wisdom.

On the boats, Gandharva couples, young men and women, were partying - some singing, some dancing and others playing instruments, keeping time, in a great variety of styles, to nature's beat of the roar of the waves. And, from the rays of the moon was coming eternally fresh music, that sounded like the hum of golden bees. At the same time, the sea breeze teased the curls of hair over Parvatakumari's forehead.

Oh my! Although I had been changed into a Gandharva in form, because my soul was human I was unable to bear such a bewildering amount of joy. My senses were overwhelmed. My mind became clouded. My soul was being tossed around like a speck of foam on the spray of the ocean of pleasure, and swirled like a mote of dust caught in the stormy wind of euphoria. Oh, this fragrance, this music, these sights!

I carried on talking to Parvatakumari about one thing and another, but my words were disjointed. All these pleasures had stunned my mind, and like a wild, unbridled horse, my tongue wandered aimlessly. Not that I had been sated with gratification. From being one who merely enjoyed pleasures, I had become completely overwhelmed by them.

In the midst of my thoughts, I dozed off. And when a little later I awoke, it was dawn. Where the sea and the sky met and embraced each other, the orb of the sun was rising like a radiant infant born of the union. The eastern sky was swathed in molten fire. The clouds appeared as flaming islands. I think clouds have human mentality, for they were about to subdue and slay that very sun which had altered their natural darkness and endowed them with light.

Did not the Jews turn hostile and kill Christ, the sage who preached to them such noble codes of life as, 'Love one another'[71] and 'God is Love',[72] and sought to bring light into their lives – Christ who, by being born among them, brought renown and honour to the Jewish race? Yet they tried to kill him. But they were unable to – Christ the Logos lives to this day. For the sake of righteousness and for his love towards others, he lives on in every person crucified on the cross of the vilification and callousness of the world.

As I looked at those clouds, for a moment I was also reminded of the Jewish priests such as the Pharisees. Then the fiery sphere began to progress upwards. With its vajra-like[73] beams having broken up the clouds, scattered them, pushed them along, shaken them, thrown them into confusion, rolled them around, and finally driven them away, the young sun diffused its magnificent rays across the world in great triumph, and blazed forth like the unfettered Absolute Truth.[74] The World was imbued with joy. The Gandharva women all sang the Gayatri Mantra[75] in worship, using the dawn melody.[76]

The Waterfall

'Up you get. Let's go for a bathe,' said the young woman who had come to be the captain of my soul.[77]

We arrived at the ridge of a waterfall. From the top of a high hill, it flowed down in two stages: first into a pond mid-way, and from there down to the ground at the bottom.[78]

Poets galore have compared a waterfall to a garland or suchlike. But I am not in agreement with them. Just as the wise say that the sky, the ocean and the Ramayana[79] are each sui generis, the waterfall should also be considered as beyond comparison.

Before we arrived, many people were already bathing[80] there. It was amazing to see their strange ways of taking a bathe. As I write about them now from the Earthly World, I am in truth somewhat embarrassed doing so. There are some folk on Earth who are utterly prudish in speech and writing – but in their thoughts and behaviour, who knows what? Down below on the ground, the waterfall flowed like a stream. Along its course, there were miniature rocks, on each of which could be seen a Gandharva couple. From there, they would fly up to the waterfall, walk around it, stand there for a while, and return to their respective rocks. To the pure-minded, all things seem pure. In the World of the Gandharvas there is no such thing as a perverse thought. Hence, they are not overly bashful in matters of clothing and so on. How admirable that is. After bathing in the waterfall, most people went to a temple nearby to worship their favourite deities in a variety of ways.

The Gandharvas, endowed with matchless artistic skills, kept some temples without any effigies. At the tops of these temples was written ஓம் (*ōm*) in bright lettering.[81] They kept idols only in the temples meant chiefly for festivities and merrymaking. They chose not to put idols in places where they would go in sincere pursuit of purity of the soul.

They worshipped their chosen deities by meditating on their images. I gradually came to an understanding of Kumari's words, 'Self-gratification and yoga meditation are related; the World of the Gandharvas and the World of Tranquillity are very close.' If you thirst after Beauty, you come to realize Truth as well. A wise man once said, 'Beauty is truth, truth beauty.'[82]

Kumari and I entered the temple.

'Kumari, you say that this temple's meant for the worship of one's favourite deity. Who is your favourite?' I asked. 'Which one are you going pray to?'

'My favourite's Manmata,' replied Kumari. 'That's who I'll meditate on. You can choose your favourite.'

I said, 'My favourite deity is you. I'm going to meditate on you.'

'Fine, fine!' she said laughing, and added, 'My friend, God is what your mind makes Him. Whichever form you worship God in, God manifests in that form to you and grants you His grace.[83] What is God after all? God is perfection.[84] God is the mind's ideal. God is truth.[85] God is beauty.'

Amen to that.

If you say, 'For one born in the world as a human being, there's no nobler practice than that one should conduct oneself like Rama,' then Rama is your God.[86] When I forget my own self, when my purpose is not my personal pleasure, when I lose my soul in the flood of beauty and take Parvatakumari for my deity, she is the means of my salvation. There is truth even in the fable our people tell of Kalidasa worshipping in a brothel.[87]

She withdrew to a quiet spot in the temple, sat in the lotus position, facing east, and chanted the mantra *Ōm Namah Prammaṇē*,[88] her eyes drifting in ecstatic emotion. And I sat in front of her, reflecting the lotus position – not playacting, but genuinely – and, directing my movements towards her, I immersed myself in meditation with *Ōm Namah Kumāriyai*.[89]

We came out of the meditation, and stood up.

'Up you go then,' said Parvatakumari, gesturing me into the air.

Off we flew, thirstily drinking up the burgeoning rays of the morning sun. Our wings took us to the art gallery. What a huge task I had taken on! Normally, if one had wanted to give even a simple description of the art gallery in Calcutta,[90] it would have been necessary to write a whole book on it. How can I write about the scenes in the art gallery of the World of the Gandharvas?

'Come on then, to the gallery,' I said. 'All day yesterday, we witnessed the beauties of nature. This morning we visited the waterfall. And now I'd like to see the finer creations of your World. This sky's immense, and very lovely. And over there, can you see how beautiful it is where the top of the distant hill meets the sky? If we keep looking at all these things, time will soon pass. So, let's go to the art gallery now.'

Parvatakumari laughed out loud, with a mischievous look in the corners of her eyes.

'Kumari,' I said, 'if you keep on laughing like that, you won't be my favourite deity. I'll still kiss you, though.'

Parvatakumari laughed twice as loudly as before. So, just as I had threatened, I gave her the punishment. She eyed me angrily.

'I did warn you right at the beginning,' I said, not disrespectfully. 'Why did you laugh a second time?'

'That wasn't the reason I got angry. When true devotees mete out such punishments to the women of the World of the Gandharvas, they don't touch their cheeks. But you— k— k—,' she faltered.

In accordance, then, with the Gandharva rules, I administered the penalty on the lips of that gorgeous wrongdoer.

With another ringing laugh, she said, 'My stupid friend, here *is* the art gallery.'

I was taken aback. 'You're having me on, Kumari! *This* is the art gallery?'

'Yes. This is the greenwood scene set up in the past in our art gallery by one Ramanath,' she said. 'It's not surprising you should think it was a real forest. Even our own folk get confused as to whether it's natural or a representation.'

We then went to the hall where statues were displayed. On one side could be seen figures of living beings. There I saw images of almost all creatures except those minute organisms invisible to the naked eye which can be seen only through a microscope. As I did not have appropriate training, or much interest, in zoology, I was unable to appreciate the finer points of those images.

On the other side were arranged the Gandharva images. I went over there eagerly. The shapeliness of women or men was depicted in exquisite statues, of which there are very few examples in our world. Even images of inanimate things, which were beautifully fashioned, were worthy of veneration. When the face of a woman or a man shows beauty mingled with the light of acumen, need we say that such beauty is very alluring? I have always been hungry to appraise the beauty of the human form, wherever it exists, but there is no woman or man on Earth with beauty to perfection. Because they lack purity of mind, and serenity, the people of the Earthly World in general appear ugly, the physical body being a reflection of their inner state.

Moreover, in my homeland, fallen prey to famine and disease and to the wellspring of these, servility, men and women look so deformed that one's eyes start at the sight of them. (This is the current condition in India. Needless to say, there are exceptions to this.)

Only artworks and figures created by competent hands keep Indians' vision of beauty from being lost. Our ancient poets and others have also come to our rescue in this regard. If we do not protect our country's profession of painting at this moment, after two or three generations every Indian will be ignorant of it.

Enough.

Standing in the art gallery, when I saw the Gandharva images there, I did not experience the ecstasy that had been generated within me at the sight of the idol of Manmata. This was because in the World of the Gandharvas, the statues, except those of gods, showed off its sculptors' skill in workmanship and did not reflect their inner quest. In that respect, in the Earthly World, the sculptures of Greece are greatly renowned. Their carvers envisaged perfect beauty and represented it in stone through their inner vision, even though what they actually saw were the defective human forms.[91] Such first-rate artists we call not only fine craftsmen, but also tradition-makers and visionaries. Because everyone in the World of the Gandharvas was endowed with perfect beauty in one way or another, there was no scope for its sculptors to use their power of intellectual refinement. It is true that the images I saw there were infinitely beautiful. But the women and men of that world were really as fine-looking as their images. I looked around for a sculpture that could be more beautiful than the living one called Beloved Kumari standing next to me. There wasn't one.

We left and set off to find something to eat. I went happily in anticipation of a delight for my palate, because that was a world which provided for the pure, uncloyed enjoyment of all five senses.

We arrived at a park. There, from a shade of a gazebo, Kumari called out, 'Ranjan, Ranjan.' Her younger brother Chittaranjan came from some way off. 'Could you bring some food for me and for our guest,' she said to him. Off went the young man, with a kind of laugh.

Some minutes later, he and one of his friends came carrying golden platters, which they put on the marble table in front of our seats. I looked eagerly to see what the food was like.

It was fruit, fruit, and more fruit. Nothing but fruits.

'My friend,' said Kumari, ever capable of reading my mind, 'we don't take much interest in food and varieties of flavour, as do the people of your world. Taste is the enemy of the other four senses. Gastronomes tend to lose the capacity to appreciate food through the intense pleasures of the divine organs called the ear and the eye. Other than eating just to stay alive, we don't seek pleasure in food. Still, the flavour of the fruits here is no everyday one. Try them, and you'll see.'

We began to tuck into those delectable and nutritious fruits.

Chittaranjan then put goblets of wine before us. I didn't touch them. Parvatakumari turned to me.

'I'm not used to drink,' I said.

'This isn't the human world,' she replied.

'But your World has so many qualities – the air, the light, the pleasant coolness, the sights, and you. Aren't these enough? Is there any need to intoxicate one's mind by drinking alcohol as well?'

I said a lot more such things but giving in to Kumari's insistence, I did down a draught of wine. I was overcome by a feeling of exuberance. Pleasure is a fever. When the temperature in a fever exceeds a certain level, a coolness develops, resulting in delirium; similarly, at the head of pleasure lies pain.

My experience continued to be that of an abundance of delights such as those I have described. Several days passed. When I look back on them now, they were all like a single moment, but in another way, each moment of those days seems like an aeon of joy.

More days passed. Kumari had become my soulmate. I felt an elation that I had never before had, even in my dreams, and became completely freed from fatigue and disease, depression and melancholy. However, my Mind remained unfulfilled. Something seemed to be missing. In the course of time, even what the World of the Gandharvas offered, although still exceptional, wore off. From the beginning, the state of ecstasy had eluded me. Although I could feel ecstatic whenever I immersed myself in the beauties of nature such as the ocean and the moon, my devious Mind lacked the strength to remain in that state in them. My Mind started loosening the hold that it had originally had, even on Kumari.

One morning, sitting alone, I thought to myself, 'Even after coming to this World, a storehouse of pleasures, my Mind remains unsatisfied. The cheery-faced folk of this World of the Gandharvas live happily in a monotonous existence. They don't seem to have grown discontent in this. I wonder why it's only my Mind that's been afflicted with this incurable sickness.'

In the midst of my thoughts, flying out of nowhere came Kumari. She embraced me, and sat proudly next to me. Then, as usual effortlessly fathoming my inner thoughts, she told me some very significant truths.

'My friend,' she said, 'you're surprised there's no originality in the activities of the people of our World.

Have you forgotten the lives of the people of the human world? Is there any novelty in them? Even among humans, certain fortunate ones perish in their youth.[92] There are others who live to the age of ninety or a hundred. The kind of food they start eating when they're eight months old, they still eat at the age of eighty, but they don't regard this as monotonous. The people living in your human world tell lies for their sustenance and their clothing; they deceive, they pretend, they cheat, they steal, they harass, they kill, they hawk their bodies, they peddle their knowledge, they become slaves, they sell their souls. Human, the poor in your world are mostly shamelessly in thrall. They'll do anything for the sake of some trivial comfort. Most of the well-to-do are thieves. In your world, people of no means are essentially hatefully unpleasant. The powerful are of an evil disposition who should be trampled underfoot. What else do all these folk do other than repeat over and again what they've always been doing? They eat, they sleep, they act out, they die.

'In our World, there's no death, no falsehood. On top of that, wicked pretence, vile hypocrisy, deception, thinking one thing and saying another – these grievous wrongs aren't in our nature; nor are all their resultant sufferings. Even so, you're not to be blamed for being dissatisfied with our life. Because however pitiable human birth may be, it's superior to ours in one important respect. That is, that human nature is perfectly designed for spiritual quest. To be dissatisfied with anything is a protective quality of human nature, and also an indication of its rare excellence.

'Man perceives an ephemerality in material things and becomes dissatisfied with them. Whilst it's true that most of you cloud your knowledge in many ways, become oblivious to reality, and perish like worms, there are still a few able to perceive the Ultimate Reality. You may have heard that even the devas[93] need to take human birth if they wish to attain moksha.[94] And it's true. It isn't possible for the great men of your world, such as Sankara,[95] Suka,[96] Janaka,[97] Krishna, Buddha or Christ, to be born in our World.

'We're bound by fetters of illusion, albeit golden fetters, which makes it difficult for us to espouse enmity. Because you remain chained in ugly shackles, your great men get annoyed easily. But one or two souls do cut and shed their bonds. When you hear me, a woman whom you seem to consider as simply fit for kissing and listening to songs from, speaking such words, like an austere renunciant, your mind is overawed. Because clarity of mind is the norm for the people of our World, these things strike our minds with ease. But turning them into experience is difficult for us. That needs human birth.'

I was not overly surprised by these words. But it was amazing that although she spoke at such length, she was able to read my mind minute by minute. And once she had finished, this hard-hearted woman adopted the look of wonderment of an innocent doe.

'That's some smart lady!' I muttered.

'Punish me again,' she pleaded, referring to the earlier penalty of a kiss.

'You're not my love, you're a wise old owl,' I said.

'It's all the same,' said she. 'Well, come on then.'

Our lips met, and for the next several minutes we remained in soulful union.

3

The World of Truth

The following day found me in the World of Truth. I saw there a light shining like the immaculate brilliance of the sun. But there was no sun in the sky. It was a divine form seated at the centre of that world. Emanating from its face were rays of light, which I saw were beaming into the sky and colliding with it. I steered my chariot in several directions. The people of that World were all going about their business as if with great diligence. A few of them went round on foot, with difficulty, sweating profusely.

Some were, like me, moving along slowly in chariots. Others were beating their wings and flying briskly. Some looked chipper, others completely worn out. Others appeared abruptly, but unable to stand the glare, shaded their eyes with their hands and disappeared again. I learnt that those who had disappeared were the ones who had recently come here on a visit as I had, but since they were unable to stay, had fled to various other worlds. Some appeared to be devas.

They wore happy, smiling faces and roamed around apace. Many of those who appeared fatigued were, again like me, in human form. I had no change of form here as had occurred in the World of the Gandharvas. The people who fled were also humans.

There came a pot-bellied man, wearing a gold bracelet on his wrist, who ran off yelling in pain. Another man came, with his family.

'Why the heck d'you bring us to this World, of all places?' shouted his wife, who looked like a pack bull. 'Are there any shops or anything like that here, or a temple, or a lake, or amusements, or sports? There's nothing worthwhile here at all. Everyone just keeps running around as if they've gone mental. I'm not going to stay here with the kids a minute longer. Come on, back home we go.'

'Hold on, hold on,' said the man. 'I'll just see this ray of moonlight and then I'll be along. No need to rush.'

'Moonbeam, shmoonbeam. Get a move on, will you,' she shouted back.

Reluctantly he vanished, unable to withstand her badgering.

Yet another man arrived, with a handcart laden with bundles of books. While no one else spoke to me, this man approached me, saying, 'Sir, all these books are very special. Would you like to look over them and buy any?' Even as he was speaking, I saw that the cart behind him had caught fire and the books were being reduced to ashes.

'Hey!' I said. 'Look there.'

The man began striking himself in the stomach and on the mouth, and, cursing all the while, quit the World of Truth.

There were many such people – those without strength of mind, those who let their mental faculties give way to their sense organs, fickle hypocrites who merely paid lip-service to Truth – there one minute, gone the next.

Whilst I was there, apart from that one man, as I mentioned, no one else spoke to me. Wise men have said that knowledge needs an aide for it to be acquired.[98] True. But only now have I seen that the pursuit of Truth requires that you go alone. You should not take anyone else along in the quest for Truth. Once you find Truth, and return, you can share it with others – indeed such is a duty. But when you start out, you must go alone. Were you to take another along, arguments might arise between you. When disputes occur, they lead to confusion of mind, not clarity, and Truth comes only through clarity of mind.

Besides, if you choose to go in search of Truth with someone else, he will pull in one direction, and you in another. Only one of these two will be the path of Truth.

But what you will do to settle this dispute is that you will likely come to a compromise such as, 'Come on, let's not adopt either your view or mine. Let's take a middle way.'[99]

Unless you make this kind of compromise, neither of you will be satisfied. And this path of compromise may lead you up to your neck in mud pits, or into lakes, river-deeps, thorn-bushes, rocks and quicksands. Of the two paths you first saw as legitimate, it may perhaps be good even to reject the right path and take the false one. You can go to the end of it, and seeing that the Truth you sought is not there, you can then go back, and along the right path. This you will not do in the case of the path of compromise, one which will only lead you into a void. Don't take this to mean that I am impugning the 'harmony' of the sages. I am emphasizing only that the 'agreement', that is the compromise, made by the man in the street is always at fault.

Thus did I come to realize that those who journey to the World of Truth do not spend their time in fruitless conversation. Therefore, so as not to trouble others, I kept my own counsel. My Mind did not direct itself to look closely at the ray of light. It seemed to me that I wanted to go straight to that divine form at the centre of this World. At that moment, there arose a sound. I listened to it attentively.

The sound declared, 'The form at the centre is Brahman, the manifestation of Truth. No one can approach it in a sudden leap. You must catch hold of a ray and move gradually toward the form, flicker by flicker. Trying to go in one bound is futile unless you want your chariot to end up in pieces.'

I am by nature very indolent. These rays are lengthy. My Mind is not inclined to crawl along them slowly like some worm.

'Fine. I'll look into this Brahman matter later. For now, I'm coming all around the border of this World.'

And with this purpose, I steered the chariot along an orbital route. After covering a short distance, I saw a differently coloured light. Viewed from there, this new colour could be seen all around.

'What a wonder,' I said in amazement. I moved on, and as I did so, newer and newer colours kept appearing. I realized that Truth is manifested in many hues.[100]

After a long journey, I arrived at the gate of the northern fort. When I looked from there, the divine form of Brahman was shining directly into my eyes. I thought over the phenomenon. I looked intently to see whether the face was the same as the one that had appeared to me earlier. Then I saw a new wonder. The more intently I looked, the brighter shone the light of that divine face. After a while, my eyes became dazzled, and I turned away from the light. Once again, there emerged a sound like the one I had heard earlier.

'Human,' it said, 'at first Truth may appear to be unclouded. If you concentrate a little, your eyes will begin to be dazzled. If you hold onto a ray, and do not slacken, and move nearer and nearer, the strain on your eyes will disappear. And finally, as you draw close, Truth will become as clear as day[101] to you.'

After hearing this, I did wish to take hold of a ray and set off. Then once more, my characteristic of sloth overtook my Mind.

'Gee, it was this wretch called Sloth,' I thought, not without feeling saddened somewhat, 'that thwarted me when I desired worldly status and wealth. But now, through the power of Fate, all those kinds of aspirations have left me. Yet even as I've crossed into this World in search of Truth, vile Sloth comes along to frustrate it.

'What's the good of crying? What good is blaming anyone? Nothing useful will come of them. You reap what you sow.[102] The fruits of one's actions alone can one enjoy. In this World governed by the flattering rule of the god of Dharma, mortals aren't entitled to benefit even one atom more, or one atom less, from their actions. In my own nature, I've nurtured lethargy. And now I'm living with the consequence of that.

'Even though the wealth and greatness attainable in the Earthly World are inferior, the person who abandons them on account of his lethargy won't achieve the path of bliss. We must seek out things by hard work, enjoy their qualities, and then renounce them. The poet doesn't disdain people who earn their wealth by hard graft, merely censures those who consider their fortunes as treasure and bury them.[103] It's not a matter here of whether the creators spend their wealth in good or bad ways. That's a different issue. The poet says only that a heinous sinner is one who, after searching for this wealth and enjoying it, craves it even more, without realizing its worthlessness and scornfully rejecting it.

'I agree. The person estranged from even the mean things on Earth because of indolence is undeserving of praise. The entire cosmos functions only by virtue of relentless labour. The darkness of sloth is the forerunner of destruction; indolence leads to ruin. The attendants of Yama, the god of Death and Dharma, are the children of Mudevi, the goddess of Misfortune and Adversity.'

After reflecting in this way for a while, I resolved, 'I need to get over this foolish bewilderment, this mental anxiety and this indolence. From now on, I must spend my whole life in the pursuit of Truth.'

My Mind intervened at this point, 'Do we have the pleasures here that we had in the World of the Gandharvas? I realize now it was wrong of us to have gotten dissatisfied with our time there. Come on, let's go there again. Are you going to gain more pleasures in this tortoise-paced business of moving along the rays of light than in the music, the sky, the water, the light, the flowers and the women of that World?'

As I listened to this, for a moment I was worried again. Then, because of past good karma, I came by a courage previously unknown to me.

'Mind,' I said, 'I understand you at last. You're out to undo all the good things I do. You're supporting all the evils that come to me. Look here, I'm gonna finish you off.'

I put my hands around its neck. My Mind began to scream.

Then once again, there came the voice from above, 'Human, don't try anything pointless. You can't kill off the mind. When you have zealously transcended the condition of the mind, it will perish by itself and pass into nothingness. You've not attained that stage of perfection. Until then, whatever you do, the mind won't die. Moreover, you began your journey strangely. Truth wouldn't be manifest to anyone who came merely after amusement. Abandon the foolish idea that you can attain Truth effortlessly here, in the same way that you obtained pleasure in the World of the Gandharvas. Because you're fortunate, your chariot has the power to stay and travel around here, unlike the ones of the many others you saw before who were chased away. Only those mortals who've passed through the six worlds – the Earth, *Bhuva*, *Sva*, *Maha*, *Jana*, and *Tapa*[104] – can find a lasting status in this World of Truth. Because you're favoured, you don't need to go through all these hardships. To benefit from the pursuit of Truth that you've had here, go once to the

World of Dharma and gain some experience of it. Then if you come back here later, you'll have understood by experience the things said here of this World. Adieu.'

My eyes eddied. I briefly passed out. When I came round, I opened my eyes and looked about me. There I was back on Earth, surrounded by bits and pieces such as newspapers, a pen, betel leaves, areca nuts and so on, upstairs in that east-facing house in Veeraraghava Mudali Street, Triplicane.

4

The Earthly World

My head was aching terribly. I got up off the couch, and walked eastwards past two or three lanes to the street, whose name escapes me, where I was renting a place. Shall I briefly describe it? You have heard all about World of the Gandharvas. You may as well hear about the comforts that we have in our Earthly World.

The front section of the house where I used to live had a vestibule, with two or three rooms around it. The house itself faced west. On the south side of the vestibule, there was an inner courtyard, with rooms on opposite sides. At the back, there were some more rooms and another courtyard, and an upper storey with two rooms. In the outside backyard, on the south side, there was a communal well and a water pipe. It was in this back section of the house that the six of us lived – my aunt, my wife, her sister, my younger brother, my child, and me.[105] The front section was occupied by a large Rayar family.[106] Rayar himself had a job somewhere in the Post Office, which kept him busy the whole day. He had as many children as the ochre sect-marks on his body.[107] And his wife was pregnant again. In the courtyard, there was also a cow. On top of all this, he had some of his relatives lodging there as co-tenants.

At least in my section, there was an upper floor and we had some breeze around. The Rayar bunch did not have even that. During the night, the mosquitoes were such an unbearable nuisance, I could not get any sleep at all. And as Rayar was asthmatic, the sound of his coughing could be heard incessantly. Then there would be the bawling of his children, one after the other. His expectant wife would wake up every now and again and, in Kannada, berate the children, or some god, or Rayar himself, or whoever, and then fall back asleep.

This is what went on in the Rayar household; how things were in my own was somewhat different.

But I have digressed mid-story. So, I had come to the house from Veeraraghava Mudali Street, had I not? After dodging such ordeals as the jutkas,[108] the carriages[109] of the affluent, the dust, the din and bustle, and the stench on the way, Rayar's cow in the front yard, and his wife and his masses of children, I managed to reach the first floor. Sitting there outside the room I used for a thousand and one things, such as sleeping, reading, writing, chatting during the day with visiting friends, and so on, I called my wife.

'My head is splitting. Could you grind me up some pepper?' I said.[110]

'Yeah, yeah. It's every other day you're shammin' a headache, just to order me about. Fine. But the milkwoman came round this morning asking to be paid. And Rayar's wife wanted me to remind you of the rent.

She said Rayar had told you about it yesterday. And talking of money, you promised me some this month for the child's protection bracelet.[III] You're making a habit of taking me in.'

All this, and a thousand more things, she laid out before me. It struck me that if I had wanted to settle all the tabs she told me about that evening, I should have needed at least three hundred thousand rupees.

She finished off her sermon: 'You'd splash out on every street mongrel, but when you're asked for housekeeping money all you do is scowl. If things keep going on like this, what're we going to end up with? Nowt but the earth under our feet, that's what!'

'Actually, my headache's cleared up now. Why don't you go downstairs again,' I said with all graciousness.

'All right, all right! It's all very well for you to parch your throat talking on and on to outsiders, but the minute *I* utter a word, you get snappy,' she said. I recall that in her mind she thought she was calming me down.

It was not until several days later that I came to a decision to set out for the World of Dharma. Let me put down the details of a few incidents, and their contexts, which occurred in the meantime. The Earth is so vast that if I had to write about all my experiences here, they would run to a volume eighteen times that of the Mahabharata. I will mention only a couple of typical scenarios.

20th: Child has a temperature. Wife, earache. And me, bilious giddiness.

21st: Last day for payment of younger brother's school fees. Forgot to draw money from my workplace, so he stops going to school. He comes to tell me that the intelligence officers, sent by the government to keep a constant watch on me because of my active participation in the nationalist movement, told him the 'auspicious' news that they were going to arrest one of my elder brother's friends.

22nd: Misunderstanding between wife and aunt. They take turns to bring accusations against me. Aunt counsels me in good faith that my principled commitment to the Swadeshi movement is misguided and futile, and my involvement in it will heap misfortunes on the family.

Keep feeling as if I have a kind of itch in my nose, and foolishly fret it may be a symptom of something serious. Try repeatedly to divert my Mind from this concern, but it keeps falling back into anxiety.

23rd: Too much lime put on a betel leaf leaves my whole mouth smarting.[112] Can't even put water to my lips.

It was normal for me to be overworked, but added to that, when I could not swallow any food, I became enervated and morose.

And on and on it went.

Not a day passes without my being beset by some money matter. Bah, is this Earth a real place? Can man actually live here? Turtles and wolves may be able to survive, but it is a place of misery, a storehouse of sorrow. A real hell, nothing more. We should not even look people in the face who are not disgusted with this world.

I have indicated some examples of the business of running the household, as well as of my personal affairs. Let me now mention some instances of matters relating to my outside activities, and some doings of my friends and others. In Triplicane, there was a patriotic association called the Che— Society.[113] Only there were no patriots in it. A few Iyengars[114] and I had got together to run some 'activities' – but none ever took place. Since nothing came of that interest, you will well appreciate that we were no patriots.

I am a devotee of sloth. All my friends were votaries of tamarind rice[115] and some few were slaves to money, the disciples of the quarter-anna.[116] But hearing each of us speak would send a frisson through your limbs. One said that it should be possible to bend the sky into a bow. Another, that we could twist sand into coir. One said, 'If we keep up at this rate, the commercial reputation of the English'll vanish into thin air in half a year.'

Another added, 'Shyamji Krishnavarma calculates we'll see Swaraj[117] in a decade. I think six years.'[118]

'Six months, more like,' said a third, a frog-looking man, correcting him.

And a mightier warrior in speech than any of us was Panathondaradipodi Alwar,[119] one of our leading lights. He would listen to all this and go into raptures of glee. Suppose one day a goddess came before him and said, 'I'll get you independence before sunrise tomorrow. In return, bring me one pagoda[120] from your house.' Alwar would reply, 'O goddess, I pay homage to you. *Ōm Śaktiyai Namaḥ, Ōm Parāyai Namaḥ*'[121] and so forth. 'Ambika, how are we going to repay this help of yours? Our body, our wealth, and our soul, all are yours. But as for your demand for one pagoda, with all due respect I'd like to say a word. Please hear me out. What you propose is for a benefit in common. It'd be only right that members of the general public should contribute towards it. It wouldn't be proper for just me to pay for that. We'll discuss the matter and come to a decision at a meeting we're calling for next week. After that you may grace us again with your appearance. For now, will you be pleased to leave us. Vande Mataram![122]' And with such a response, he would dismiss her.

Jeez, what a world this is, this Earth! Nothing but cheating, constant deceit, interminable worries. There is no substance, no truth. Life is as if gnawed away within by insects, and left hollow. Everyone is in the blame game. They firmly believe everything will come right if one is left to oneself. But each one thinks, 'Is it enough to be the only one in the right? Others aren't to be trusted.' Thinking that other people are untrustworthy, they themselves are dishonest with them. Fools! Do you think that deceiving others is going to bring about any more mutual trust than before? Humanity suffers from an incurable disease. An unremitting bane. An eternal venom. Its name is 'money'. The human race has been bewitched by a malign rat able to bite through the web of divine love – its name is 'money'.

And what induces man to esteem this demon is desire. Desire, that is, minus good taste; desire devoid of wisdom. For the Gandharvas, desire is accompanied by taste; such is the instrument of the World of Truth.

I had wished to present many more such tableaux of the Earth. However, I realized that it would not be worthwhile to elaborate further on this useless world, so I will stop here.

5

The World of Dharma

Some days later, I journeyed in my Chariot of Wisdom to the World of Dharma. On my arrival, I was preparing to alight, intending to go round freely and see things, as I had done in the World of the Gandharvas, when just then, a clear-faced young man with wide eyes, and a dark, curly beard, and holding a book in his right hand, appeared before me.

'Don't leave your chariot,' he said. 'Stay there. I'll join you. The goddess of Dharma has commanded me to show you around this land.'

The moment I saw him, I began to feel a kind of awe and respect towards him. For some reason, I thought that by having a companion like him I would be certain to learn some valuable things, as well as achieve mental liberation.

The young man got aboard the chariot. I looked him up and down once again. And indeed what a marvellous figure he had – not one wrinkle, nor a single defect. His body conformed to nature, as if formulated by the goddess of Mathematics herself. He had an all-over glow, but not of the intoxicating kind as with the Gandharva people; it was the very lustre of nature, as it were, the type of radiance seen in nature itself, such as exhibited by a flower or a plant, or some such, earnestly fulfilling its role there. His glow was of this kind. I prostrated myself[123] at his feet.

He gave me his blessing, 'Abide by your dharma.'[124] He then said, 'My son, my name is Tapas.[125] It's my job to guide visitors to this land. I show people whatever dharmas of this World they wish to know about. From the whale to the amoeba, all creatures have their particular dharmas. Every object, from the great suns right down to atoms, has its own dharma.[126] And, even in the case of an individual entity, dharmas vary, too, according to the conditions of time, place, and situation. If you wanted to observe them all one by one, you'd need ten thousand years. So, I'll show you only the dharmas you'd most like to know about. You can also have an overview of many other things as we go around.'

'I'd like to know about the dharmas of the brahmins and the kshatriyas,' I replied.

'Good. Come with me then,' he said. 'First of all, let's go and pray at the temple of Yama.'

We went off together, and even before the blink of an eye, so that we had not been able make out any of the things along the way, we reached a very spacious temple built of pure white crystal. Tapas got down out of the back of the chariot, and I followed his lead as we made our way into the temple, where we could hear the chants of *Jaya Tarma Rājāya*, *Jayayamāya*, *Jaya Vaivasvatāyā*, *Jaya Sūrya Tējasviṉē*, *Jaya Mahōkrāya*, *Jaya Mahācantāya*.[127] My Mind was startled. My limbs shook, and my whole body was bathed in sweat.

'Sage,' I asked in panic, 'where are you taking me?'

'Into the presence of Yama,' he replied.

'Why? What for?' I screamed.

The sage turned toward me, passed his hands over me, and directing his wide, gracious eyes toward mine, said in a reassuring tone, 'Don't be afraid. Should we be afraid of dharma?'

My unbearable fear seemed to be fading, but then I passed out and fell to the ground. I began to dream.

'Oh, what terrible dreams!' I cried. 'It's as if gigantic worms are coming to swallow me up. No! I've fallen into hell on account of some past grave sin. Hasn't it been said that in hell one'll be consumed in fire and tortured by one's body being hacked limb from limb? Even with all that, flung into the midst of beings and matter of the grossest impurity, I'm being subjected here to agonizing torment! Lord, is this my punishment for wallowing in unclean thoughts and desires!

'I'd continued in that fashion oblivious to right and wrong. I'd become tarnished too through my association with relatives, friends, neighbours, and everyone, who themselves were absorbed in impure thoughts. I knew nothing of all this! Nothing at all! Look there! Look around there! So many people I know have also been experiencing the anguish I'm suffering. Some of them look at me and feel ashamed and hide their faces under the horns of a huge carapaced insect. Others cry when they see me. Infamy! Snails, crabs, cockroaches, lizards – all of monstrous appearance. How it discomfits me to write here of my experiences among these and other such grisly creatures. O humans! Rid yourselves of impure thoughts. I say this in love. Don't entertain unclean thoughts. Lord above, cast me into the fire, into the fire! This is enough for me; enough is enough. Never will I sin again.'

I broke down in floods of tears. 'Then I look around. I had been put in another place. All over me there were signs of diseases. Black leprosy, elephantiasis, hemiplegia, tuberculosis, chronic dyspepsia – just one, or two? Fools, I warn you, who, out of love for your bodies, care for them by engaging in adharma. Why on earth should you ruin yourselves?'

Some time passed.

I had been grabbed by demons, who were pushing me into fires. At first, I had thought that fire was nothing to fret about, but as soon as I saw the blazing pit, I kicked and bit and punched those fiends in a struggle to free myself from them.

'But what strength they possessed! Into inferno after inferno they flung me. Seared through, every part of me is roasting. They chop off my limbs and hang them up like joints of mutton! They dash my torso against scorching rocks! Is there no one to come to save me? Tapas, won't you come to my rescue?' I wailed.

I came round, and opened my eyes and looked about me. Tapas dabbed water on my face, stood me up, and, with tears flowing from his gracious eyes, 'My son,' he said, 'from now on, all will be well with you. The consequences of deeds in previous births aren't spent unless they're gone over again. Forget everything you've seen in your dreams. Lamenting in the present the miseries of the past is mere folly. From now on, I'll lead you along the right path. Say *Jaya Tarma Rājāya*.'

'*Jaya Tarma Rājāya*,' I reprised.

The sage then took me through countless winding paths, to bring me to the court of Yama, the god of Dharma, where the floor, the walls, and the pillars were all crystalline. The throne was of diamonds, and at its foot lay the crushed figures of a serpent and a tiger in gold. The hall itself had no canopy; the sky alone was its roof. The sun's rays shone directly down on the Dharma god's gem-studded crown, lending it a certain splendour. I learnt that because he was the child of the Sun, its rays did not burn him or his courtiers. Fire doesn't burn fire, does it? Right above the Dharma god's crown, a sword of fire hanging in the air, gleaming and flashing with fiery light, acted as dharma's protection. I was given to understand that if anyone came to harm dharma, it would fall on his head and kill him; or if dharma itself should go at all astray, there would be a similar outcome.

I looked at the face of Yama. It bore not a little resemblance to that of Bal Gangadhar Tilak.[128] However, because the god of Dharma himself was Time, on his divine face there were to be seen none of the ravages that time wreaks on a human face. Seemingly cast in a superior metal, golden and with a diamond core, he shone forth as if infused with the living splendour of Maha Shakti.[129] Beyond this, the light of grace gave him a vibrancy.

I often used to think that dharma was merciless, that its heart would be just as unyielding as the substance of its throne. But that is wrong. Dharma is impartial, and is not for anything blinded by love. Rather, dharma is an idol of grace and acumen united.

Tapas took me into the divine presence of Yama, the god of Dharma.

'Welcome,' he said cheerily, and then *ōm* as a blessing.

Before he had even opened his lips, I had prostrated myself at his feet in adoration, drenched them with my tears, and stood up again.

He looked at me and said, 'All your sins are remitted. You're absolved of all your imperfections and you've become worthy to journey on the path toward fulfilment. From now, your Mind will no longer be directed toward sensual pleasures. You'll have no fondness for the trivial. You won't yield to vanity. Your Mind will come into your possession and do all you ask of it. Tapas will show you everything you desire to see. May I wish you success!'

I bowed to him again, and withdrew.

Tapas took me to a dense forest, close to which there was a village of about twenty cottages, each surrounded by a garden. The houses were not huddled together, but had been spaced out among one another. Each one shone as a model of the three qualities of beauty, cleanliness, and serene simplicity. Even on close inspection, no trace of filth or stench could be found there.

The sage and I entered a spotless house in that wooded clearing, where we found seated a broad-shouldered, wide-eyed brahmin with a long, hoary beard, and whose face radiated wisdom. Sitting in front of him were some five or six pupils, palm leaves in hand,[130] listening to his teaching. As Tapas and I entered, he welcomed us with customary courtesies, and had us take seats.

'Children,' he said to the students, 'that's enough for today's lessons. Dismiss.'

'Do go on with your class,' I said. 'We don't want to interrupt you.'

'No problem,' replied the brahmin. 'You've come just at the moment when it's time to stop. Your arrival affords no hindrance to our teaching. In this World, no obstacle to one's dharma will arise.'

'Kanvachariar, what subject were they studying?' Tapas asked the teacher.

'Mathematics,'[131] replied Kanvar.

'When I was last here, weren't you teaching sculpture?'

'Yes, those students were labourers. These ones are brahmins and kshatriyas.'

'Such an ocean of knowledge!' I murmured to myself.

'Not at all,' said Kanvar, who had overheard me. 'Other than the fields of Vedanta and Dharma, I have knowledge of only two – Sculpture and Mathematics. When students come to me for lessons, I teach them what I know. That is my dharma.'

It was only after this that Tapas introduced me to Kanvachariar.

'He wants to be shown brahminical dharma, so I've brought him to you,' he said.

'Honestly, I'm amazed that you, yourself the fountain of all dharma, should consider me worth coming to for that,' said Kanvar with a smile. 'But since you wish it, in all humility I'll take on the task of addressing his questions.'

I had been holding back my curiosity till then. Now, delighted at hearing his words, I showered the master with questions, much like examining a witness in court, but rather with reserve, devotion, and diligence.

And he, in his replies, tirelessly explicated things clearly and succinctly. Here I mention some of these questions and replies.

Question: Master, is one a brahmin by birth or through training?

Answer: Humans are all born as animals. It's through training, qualities, and deeds that they come to belong to the different castes. God has said, 'I brought forth the four-class system according to the division of properties and actions.[132]'

Q.: Master, is this code in operation now?

A.: Yes. My father's a kshatriya, I'm a brahmin. But I've selected just one of my twelve children to take up the functions of a brahmin. The rest I've had learn those of brahmins, kshatriyas, and vaisyas according to their individual aptitudes, personalities, and so on.

Q.: In the human world, it's only in India that there are caste-based distinctions, but things there aren't as you said, are they?

A.: No, it's wrong to say that caste-based distinctions are practised only in India. They exist in every country. But in India the caste code has become distorted. In ancient India, it was indeed as I said, to wit in all the Vedas, Upanishads, Puranas,[133] Itihasas[134] and so forth of that country. Nowadays, what God said is being followed in all countries except India, where it has been lost. Because of that, its people have fallen into the disgrace of poverty, disease, and slavery.

Q.: I wish to acquire knowledge of the brahminic dharmas.

A.: Briefly, then, brahmins are the custodians of a community's preserved wealth of knowledge; they're the farmers of the crop of learning, if you will. They should study the scriptures according to their abilities, and dutifully teach them to people of other castes. For this, they should charge no more than the food they need. Yajnavalkya says that one in whose house rice is stored today for tomorrow's meal won't be a brahmin.[135] Brahmins must take the responsibility inasmuch as the cause of all the misery that can befall people is ignorance, and it's the duty of a brahmin to protect them against that ignorance. If there's a decline in the sudra dharma among the people, then the brahmins' primary task must be to teach that dharma, to increase the number of the genuine sudras in the country. If the vaisya dharma declines, the intellectuals will have it as their primary duty to learn and teach vaisya scripture, and make everyone they run into, true vaisyas. The kshatriya and brahminic dharmas should never suffer any hurt. If they do, human society as a whole will wither. In the event of such a calamity, we oughtn't simply to stand idly by and say, 'We'll just take care of our own dharmas. Why should we bother about those of others?' When a house is on fire, can the father go cheerfully off to the office, the son to school, the girls to a park, the mother to the temple, the servant to the market to buy vegetables, and the cook to fetch water for the kitchen? No. It's everyone's duty to try and put out the fire. The office can wait. And temples and schools won't be thieved away. There's always tomorrow. Picking flowers for fun is trifling; vegetables and cooking are unimportant. What *is* important is quenching the fire – that's what everyone should work at. In Kaliyuga,[136] caste distinctions are false, nothing but deception. You asked me about India. Now, it's the Kaliyuga period in that country.[137] But in two or three generations' time, Kaliyuga will end, and Kritayuga[138] will emerge. Then will the true caste distinctions arise there, and the current phoney ones cease to be. Only one who has brahminic wisdom of the Ultimate Reality is fit to be called a brahmin. This is elegantly elucidated in the Vajrasuchi Upanishad.[139] However, in this matter, it's the brahmin caste which gives intellectual training to the world. Being au fait with all the various scriptures, teaching them to the world, helping in the effective operation of all societal affairs, and having no desire for material honours – these, in short, are the essential aspects of brahminic dharma.

He stopped speaking, and suddenly stood up and went outside. But he shortly came back, and told us it was time for evening prayers.[140] The three of us rose, and went to the riverbank by a mango orchard a short distance beyond the village.

Half of the sun's orb had disappeared in the western empyrean, and with all the clouds resembling islands of fire, Mother Nature radiated an amazing loveliness.

At that moment, after their ritual bathe, Kanvar and Tapas sat away from each other, and set themselves to meditate on Brahman. I chanted '*ōm*' and invoked the goddess of Tranquillity.[141]

When we had finished our devotions, we returned to Kanvar's house, and with a few friendly words Tapas and I bade him goodbye.

'But it's already dark,' said Kanvar. 'You should both spend the night in my little hut, and go on your way later.'

I was immediately reminded of his quotation that one in whose house rice is stored today for tomorrow's food won't be a brahmin. Therefore, thinking that he might be fairly hard up, I said, 'No need. Sorry, but we'll be off.'

Realizing what was in my mind, he replied, 'Brother, where there's dharma, there's no poverty. You don't have to be concerned about that. Do stay over for the night.'

I hung my head in embarrassment.

The two sages smiled.

After that, Tapas and I resolved to spend the night there.

As we were sitting on a mat at the entrance to Kanvar's house, my Mind appeared more serene than it had been when I was seated on the couch with Parvatakumari on the balcony of the Fragrant Mansion in the World of the Gandharvas.

Kanvar and Tapas began on an analysis of Vedanta, which Tapas punctuated with some interesting comments. Then Kanvar's wife also came and sat with us to listen to the conversation. When I looked at her, there came into my mind's eye an image of women such as Maitreyi,[142] educated in the Vedas. All such noble qualities as fidelity, perspicuity, modesty, intelligence, and compassion were come into play in that goddess. As I saw it, the charm of the dialogue bringing out the inner lustre of the two sages, and the radiance in the modest bearing of Kanvar's wife vouchsafing her glow of life, complemented each other well.

Shortly afterwards, Kanvar's son came in too, and sat down beside his mother. But my Mind could not bear the sight of this young man dressed in the garb of an ascetic. One should rather picture him as a prince, enchanting lovely-eyed ladies. Or as a general at the head of an army of youthful warriors. Should this man, who resembled the radiant rising sun, be clothed in mere bark?[143] Should he eat just grains and fruits? Should he be drinking only spring water? Is he to be forever immersed in the minutiae of book-learning and metaphysical jargon? I felt that it was obviously a mistake for Kanvar to have chosen this one from his twelve children for the life of an ascetic.

While these thoughts were racing through my head, the sages concluded their Vedanta discussion.

And as if having literally read my mind, Tapas asked Kanvar, 'What was the reason you picked out this very regal son of yours for the dharma of a brahmin, at the same time sending all your other children elsewhere?'

'My boy,' said Kanvar to his son, 'today we're doing astrology, that is the science of calculating the planetary stars of the zodiac, and not everyday forecasts such as the study of what to do if a buffalo or a cow strays. Out you go by yourself, and make a note of the exact positions of the stars.' And with that, he sent him on his way. Kanvar did not want his son to hear himself having his praises being sung. The son left. Then what the sage said was this.

'It takes more fortitude to kill ignorance than to kill adharma. It's the duty of the sudras and vaisyas to save people from physical ailments. The kshatriya protects the dharma. The brahmin, as I said earlier, is concerned with the preservation of wisdom, and for this he needs boundless strength, boundless radiance, and boundless courage and prowess. The forces of ignorance are legion. The fountain of ignorance is inexhaustible. The roots of the tree of ignorance extend up to the crown of Adishesha himself. To conquer those forces, to drain that fountain, and to uproot that tree, are no ordinary undertakings. In the Mahabharata war, Krishna's task was heavier than Arjuna's, and Vyasa's was the equal of Krishna's.'[144]

We continued our conversation, covering a number of different topics; then, after a light supper, we retired for the night.

Next morning, after going through our daily devotions, Tapas and I headed for the mansion of a kshatriya warrior named Satyaraman.

When he heard of Tapas's visit, Satyaraman came out and greeted us. He led us to a hall, and after showing us where we could sit, proceeded to take a seat too. Tapas then quietly began to tell him my story.

Satyaraman laughed, shaking his strapping shoulders. 'I'm just a guardsman,' he said. 'I can't claim to be able to offer advice on any subject with skill or clarity. Besides, among Yama's military commanders, there are many better endowed with kshatriya qualities than I am. Even as I regard it as great good fortune that you should've thought of little ol' me as above all others exemplifying dharma, I still can't get rid of the feeling of being quite unworthy.'

Then, looking at me, he averred, 'If you ask your questions, I'm ready to provide answers and clear your doubts as best I can.'

'Can you explain clearly to me,' I ventured, 'what a kshatriya's primary obligation is that serves as the basis of all others?'

The majestic face of the warrior seated before me lit up. His very eyes appeared to radiate wisdom. I saw that his entire body took on a whole new glow and sense of elation. I began listening to him with an unquenchable thirst, like a seasoned disciple engrossed in the pronouncements of his teacher.

'My friend, you asked me what the mother of all the duties of a kshatriya is,' he replied. 'And you enquired about the spring at the root of all a kshatriya's endeavours. Listen to what I say. That duty is *war*. War is the kshatriya's first dharma. It's war which is the life-breath of the true kshatriya. War alone is his soul. The moment he stops waging war, the kshatriya is emasculated. After that, he's nothing more than a log of wood, a corpse, a contemptible sham. My friend, I'm not the one to tell you what's in the Vedanta scriptures. You can go and learn from wise men like our sage here how adharmas originally came about. But there's one thing I do know: adharma is always there in front of us. Why's that the case? It's so as to be killed by your hand, and to die out. What does it say? "Come on," it says, "wield the axe you're holding, and strike and split open my head." Adharmas are seeded with blood; as you keep killing them, they regenerate.[145] It's a kshatriya's duty to have to go on cutting them off till his last breath.[146] Day after day, the sun chases around and around after darkness, continually killing it. The sun was the first kshatriya, the progenitor of our caste. I told you that it was the dharma of kshatriyas to go on waging war to destroy adharma. Needless to say, one should acquire the proper training and means for this task.' And with that, he concluded his answer.

I was confused, I thought, what is the use of our continuing to destroy adharmas which have an eternal existence? I put that question to Satyaraman.

'That's a question born of the darkness of ignorance,[147]' he replied without the least hesitation. 'My friend, a man can't exist even for half a moment without the duty of action. Whether you like it or not, you must keep on engaging in some activity. It's the law of nature. Isn't it more honourable to carry out that duty, like the sun, rather than like a piece of chaff tossed about on the ocean's waves? But even in behaviours related to ordinary bodily pleasures, a man doesn't think in this way. The body is constantly getting dirty, why should we keep washing it every day? Would anyone stop bathing just because he thinks the body still keeps getting dirty even though we carry on washing it? Shouldn't we extend the same courtesy to the perdurable dharma as to the body which comes into being and perishes in an instant? What's more, dharma feeds off adharma. So, as long as dharma exists, certainly adharma will too. This is only right. If adharma were to die out completely, leaving a void, then dharma would perish through lack of any sustenance.'

I did not have the good fortune to stay for very long in the World of Dharma. After we had left the kshatriya warrior's house, Tapas took me to several other places.

Then, like some piece of long undigested food triggering a stomach pain, a karma which had not been consumed in the fires of my expiation emerged from some corner, and aroused in my Mind a desire quite contrary to the fulfilment of dharma. And even as Tapas would show me many new things concerning dharma, that desire would repeatedly well up in my heart.

A few days later, there was an occasion when Tapas had gone off on some errand, leaving me on my own. Ah, the consequence of past karma! When I was alone, my wretched Mind brought before me a subtle vision of Parvatakumari.

'Oh, what a joyful time that was,' I thought back.

The alluring form before my eyes came yet closer. I rose to embrace it. And Parvatakumari flew into my arms like a bolt of lightning. We held our lips in union, and for a moment I remained in a rapture of passion – only then to hear a deafening roar as if two or three Earths had come crashing down. I let out a yell, and collapsed to the ground in a faint.

When I came to and looked around, I found myself in the same old place, the same old Triplicane,[148] with some people standing about and fanning me. I asked them what they were doing.

'You shrieked as if you'd seen a ghost,' they said. 'When we came to see what was up, you were absolutely winded. We cooled you down, and you're breathing again now.'

'Even if all my breath had left me completely,' I sobbed, 'it wouldn't have been such a great matter. What *is*, though, is that I've failed in dharma!'

Translator's Acknowledgements

I should like to thank Professor P. Marudhanayagam for his initial suggestion that I might undertake a translation of *Ñāṉaratam*; and Professor V. Jayadevan, who good-naturedly tolerated my frequent excavations of his deep knowledge of Tamil to help solve my problems of syntax, morphology, and cultural allusion encountered en route. Errors and misinterpretations are uncompromisingly attributable to me alone.

I am grateful to Professor R. Azhagarasan for his recommendation; Professor Olivia Cattedra for generously sending me a copy of her now scarce book *El carro*; Mini Krishnan for opening the doors to publication for me, and for her advice and help; Dr Li Polung for assistance with library searches; G. Sundar and the Roja Muthiah Research Library, Chennai, for furnishing me with a copy of the first printing of *Ñāṉaratam*; and Abhivyakti Singh, commissioning editor at Hachette India, for her patience and good grace during the production process.

Notes

1 Jalal Uddin Khan, 'Shelley's Orientalia: Indian elements in this poetry'. *Journal of the Spanish Association of Anglo-American Studies,* 30 (1) (2008), p. 42

2 From 'Recessional', in *The Times*, 17 July 1897.

3 'Ozymandias', in *The Examiner*, 11 January 1818.

4 D. Gnana Sambandan, 'Shelley and Bharati: Comparative study of their poetic creed' (PhD, University of Madras, 1980, p. 92).

5 Indian National Congress, *The Twenty-Second Indian National Congress* (*Held in Calcutta, December 26-29, 1906*) (Calcutta, 1907, p. 64).

6 See India (Magazine). *Tamil Wiki*, https://tamil.wiki/wiki/India_(Magazine), last accessed 15 February 2023.

7 Although Bharatiyar was the de facto editor, he was uncredited, and M. Srinivasa Iyengar lent his own name as editor because *India*'s owners feared that Bharatiyar's involvement would draw unwarranted attention from the authorities. Srinivasa Iyengar was sentenced to five years' transportation for sedition. See S. Mohan Ram, *Tamil Press and Colonial Rule* (Madurai, 2003, p. 92).

8 Lion M.G. Agrawal, *Freedom Fighters of India* (New Delhi, 2008, Vol. 3, p. 237).

9 The genre has a distinguished pedigree in European literature. Among the most well-known examples are, in Latin, M. Tullius Cicero's *Somnium Scipionis* (The Dream of Scipio) in Book VI of *De Republica* (On the Commonwealth) (*c.*50 BC); in French, *Le Roman de la Rose* (The Romance of the Rose) by Guillaume de Lorris (*c.*1230) and Jean de Meun (*c.*1275); and in English, Geoffrey Chaucer's *The Parlement of Foules* (*c.*1382), which begins with the narrator falling asleep while reading *Somnium Scipionis*; John Bunyan's *The Pilgrim's Progress* (1678); and Percy Bysshe Shelley's *Queen Mab* (1813) and *The Triumph of Life* (1822). A related *visio* work is Dante Alighieri's Italian (Florentine) *Divina Commedia* (*c.*1308–1320).

10 Marina Beach is Chennai's natural urban beach, stretching some six kilometres along the coast from the mouth of the Cooum River in the north, to the Adyar Estuary in the south. A promenade was built in 1884. The beach was a popular locale for public meetings during the Indian independence movement.

11 See Bharatiyar's description of a daydream:

விந்தைகளை *vintaikaḷai*

முன்னிக் கவிதைவெறி மூண்டே நனவழியப்

muṉṉik kavitaiveṟi mūṇṭē naṉavaḻiyap

பட்டப் பகலிலே பாவலர்க்குத் தோன்றுவதாம்
paṭṭap pakalilē pāvalarkkut tōṉṟuvatām
நெட்டைக் கனவின் நிகழ்ச்சியிலே
neṭṭaik kaṉaviṉ nikaḻcciyilē

that rare other sight which greets the poets
when their imagination removes them
from the world of everyday action.

From 'The kuyil' (1912). In Prema Nandakumar (tr.), *Poems of Subramania Bharati*. Second edn (New Delhi, 1982, p. 133).

12 Maurice Bloomfield, 'The mind as wish-car in the Veda'. *Journal of the American Oriental Society*, 39 (1919), pp. 280–81.

13 In Edwardian Britain itself, the élite tyrannized the powerless underclasses: for a damning indictment, see Robert Tressell, *The Ragged Trousered Philanthropists* (London, 1955[1914]).

14 We find an interesting parallel to this in Cicero's *Somnium Scipionis*, in which the narrator, in awe of his dream universe, enquires of his guide, 'As I wondered at these things, when I recovered myself, "What," I asked, "is this loud and so sweet a sound that fills my ears?"' (*De Republica*, VI.18). The guide replies that the sound infusing the atmosphere is generated by the impetus and motion (impulsu et motu) of the moon and the planets,

which gifted musicians have been able to imitate, but to other people are deaf.

15 An echo, perhaps, of the Hegelian precept, 'But to seek to know before we know is as absurd as... not to venture into the water until he had learned to swim' (William Wallace, *The Logic of Hegel translated from The Encyclopaedia of the Philosophical Sciences*. Second edn [Oxford, 1892, Introduction, §10]).

16 See also Sumathi Ramaswamy, *Passions of the Tongue: Language Devotion in Tamil India, 1891–1970* (Berkeley, 1997, p. 203): 'Much of his later life was marked by poverty, even destitution; poor health; the burdens of taking care of his family; and the attempts to find patrons who would publish his work. Yet the stories that circulate about Bharatiyar today emphasize that he did not let any of these stand in the way of expressing and pursuing his primary passions – devotion to India and to Tamil.'

17 Sumathi Ramaswamy, *Passions of the Tongue*, p. 204.

18 Cf. Cicero (*c*.45 BC), citing the Greek philosopher Epicurus (fourth/ third century BC), 'It is impossible to live pleasantly without also living morally (honourably)' (Cicero: *On ends*, tr. H. Rackham [Cambridge MA, 1914, II.xv.49]).

[19] Paolo Magnone, 'Soul chariots in Indian and Greek thought: Polygenesis or diffusion?'. In Richard Seaford (ed.), *Universe and Inner Self in Early Indian and Early Greek Thought* (Edinburgh, 2016, p. 160).

[20] Marcus Sparreboom, *Chariots in the Veda* (Leiden, 1983).

[21] Jean Filliozat, *Les Philosophies de l'Inde* ['The philosophies of India'] (Paris, 1970, p. 7). More recently, however, a much later dating, of up to the first century BC, has been suggested: see Patrick Olivelle, *The Early Upanishads* (Oxford, 1996, p. xxxvii). Upanishads (Tam. உபநிடதம் *upaniṭatam*, Skt उपनिषद् *upaniṣad*) are Sanskrit scriptures, the earliest dating possibly from the ninth century BC, on philosophical, ontological and religious topics which form the foundations of the traditions of Hinduism.

[22] See Joseph Rawson, *The Kaṭha Upaniṣad* (Oxford, 1934, p. 125): 'the *manas* is central organ of the conscious life which shapes into perceptions the impressions of the senses, and also translates these perceptions into conative acts expressed through the organs of action.'

[23] §1.3.3–4, from *The Katha and Prasna Upanishad and Sri Sankara's Commentary*, tr. S. Sitarama Sastri (Madras, 1928, pp. 46–47). Famously, this verse has been compared to Plato's *Phaedrus* (fourth cent. BC), 246a–b (et seq.): 'We will liken the soul to the composite nature of a pair of winged horses and a charioteer. Now the horses and charioteers of the gods are all good and of good

descent, but those of other races are mixed; and first the charioteer of the human soul drives a pair, and secondly one of the horses is noble and of noble breed, but the other quite the opposite in breed and character' (from *Phaedrus*, in *Plato in twelve volumes,* Vol. 9, tr. Harold N. Fowler [Cambridge MA and London, 1925]; see also Elizabeth Belfiore, 'Dancing with the gods: The myth of the chariot in Plato's "Phaedrus"'. *American Journal of Philology*, 127 [2] [2006], pp. 185–217). The similarity of the imagery could, of course, be coincidental, but scholars posit the greater likelihood of an east-west influence: see, for example, K.A. Nilakanta Sastri, 'The beginnings of intercourse between India and China'. *Indian Historical Quarterly*, 14 (1938), pp. 380–87; *idem*, 'Ancient Indian contacts with Western lands'. *Diogenes*, 7 (28) (1959), pp. 40–62; Nicholas Kazanas, 'The dialogues of Plato and the Upanisads'. *Adyar Library Bulletin*, 67 (2003), pp. 1–35; Silviu Lupaşcu, 'The chariot of the soul. A commentary on Plato, *Phaedrus*, 246a–254b and *Katha-Upanishad*, I, 3. 3-9'. *Archaeus,* 11/12 (2008), pp. 337–50; Paolo Magnone, 'La alegoría del carro del alma en Platón y en la Kaṭha Upaniṣad' ['The allegory of the soul-chariot en Plato and the Kaṭha Upaniṣad'], in Olivia Cattedra (ed.), *El carro: Imágenes y símbolos en oriente y occidente* ['The chariot: Images and symbols in the East and the West'] (Mar del Plata, 2009, pp. 133–64). Tiago Lier, in *Reason, Rhetoric, and the Philosophical Life in Plato's* Phaedrus (Lanham, 2019, p. 209, n. 63), shows that Plato's image of a winged chariot is not unique, but is 'pervasive' in ancient Greek literature.

24 *The Upanishads*, tr. F. Max Müller (Oxford, 1884, Part II, p. 164).

25 Patrick Olivelle, 'The date and provenance of the Viṣṇu Smṛti'. *Indologica Taurinensia*, 33 (2007), pp. 149–63.

26 *The Institutes of Vishnu*, tr. Julius Jolly (Oxford, 1880, lxxii.6); *The Institutes of Vishṇu* (Calcutta, 1881, lxxii.6).

27 See, for example, Teun Goudriaan, 'The Ātman as charioteer: Treatment of a Vedic allegory in the Kulālikāmnāya'. In *idem* (ed.), *The Sanskrit Tradition and Tantrism* (Leiden, 1990, pp. 43–55).

28 V. Sachithanandan, *The Impact of Western Thought on Bharati* (Annamalainagar, 1970, p. 43).

29 In *Posthumous Poems* (London, 1824, pp. 73–75).

30 Rousseau's key texts are *Discours sur l'origine et les fondemens de l'inégalité parmi les hommes* [Discourse on the origin and foundations of inequality among men] (Amsterdam, 1755); and *Du contrat social; ou, Principes du droit politique* [The social contract, or Principles of political right] (Amsterdam, 1762), with its famous introductory sentence, 'L'Homme est né libre, & par-tout il est dans les fers' [Man is born free, but everywhere he is chains].

31 For a comparative study of Bharatiyar and Shelley, see G. John Samuel, *The Harp and the Veena* (Madras, 1993).

32 William Shakespeare, *The most excellent and lamentable tragedie, of Romeo and Iuliet.* Second quarto (London, 1599 [c.1591], I.iv.65, 68–69).

33 Jalal Uddin Khan, 'Shelley's Orientalia', p. 47.

34 Ann Wroe, 'Good self, bad self: The struggle in Shelley', in Mark Sandy and Sarah Wootton (eds), Modelling the Self: Subjectivity and identity in Romantic and post-Romantic thought and culture. *Romanticism and Victorianism on the Net*, 51 (2008). https://www.erudit.org/en/journals/ravon/2008-n51-ravon2473/019259ar/, last accessed 15 February 2023.

35 D. Gnana Sambandan, 'Shelley and Bharati', p. 73.

36 2 March 1822, cited in Donald Reiman, 'Shelley's "The Triumph of Life": The biographical problem'. *Proceedings of the Modern Language Association of America*, 78 (5) (1963), p. 549. The phrase is from *Saint Augustines Confessions*, tr. William Watts (1631, Book 6, p. 267): 'I groped out of my selfe after thee, but found not the God of my heart.'

37 Sister Nivedita, born Margaret Noble, was an Irish teacher, author, social activist, whom Bharatiyar met in 1906. See *Prabuddha Bharata* 122 (1) (January 2017), Special issue, 'Sister Nivedita: Offered to India'. A disciple of Swami Vivekananda – Hindu nationalist, and a leading

figure in the introduction to the Western world of the schools of the Vedanta tradition of Hinduism and the practices and disciplines of Yoga – Sister Nivedita exerted great influence over Bharatiyar, shaping his philosophical thought, and vitalizing in him his concepts of social equality, the emancipation of women, secularism, and nationalism. In a later edition of *Ñāṉaratam*, Bharatiyar included a short ode, which he had composed for her:

அருளுக்கு நிவேதனமாய், அன்பினுக்கோர்
aruḷukku nivētaṉamāy, aṉpiṉukkōr
கோயிலாய், அடியேன் நெஞ்சில் *kōyilāy, aṭiyēṉ neñcil*
இருளுக்கு ஞாயிறாய், எமதுயர்
iruḷukku ñāyiṟāy, ematuyar
நாடாம் பயிர்க்கு மழையாய், இங்கு
nāṭām payirkku maḻaiyāy, iṅku
பொருளுக்கு வழியறியா வறிஞர்க்குப்
poruḷukku vaḻiyaṟiyā vaṟiñarkkup
பெரும்பொருளாய்ப் புன்பைத் தாதச்
perumporuḷāyp puṉpait tātac
சுருளுக்கு நெருப்பாகி விளங்கிய தாய்
curuḷukku neruppāki viḷaṅkiya tāy
நிவேதிதையைத் தொழுது நிற்பேன்
nivētitaiyait toḻutu niṟpēṉ

Mother Nivedita full of grace,
Thou temple of love,
Sun to the darkness in my heart,
Rain to the crops of our noble land,

Liberating wealth to the lost and destitute,
Flame to the compendiums of iniquity,
Mother Nivedita, I stand in adoration before thee.

38 The seeming incongruity of this is explained by the appearance (at **), in a later edition of *Ñāṉaratam*, of these two sentences, which presumably had been inadvertently omitted from the first printing: எனக்குப் போதிய வெளிவும், திறனும் கொடுத்து இதன் இரண்டாம் பாகமும் எழுதி முற்றுவிக்கும்படி அவன் புரிந்தால் அது செய்வேன். இல்லாவிட்டால் நானாக முண்டு ஒன்றும் செய்ய மாட்டேன். 'If he grants me sufficient fluency and skill to write up the second part, I shall do it. Otherwise, I shall not proceed with the task by myself.'

39 Mahesh Kumar Sharma was the adopted Bengali name of M. Kuppuswamy Iyer, a renowned translator of contemporary Bengali literature into Tamil.

40 That is, *India*, in which the first parts of *Ñāṉaratam* appeared in instalments.

41 The title of a Bengali poem written by Bankim Chandra Chattopadhayay (Chatterjee) in 1875, and set to music by Jadunath Bhattacharya. Bharatiyar was inspired by this song, first sung by Rabindranath Tagore at the 1896 session of the Indian National Congress, and his Tamil version of it was published in ஆனந்த மடம் *Āṉanta*

maṭam (1908), Mahesh Kumar Sharma's Tamil translation of Chattopadhayay's 1882 novel *Ananda Math* (আনন্দ মঠ *Anondo môṭh*, 'The abbey of bliss'). Set during the famine in Bengal in 1770, and a rebellion against the rule of the East India Company there, *Ananda Math* became a motivational work in the nationalist struggle. *Vande Mataram* was to be a popular anthem for the Indian freedom movement, and was banned by the colonial government from 1905 until 1911 (thus, during the period of the writing of *Ñāṉaratam*), and again from 1930 to 1937. From 1950, it has been the national song of India, enjoying equal honour with the national anthem, Rabindranath Tagore's *Jana Gana Mana* (சன கண மன *Caṉa kaṇa maṉa*, Hindi जन-गण-मन *Jana-gaṇa-mana*).

42 Bharatiyar gives the date according to the Tamil calendar, as the fifteenth day of Tai (tenth month) in Saumya (forty-third year of the sixty-year cycle). This was the day of Sankatahara Chaturthi (சங்கடஹர சதுர்த்தி *Caṅkaṭ ahara caturtti*), an auspicious festival for Hindus, when devotees fast, and pray to Ganesha – god of Intellect and Wisdom, revered as the remover of impediments – to help them overcome the obstacles in their lives.

43 Bharatiyar uses the term பின்மாலைப் பொழுது *piṉ mālaip poḻutu* 'dawn' (பின் *piṉ* 'after' + மாலை *mālai* 'evening, night' + பொழுது *poḻutu* 'time'), referring to Brahmamuhurta (Sanskrit ब्रह्म मुहूर्त *Brahma muhūrta*

lit. 'time of Brahma'), the 48-minute period beginning 96 minutes before sunrise, in correlation with the constellation Cygnus. The serenity of the atmosphere at that time of day is considered conducive to bodily health, emotional strength and spiritual practices, and as a highly auspicious moment for worship or meditation, or beginning a task.

44 Veeraraghava Mudali Street (வீரராகவ முதலித் தெரு *Vīrarākava Mutalit Teru*) is now known as Big Street (பெரிய தெரு *Periya Teru*). Triplicane is the anglicized form of Tiruvallikkeni (திருவல்லிக்கேணி *Tiruvallikkēṇi*), a coastal neighbourhood of central Chennai. Big Street runs north to south from Bharathi Salai (பாரதி சாலை *Pārati Cālai*) to B.V. Naicken Street (பி.வி. நாயக்கன் தெரு *Pi Vi Nāyakkaṉ Teru*).

45 Adyar is the anglicized form of Adaiyaaru (அடையாறு *Aṭaiyāṟu*), a residential neighbourhood in Chennai, on the southern banks of the Adyar River, a 42-km waterway flowing from Malaipattu tank, near Chembarambakkam Lake, north/north-westwards through Kancheepuram, Tiruvallur and Chennai districts, to join the Bay of Bengal at the Adyar estuary.

46 Kalidasa (कालिदास *Kāḷidāsa*) was a Sanskrit playwright (fl. fourth–fifth century AD), often considered ancient India's greatest dramatist. *Shakuntala* (शकुन्तला *Śakuntalā*) is one of his three surviving plays. Almost nothing is

known of his life, but legends abound. In one, he was a bullock-cart driver in Benares (Varanasi). The princess of the region wanted to marry a scholar and poet, but rejected suitor after suitor, including the king's counsellor, as second-rate. In revenge, the counsellor grabbed the uneducated, but good-looking, Kalidasa off his bullock cart, had him dress in a scholar's robes, and after warning him that he was to remain silent at all times, presented him to the princess. Smitten not only by his handsome features, but also by his silence, which she took to be evidence of profound learning, she chose him as her groom. They were married, and eventually the truth came out. At first the princess was angry, but later she advised her husband to pray to the goddess Kali for learning. His plea was granted, and in gratitude, he assumed the name Kalidasa (काळि *Kāḷi* + दास *dāsa* 'devotee') 'devotee of Kali'; and to the princess, he vowed to treat her henceforth as his teacher rather than as his spouse. In response at being spurned as a wife, the princess put a curse on Kalidasa that he would meet his death at the hands of a woman. The legend has him later reduced to vagabondage in Colombo, where the king announced a large prize for anyone who could masterfully complete a stanza of Sanskrit verse. Kalidasa fulfilled the task, but the courtesan he was frequenting at the time discovered his work and, aiming to claim the prize herself, murdered him for it.

47 Although singularly reminiscent of the mind-body dualism in Cartesian philosophy (René Descartes, *Meditationes de Prima Philosophia* [Meditations on first philosophy] [Paris, 1641], Bharatiyar's allusion here is, however, rather to the Vedanta, a tradition of Hindu philosophy reflecting ideas contained in the Upanishads. Advaita (அத்வைத *atvaita*, Skt अद्वैत *advaita* 'non-duality') refers to the idea that the phenomenal transient world is merely an illusory appearance of Brahman (பிரமம் *Piramam*, Skt ब्रह्मन् *Brahman*), the metaphysical Ultimate Reality, that all things are interconnected and that the individual is one with everything in the universe. Dvaita (duality) is the belief that God and individual souls exist as distinct, independent realities.

48 அ is the first syllabic character (representing the vowel/a/) in the conventional order of the components of the Tamil script. My loose translation here is an attempt to reflect Bharatiyar's play on the words ஆநா *ānā* 'the letter அ' and ஆனை *āṉai* 'elephant'. Parallel metaphors could perhaps be found in the Roman alphabet, with English examples, such as *B – bee*, *I – eye* or *U – you*, but I have preferred not to superpose an alternative cultural analogy.

49 The four main social divisions discussed in ancient Hindu texts and observed in traditional Hindu society, namely brahmins (priests, teachers, scholars), kshatriyas (warriors, officials), vaisyas (traders, bankers,

agriculturists), sudras (labourers, servants), were termed *varnas* (Skt वर्ण *varṇa* 'colour'), in contradistinction to *jatis* (Skt जाति *jāti* 'kind, class', cognate with *genus*, *kin*), which emphasized hereditary function, and whose status in relation to the varnas is often disputed. In English, the term *caste* is often used to denote both varnas and jatis. Higher castes were polluted by contact with lower castes; thus, members of a given caste would not take food from those of a lower caste to theirs, but would do so from ones of a similarly ranked or higher caste. Hence brahmins, the highest-ranking on the social scale, were in demand as cooks, since their food was acceptable to all other castes.

50 A trapezoid tower at the entrance of a temple, characteristic of Hindu monumental architecture in southern India.

51 வீணை *vīṇai* (cf. Skt वीणा *vīṇā*, a generic term for plucked musical instruments). The South Indian veena is a seven-stringed, pear-shaped lute, with a second resonance chamber made from a gourd.

52 Bharatiyar's expression is மூன்று விரல் *mūṉṟu viral* 'three virels': 1 virel (finger) = 1.94 cm (≈ ¾ in).

53 பர்வத குமாரி *Parvata Kumāri* < Skt पर्वत *parvata* 'hill, mountain' + कुमारी *kumārī* 'daughter'. It is believed that in the last Kritayuga (see note 138 below) mountains

had wings. Because of this, all beings lived in a state of insecurity since at any moment a mountain might fly and land on their heads. See *The Skanda Purana*, tr. G.V. Tagare (New Delhi, 1950, Book III, §1.4.53b–58): 'Formerly all the mountains had wings.... They glided and flew along and settled on cities and countries, villages and forests. Wherever these mountains settled down like this, men, cows and other living beings were crushed by them. They met with instantaneous death. When Brāhmaṇas and peoples of other castes too perished thereby, this prevented the performance of [sacrifices]... and other rites... [and Indra, the king of the gods] became infuriated. Seizing the thunderbolt he cut off the wings of the powerful mountains.'

54 Stanza 1100 of the *Tirukkuṟaḷ* (திருக்குறள்), the ancient Tamil classic on ethics and morality: கண்ணொடு கண்ணிணை நோக்கொக்கின் வாய்ச்சொற்க | ளென்ன பயனு மில *kaṇṇoṭu kaṇṇiṇai nōkkokkiṉ vāyccoṟka* | *ḷeṉṉa payaṉu mila* (from A.A. Manavalan [ed.], *A Compendium of* Tirukkuṟaḷ *Translations in English* [Chennai, 2014, Vol. 3, pp. 29–30]). The English rendering I have cited is from P.S. Sundaram, *The Kural* (New Delhi, 1990).

55 அபேதம் *apētam*, Skt अभेद *abheda* 'non-difference, indistinction', in contrast to பேதம் *pētam*, भेद *bheda* 'difference, dissimilarity'.

56 போகம் *pōkam*, Skt भोग *bhoga* 'sensual enjoyment, self-gratification', as complementary to யோகம் *yōkam* (योग *yoga* 'union') 'meditation'.

57 Palm trees, that is species of trees of the Arecaceae family, mostly native to tropical and subtropical climates, typically grow to a height of between nine and fifteen metres. The formulation *as high/tall as a palm tree*, meaning 'very high' or 'very tall', is a commonly occurring simile in many languages of India, as well as of western Asia, Africa, and Central and South America.

58 The first hostile use of aircraft in war, however, was on 1 November 1911 – some time after the publication of *Ñāṉaratam* – when four grenades were dropped from an Italian monoplane onto a Turkish camp at Ain Zara in Libya, during the Italo-Turkish War. The Declaration Prohibiting the Discharge of Projectiles and Explosives from Balloons, XIV of the 1907 Hague Convention, had banned aerial bombardment, but Italy was not a signatory to this, and countered protests by arguing that in any case, the ban referred only to missiles ejected from balloons. See Gerard DeGroot, *The Bomb* (London, 2004, p. 2); Charles Stephenson, *A Box of Sand: The Italo-Ottoman War 1911–1912* (Ticehurst, 2014, p. 107).

59 யக்ஷன் *yakṣaṉ*, Skt यक्ष *yakṣa* 'a class of generally benevolent but sometimes mischievous, capricious, sexually rapacious, or even murderous nature spirits

who are the custodians of treasures that are hidden in the earth and in the roots of trees. They are powerful magicians and shape-shifters' (*Encyclopaedia Britannica*).

60 Manmata (மன்மதன் *Maṉmataṉ*, Skt मन्मथ *Manmatha*), also known as Kama (காமன் *Kāman*, काम *Kāma*), is the Hindu god of Love – cf. Eros in the Greek tradition, Cupid in the Roman. His consort is Rati (இரதி *Irati*, रति *Rati*); and from a sugar-cane bow, he shoots floral arrows which can make his target fall in love. (Eros's quiver held two types of arrow: gold-tipped, which kindled passion, and lead-tipped, which doused amorous advances.) In one of the principal Manmata legends, of which there are several versions, Indra – the king of the gods, ruler of heaven, and god of Thunder, Storms, Rain and War – and the other gods are suffering at the hands of a demon who can be defeated only by Shiva's son. So that the ascetic Shiva can produce children, Indra assigns Manmata to interrupt his meditation, and invoke desire in him. Manmata creates a false spring season by taking the form of a fragrant sea breeze, enters Shiva's abode and awakens him with a love-arrow. Shiva, in a fury, opens his third eye, and incinerates Manmata on the spot. At the same time, affected by the arrow, he becomes enamoured of Parvati. Rati undertakes a severe penance and pleads with Parvati to intercede with Shiva to resurrect her husband. Parvati does so, and in response to her request and to Rati's penitential

pleas, Shiva agrees to let Manmata live again, but in a disembodied form.

61 There is perhaps something of an autobiographical element in this description. See S. Vijaya Bharati, *C. Subramania Bharati* (New Delhi, 1972, pp. 1–2): 'Bharati hated English school education and was for ever day-dreaming and writing poetry in Tamil. ... [His] wife, Chellammal, relates how fond he was of "dreaming enchanting day-dreams": Bharati could not concentrate on his studies. Even when he was seven or eight years old he had dreams of an enchanting nature and started writing poems of love and romance.'

62 Bharatiyar's action verb here is உச்சிமோ *uccimō*, defined in the *Tamil Lexicon* (Madras, 1923–1939) as 'To smell the crown of the head, especially of a child, from affection' and in the *Cre-A: Dictionary of Contemporary Tamil* (Chennai, 1992), cross-referenced to உச்சிமுகர் *uccimukar*, as 'kiss the forehead (as a way of showing one's affection)'. Typically, an adult might respond to a young person's greeting with this gesture, or a pat on the head, with a wish for the recipient's good fortune.

63 A group of vernacular Middle Indic languages spoken in India from around the third century BC to the eighth century AD. For long, the popular perception of the Prakrits was that they were deviant forms of Sanskrit,

and they were not recognized as distinct languages. In Sanskrit plays, such as Kalidasa's *Shakuntala*, the main characters typically speak in Sanskrit, while the lesser, and most female, characters typically use a Prakrit.

64 வாகனம் *vākaṉam*, here வாஹனம் *vāhaṉam*, Skt वाहन *vāhana* 'conveyance, carrier, mount', that is, a vehicle, typically an animal or bird, used by a Hindu deity.

65 Brahma (பிரமா *Piramā*, here ப்ரம்மா *Prammā*, Skt ब्रह्मा *Brahmā*), the god of Creation and Knowledge, one of the Hindu divine trinity (திரிமூர்த்தி *tirimūrtti*, त्रिमूर्ति *trimūrti*) of Brahma, Vishnu and Shiva, the respective personifications of the cosmic functions of creation, preservation, and destruction.

66 The determinative faculty or intellect (சித்தம் *cittam*, Skt चित्त *citta* 'intellect, thought') is the aspect of mental function responsible for planning, thinking, and making choices and decisions.

67 Durga (துர்க்கை *Turkkai*, Skt दुर्गा *Durgā*), an aspect of the supernatural creative force, or the primordial mother-goddess Shakti (சக்தி *Cakti*, शक्ति *Śakti*), is associated with truth, purity, motherhood, strength, power, energy protection and war. She is believed to unleash her divine wrath against evildoers for the liberation of the oppressed, and to protect peace and prosperity.

68 The yazh (யாழ் *yāḻ*) was a type of harp, often mentioned in ancient Tamil literature, and depicted in early temple sculptures.

69 Bharatiyar's expression is நான்கு முழம் *nāṉku muḻam* 'four cubits': the *muḻam* (cubit) is based on the distance from the elbow to the tip of the middle finger. The underlying sense of *muḻam* is 'elbow'; cf. cubit < Latin *cubitum*, lit. 'for leaning on', thus 'elbow'. Known as a unit of measurement as far back as in the most ancient human cultures, it varied at different times and in different places, between 45.75 and 55.75 cm. The *muḻ am* of 46.66 cm is used nowadays in commerce in Tamil Nadu for measuring certain items of clothing or strings of jasmine flowers.

70 Bharatiyar's expression is அரை நாழிகை *arai nāḻikai* 'half a nalikei': the nalikei was the sixtieth part of a day, 24 minutes, in the ancient Indian system of time measurement; thus ½ x 24 = 12 minutes. The root of *nāḻ ikai* is *nāḻi*, a unit of capacity, relating to the measurement of time by clepsydras. The twelve-minute period, used in measuring the course of the moon, was known in medieval Europe as a *punctus* 'point'.

71 John 13:34–35 (this and other biblical citations in these notes are taken from the New International Version, 1973–2011): 'A new command I give you: Love one another. As I have loved you, so you must love one another. By this

everyone will know that you are my disciples, if you love one another.'

72 1 John 4:8, 16: 'Whoever does not love does not know God, because God is love.... And so we know and rely on the love God has for us. God is love. Whoever lives in love lives in God, and God in them.'

73 A vajra (வஜ்ரா *vajrā*, Skt वज्र *vajra*) was a powerful, ritual battle-club, which symbolized the properties of a thunderbolt (overpowering energy) and diamond (indestructibility). The iconography of Indra shows him wielding a vajra, which he uses to combat evil: cf. the club of the divine hero Heracles in Greek culture – Hercules in Roman – and the hammer of Thor, the god of Thunder, Lightning and Storms, in Germanic and Nordic cultures.

74 That is, Brahman, the Ultimate Reality.

75 The Gayatri Mantra (காயத்ரி மந்திரம் *Kāyatri mantiram*, Skt गायत्री मंत्र *Gāyatrī mantra*) is recorded in the Rig Veda (இருக்கு வேதம் *Irukku vētam*, ऋग्वेद *Ṛgveda*), a canonical Sanskrit Hindu text, dating from perhaps 1400 BC, and is widely cited in later classical Hindu texts:

> ॐ भूर्भुवः स्वः । तत्सवितुर्वरेण्यं । भर्गो देवस्य धीमहि । धियो यो नः प्रचोदयात् ॥
>
> *Ōm bhūr bhuvaḥ svaḥ | tatsaviturvareṇyaṃ | bhargo devasya dhīmahi | dhiyo yo naḥ prachodayāt*

Om. We meditate on the glory of that Being who has produced this universe; may He enlighten our minds.

English version by Swami Vivekananda, in *The Complete Works of the Swami Vivekananda. Part 1.* Second edn (Lohaghat, 1915, p. 211).

By having the Gayatri Mantra sung by women, Bharatiyar highlights the lack of caste differentiation among the Gandharvas, since in the real world the recitation of such mantras was conventionally the preserve of male brahmins, kshatriyas and vaisyas who had been properly initiated for formal Vedic study. (Not all traditions of Hinduism espouse this restriction, however.)

76 Bharatiyar's term is பூபாள ராகம் *pūpāḷa rākam* 'bhupala raga', that is, a mode or melodic type in Carnatic (South Indian) classical music, specifically used as an aubade. Bhupala raga is a pentatonic scale ascending (in Western notation) C D^b E^b G A^b C, that is, five notes, as the second C is a repetition of the first in a higher octave. See S. Bhagyalekshmy, *Ragas in Carnatic Music* (Trivandrum, 1990).

77 Bharatiyar's phrase is எனது உயிர்ப்படகிற்கு மீகாமன் *eṉatu uyirppaṭakiṟku mīkāmaṉ*, lit. 'master of the boat of my life'. As உயிர் connotes both 'life' and 'soul', I have adopted the wording from the oft-quoted final line of the poem, 'Out of the night that covers me' (later

entitled 'Invictus') (1875) by William Henley, published in his collection, *A Book of Verses* (London, 1888, pp. 56–57), which I feel captures the sense well – and which could indeed have been Bharatiyar's own source text for his imagery.

78 The image is perhaps based on the two-stage Suruli Falls (சுருளி அருவி *Curuḷi Aruvi*), about 10 km south of Cumbam, in Theni District in the western part of Madurai Region. The waterfall mentioned the fifth/ sixth century AD Tamil epic *Silappathikaram* (சிலப்பதிகாரம் *Cilappatikāram*) has been tentatively identified as the Suruli Falls.

79 Dating from perhaps the seventh to the fourth centuries BC, the 24,000-verse Ramayana (रामायणम् *Rāmāyaṇam*), or life of Rama, is one of the two major Sanskrit epics of ancient India, the other being the 100,000-couplet Mahabharata (महाभारतम् *Mahābhāratam*). There are many versions of the Ramayana in Indian languages, including Kamban's retelling, *Ramavataram* (இராமாவதாரம் *Irāmāvatāram*) (*c.* eleventh/twelfth century AD), considered among the greatest literary works in Tamil literature.

80 ஸ்நாநம் *snānam*, Skt स्नानम् *snānam* 'bathing, ablution, immersion in water'. This word had also been adopted into early Christian usage, to translate 'baptism'.

81 ஓம் *ōm*, Skt ॐ *ōṃ*, is a sacred symbolic sound signifying the essence of the Ultimate Reality or consciousness (combining அ *a* denoting Vishnu, உ *u* Shiva (*a* + *u* = *ō*) and ம் *m* Brahma: see note 65 above). Considered as a monosyllabic mantra, it is chanted independently, or before a spiritual recitation, such as the Gayatri Mantra; it is also part of the iconography found in ancient and medieval manuscripts, temples and monasteries.

82 From the penultimate line of John Keats's *Ode on a Grecian urn*:

> ...When old age shall this generation waste,
> Thou wilt remain in midst of other woe
> Than ours a friend to Man, to whom thou say'st
> Beauty is Truth, Truth Beauty. – That is all
> Ye know on Earth, and all ye need to know.

From *Annals of the Fine Arts for MDCCCXIX* (London, 1820, Vol. IV, Art. xvi, p. 639).

These final lines have proved an enigma to critics: for example, Arthur Quiller-Couch, in *Charles Dickens and Other Victorians* (Cambridge, 1925, pp. 146–47), called them 'vague' and 'uneducated'; for T.S. Eliot, in *Dante* (in *Selected Essays*, London, 1932, p. 270), they were 'meaningless'. However, such criticisms misconstrue the depth and complexity of the sentiment. Mahatma Gandhi, I feel, affords a clearer understanding: 'I see and find beauty in Truth or through Truth. All Truths, not merely true ideas, but truthful faces, truthful pictures, or songs are highly beautiful. People generally fail to see Beauty in Truth, the ordinary man runs away from and becomes blind to the beauty in it. Whenever men begin to see Beauty in Truth, then true art will arise. To a true artist only that face is beautiful which, quite apart from its exterior, shines with the Truth within the soul. There is... no Beauty apart from Truth. On the other hand, Truth may manifest itself in forms which may not be outwardly beautiful at all. Socrates we are told, was the most truthful man of his time, and yet his features are said to have been the ugliest in Greece. To my mind he was beautiful because all his life was a striving after Truth' (*Young India*, 13 November 1924, cit. R.K. Prabhu, *Truth is God* [Ahmedabad, 1955, pp. 102–3]).

83 The oneness of existence and the unity and truth of all religions were major precepts of Sri Ramakrishna, the well-known nineteenth-century Bengali mystic.

84 The standard of a perfect God is perfection; see Matthew 5:48: 'Be perfect, therefore, as your heavenly Father is perfect.'

85 Avowing that God is Truth refers to Truth as a moral attribute of God, that Truth is itself in God's very nature. In many places in the Bible, God is defined thus. In John 14:6, 10 & 11, for example, Christ declares, 'I am the way

and the truth and the life.... The words I say to you I do not speak on my own authority. Rather, it is the Father, living in me, who is doing his work. Believe me when I say that I am in the Father and the Father is in me'. Compare Christ's dialogue with Pontius Pilate, the Roman governor of Judaea (in John 18:36–38): 'Jesus said, "My kingdom is not of this world... my kingdom is from another place." "You are a king, then!" said Pilate. Jesus answered, "You say that I am a king. In fact, the reason I was born and came into the world is to testify to the truth. Everyone on the side of truth listens to me." "What is truth?" retorted Pilate.'

86 Rama (இராமன் *Irāmaṉ*, Skt राम *Rāma*), the seventh avatar of Vishnu, personifies the characteristics of an ideal person, having the full panoply of desirable virtues, and fulfilling all the requisite moral and social responsibilities.

87 See note 46 above.

88 ஓம் நம: ப்ரம்மணே *Ōm Namah Prammaṇē*, Skt ॐ नमो ब्रह्मणे *Ōṃ Namo Brahmaṇe*, an invocation to Brahman.

89 ஓம் நம: குமாரியை *Ōm Namah Kumāriyai*, Skt ॐ नमः कुमार्यै *Ōṃ Namaḥ Kumāryai*, in imitation, an invocation to Parvatakumari.

90 In December 1906, Bharatiyar attended the session of the Indian National Congress in Kolkata. The reference here is to that city's Government Art Gallery established

in 1876, and which he would have visited. Inspired by Sister Nivedita, Ernest Havell, appointed Principal of the Government School of Art in 1896, oversaw the sale of much of the Gallery's collection of European paintings, and in turn the purchase of original Indian art works. He collaborated with Nivedita and Abanindranath Tagore in the revival of Indian traditions of painting and sculpture, and an approach to fine art education based on Indian rather than Western models.

91 Mahatma Gandhi was to write, 'All true art is... the expression of the soul. The outward forms have value only in so far as they are the expression of the inner spirit in man... All true art must help the soul to realize its inner self' (*Young India*, 13 November 1924, cit. R.K. Prabhu, *Truth is God* [Ahmedabad, 1955, p. 102]) and 'True art takes note not merely of form but also of what lies behind. There is an art that kills and an art that gives life. True art must be evidence of happiness, contentment and purity of its authors' (*Young India*, 11 August 1921 [Prabhu, *Truth is God*, p. 104). This is an echo of the perception, attributed to Aristotle, that the aim of art is to represent not the outward appearance of things, but their inward significance, thus expressing through physical reality a psychological insight and perceptiveness. The principle thus expressed is, however, an extended generalization to all art of Aristotle's actual statement that poetry tends to express the universal,

history the particular: 'for poetry tends to give general truths while history gives particular facts' (*Poetics* 1451b1.5, in *Aristotle*, tr. W.H. Fyfe [Cambridge MA, 1932, Vol. 23]). The pediment sculptures and the metopes of the Parthenon in Athens, as well as the monumental frieze that portrays the procession of the annual Panathenaic festival, sculpted between *c.*443 and 437 BC, are regarded as the zenith of European classical art and altogether an exquisite example of poetry in marble.

92 Cf. Menander (fourth century BC): 'He whom the gods love dies young.'

93 Supernatural celestial beings, angels, deities.

94 மோக்ஷம் *mōkṣam*, Skt मोक्ष *mokṣa*, the ineffable experience of pure consciousness and bliss, after final liberation from the cycle of death and rebirth or reincarnation and the sufferings and limitations of worldly existence.

95 Sankara ([?]eighth century AD), a philosopher who had an important influence on the development of the doctrine of Advaita Vedanta.

96 Suka features in the Mahabharata as an ascetic who attains *moksha*.

97 Janaka ([?]seventh/eighth century BC), a king of Videha, in the foothills of the Himalayas, now revered as an exemplar of non-attachment to material possessions, and freedom from worldly illusions.

98 This is perhaps an allusion to the dialogic form typically employed in specialized Sanskrit treatises, where knowledge is presented through prima facie argument (पूर्व पक्ष *pūrva pakṣa*) and rejoinder (उत्तर पक्ष *uttara pakṣa*); or, to Greek classical dialectics, for example, Socratic and Platonic forms of reasoning and learning based on dialogue.

99 In this situation, of taking either one path or the other, there is no logical *via media*. 'Compromise' in this case is agreeing on a choice between alternatives, as there is no third way.

100 The theme of social discrimination based on colour, and by extension caste etc., is echoed in Bharatiyar's delightful lines in முரசு பாட்டு *Muracu pāṭṭu* 'Drum song' (1917):

வெள்ளை நிறத்தொரு பூனை *veḷḷai niṟatoru pūṉai*
எங்கள் வீட்டில் வளருது கண்டீர் *eṅkaḷ vīṭṭil vaḷarutu kaṇṭīr*
பிள்ளைகள் பெற்றதப் பூனை *piḷḷaikaḷ peṟṟatap pūṉai*
அவை பேருக்கொரு நிறம் ஆகும் *avai pērukkoru niṟam ākum*
சாம்பல் நிறத்தொரு குட்டி *cāmbal niṟattoru kuṭṭi*
கரும் சாந்தின் நிறம் ஒரு குட்டி *karum cāntiṉ niṟam ōru kuṭṭi*
பாம்பின் நிறமொரு குட்டி *pāmpiṉ niramoru kuṭṭi*
வெள்ளை பாலின் நிறம் ஒரு குட்டி *veḷḷai pāliṉ niṟam ōru kuṭṭi*

எந்த நிறமிருந்தாலும் *enta niṟamiruntālum*
அவை யாவும் ஒரே தரம் அன்றோ
avai yāvum orē taram aṉṟō
இந்த நிறம் சிறிதென்றும் *inta niṟam ciṟiteṉṟum*
இஃது ஏற்றம் என்றும் சொல்லலாமோ
iḵtu ēṟṟam eṉṟum collalāmō
வண்ணங்கள் வேற்றுமை பட்டால்
vaṇṇaṅkaḷ vēṟṟumai paṭṭāl
அதில் மானுடர் வேற்றுமை இல்லை
atil māṉuṭar vēṟṟumai illai
எண்ணங்கள் செய்கைகள் யாவும்
eṇṇaṅkaḷ ceykaikaḷ yāvum
இங்கு யாவர்க்கும் ஒன்றென காணீர்!
iṅku yāvarkkum oṉṟeṉa kāṇīr

You've seen that in our house
We have a pet white cat.
That queen gave birth to kittens,
Each of a different colour.
One of the kittens was ash-grey
Another kitten jet-black,
Yet another kitten the colour of a snake,
And one more kitten as white as milk.
Whatever may be their colour,
Are they not all of the same blood?
How can we say that any one colour
Outclasses any other?

Their colours may be different,
But human beings do not differ;
You can see that, in thoughts and deeds,
We are all one.

101 Bharatiyar's simile is நெல்லிக் கனிபோல் *nellik kaṉipōl* 'like myrobalan', taken from the Vajrasuchi Upanishad, of uncertain date, a philosophical critique of the division of human beings, and the assertion that anyone can achieve the highest spiritual state of existence. The emblic myrobalan, or Indian gooseberry (*Phyllanthus emblica*), is a small fruit which, according to legend, Buddha received from Indra after attaining enlightenment. In Ayurvedic medicine, it is considered to stimulate the brain to rebalance the water, fire, and air elements within the body.

102 Cf. Paul to the Galatians, 6:7: 'Do not be deceived: God cannot be mocked. A man reaps what he sows.'

103 This refers to stanza 22 in Avvaiyar's *Nalvaḻi*:

பாடுபட்டுத் தேடிப் பணத்தைப் புதைத்து வைத்துக்
pāṭupaṭṭut tēṭip paṇattaip putaittu vaittuk
கேடுகெட்ட மானிடரே கேளுங்கள்; கூடுவிட்டு இங்கு
kēṭukeṭṭa māṉiṭarē kēḷuṅkaḷ; kūṭuviṭṭu iṅku
ஆவிதான் போயின பின்பு யாரே அனுபவிப்பார்
āvitāṉ pōyiṉa piṉpu yārē aṉupavippār
பாவிகாள் அந்தப் பணம்? *pāvikāḷ antap paṇam?*

Ignoble ones, o hear me out –
Your wage as rate for work is earned,
Why go and that in earth conceal,
As once your soul ayond has turned
Who else is there to reap that weal?

104 The six worlds, or planes of existence (லோகம் *lōkam*, Skt लोक *loka*), in the Hindu cosmology – interpreted diversely in different texts, with the numbers and configurations variously delineated – are the Earth (பூ *pū*, भू *bhū*); *Bhuva* (புவ *puva*, भुव *bhuva*), the atmosphere; *Sva* (ஸ்வ *sva*, स्व *sva*), the solar system; *Maha* (மஹ *maha*, मह *maha*), interstellar space; *Jana* (ஜன *jaṉa*, जन *jana*), intergalactic space; and *Tapa* (தப *tapa*, तप *tapa*), extra-universal space. Beyond these is *Satya* (சத்திய *cattiya*, सत्य *satya*) or Truth, the abode of Brahma, the highest plane of consciousness, where the yogi achieves *moksha*. The Gayatri Mantra features the first three, *Bhū*, *Bhuva* and *Sva*, that is, the physical, astral and celestial planes.

105 India has a robust joint family system with different generations – including grandparents, parents, aunts and uncles, nephews and nieces, and others – often living with a couple and their children in the same household.

106 Rayars are an ethnolinguistic group descending from Maharashtrians who migrated to Thanjavur during the eighteenth century AD. Their mother tongue is a Tamilized dialect of Marathi, and they live largely in the central and

northern parts of Tamil Nadu. Prominent members of the Rayar community include T. Madhava Rao, one of the early pioneers of the Indian National Congress, who served as Diwan (Premier) of the Kingdom of Travancore and the Gaekwarship of Baroda; and his eldest son, T. Ananda Rao, who was Diwan of the Kingdom of Mysore at the time of the publication of *Ñāṉaratam*.

107 Some Vaishnavite brahmins impress marks in ochre paste on their foreheads, comprising vertical streaks from the hairline to the bridge of the nose. Similar symbols can also be applied to the shoulders, arms, chest and back.

108 ஜட்கா *jaṭkā* (< Marathi झटका *jhaṭkā* 'jerk, jolt'). See Henry Yule & Arthur Burnell, *Hobson-Jobson* (London, 1886, p. 362): 'The native cab of Madras, and of Mofussil [= provincial] towns in that Presidency; a conveyance only to be characterised by the epithet *ramshackle*... It consists of a sort of box with venetian windows, on two wheels, and drawn by a miserable pony. It is entered by a door at the back.'

109 கோச்சு *kōccu* (< English *coach*): a four-wheeled, horse-drawn carriage.

110 Ground peppercorn in water is an Ayurvedic remedy for headache.

111 காப்பு *kāppu* 'protection bracelet', a metal wristband or anklet traditionally given to infants or young children to

wear to shield them against disease, negative energy and malevolent spirits.

112 சுண்ணாம்பு *cuṇṇāmpu* 'slaked lime', $Ca(OH)_2$ calcium hydroxide, historically known in India as chunam, is commonly added as a digestive aid to paan (பீடா *pīṭā*), a preparation of areca nuts, and sometimes other ingredients such as fennel seeds, chewing tobacco or chopped coconut, wrapped in betel leaves.

113 In 1907, Bharatiyar was a founder of the Chennai Jana Sangam (சென்னை ஜன சங்கம் *Ceṉṉai Jaṉa Caṅkam*) Madras People's Society, whose 'special purpose was to train young men to preach Swadeshism and Boycott.... The founding of the Chennai Jana Sangam intensified agitational politics' (N. Rajendran, 'Agitational politics and methods of mass political mobilisation in Tamil Nadu, 1905–1908', in *Proceedings of the Indian History Congress, 58th Session, Bangalore, 1997* [Aligarh, 1998, p. 504]). The members campaigned extensively in the towns and villages of Tamil Nadu.

114 Iyengars are a brahmin ethnoreligious group whose members follow Sri Vaishnavism (a denomination claiming that the Vedas, the most ancient scriptures of Hinduism, are dedicated exclusively to the worship of Vishnu) and the Visishtadvaita (விசிஷ்டாத்வைத *viciṣṭātvaita*, Skt विशिष्टाद्वैत *viśiṣṭādvaita*) 'qualified non-dualism', characterized by diversity subsumed by the

underlying unity of Brahman, and propounded by the eleventh-century sage, Ramanuja.

115 That is, they were gourmands. Tamarind rice (புளியஞ்சோற்று *puḷiyañcōṟṟu*) is a traditional dish common in South India.

116 The ¼ anna (அணா *aṇā*), or 1 pice (பைசா *paicā*), was a coin in the currency of British India. In 1909, the lowest denomination coin in general circulation was 1 pie (பை *pai*): 3 pies = 1 pice, 4 pice = 1 anna, 16 annas = 1 rupee (ரூபாய் *rūpāy*). The cover price of the first edition of *Ñāṉaratam* was one anna. In Pondicherry, the currency was 24 caches (காசு *kācu*) = 1 fanon (பணம் *paṇam*), 8 fanons = 1 roupie. The roupie and the rupee circulated at par.

117 Swaraj (ஸ்வராஜ்யம் *svarājyam,* Skt स्वराज *svarāj*) 'self-rule', or independence. In its fullest sense, Swaraj is based on the utopian vision of sovereignty of the people based on moral rather than state authority, and freedom from governmental domination, whether foreign or national.

118 Shyamji (or Shyamaji) Krishnavarma was a barrister and journalist, who edited *The Indian Sociologist*, a pro-independence broadsheet printed in London (1905–1907) and Paris (1907–1914, 1920–1922). In 1905, he founded the Indian Home Rule Society in London, where he opened India House, a hostel for Indian students, among whom

he propagated nationalist views. See Ganesh Lal Varma, *Shyamji Krishna Varma* (New Delhi, 1993); Harald Fischer-Tiné, *Shyamji Krishnavarma* (New Delhi, 2014).

119 The name comes from the story of Thondaradipodi Alwar, one of the twelve Alwars, ancient Tamil poet-saints of uncertain date. Thondaradipodi Alwar was an acolyte of Sri Ranganatha, a form of Vishnu reclining on his *vahana*, Adishesha (आदिशेष *Ādiśeṣa*), the multi-headed, snake-like divinity, who is said to hold all the planets of the universe in his hoods. Legend has it that to atone for a fault he had committed, Thondaradipodi Alwar picked up dust from the footprints of Sri Ranganatha's devotees, and put it on his head. Hence, his name தொண்டரடிப்பொடியாழ்வார் *Toṇṭar-aṭip-poṭiy-ālvār* 'Alwar of the dust from the feet of devotees'. Bharatiyar and his companions nicknamed their friend பணத்தொண்டரடிப்பொடியாழ்வார் *Paṇat-toṇṭar-aṭip-poṭiy-ālvār* 'Alwar of the dust from the feet of devotees of money'.

120 The pagoda, an Indian dynastic, and later colonial, coin, was by the early nineteenth century the major gold denomination of the Madras Presidency. Mintage was discontinued in 1817, when the rupee standard was introduced. Its Tamil name is வராகன் *varākan̲*, Skt वराह *varāha* 'boar', from the boar avatar of Vishnu which figured on several coins of South India from as early as the Chalukya dynasty in the sixth century AD.

121 ஓம் சக்தியை நம: *Ōm Caktiyai Namah*, Skt ॐ शक्त्यै नमः *Ōṃ Śaktiyai Namaḥ*, an invocation to Shakti (Ambika), the primordial cosmic energy, the dynamic feminine aspect of Shiva, goddess of Supreme Power and Invincibility; ஓம் பராயை நம: *Ōm Parāyai Namah*, ॐ परायै नमः *Ōṃ Parāyai Namaḥ*, an invocation to Saraswati, the mother goddess and goddess of Knowledge, Wisdom, Music, Arts and Speech.

122 'Hail to thee, Mother.' The double entendre here is through an allusion to the nationalist song, *Vande Mataram*.

123 ஸாஷ்டாங்கம் *sāṣṭāṅkam*, Skt साष्टाङ्ग *sāṣṭāṅga* 'eight parts of the body', that is, as a reverential posture of prostration, with the forehead, chest, hands, knees and feet touching the ground.

124 *தர்மம் சர tarmam cara*: this is a transliteration of Sanskrit of part of a Vedic instruction, from the Taittiriya Upanishad (*c.* sixth century BC): सत्यं वद। धर्मं चर। *satyaṃ vada, dharmaṃ cara* 'Speak the truth. Perform dharma' (*Taittiriya Upanisad,* tr. Swami Sharyananda [Madras, 1921, pp. 40–41]). Bharatiyar adds a Tamil translation in parentheses: *அறத்தை ஒழுகு aṟattai oḻuku* 'practise virtue'. The Sanskrit dictum has been adopted over the years as a motto by several institutions and corporations; translations used include 'be righteous', 'follow the path of righteousness', 'lead a righteous life', 'offer your duty'.

125 தபஸ் *tapas*, Skt तपस् *tapas*; see Arthur A. Macdonell, *A Practical Sanskrit Dictionary* (London, 1929): 'heat; fire; torment; penance, self-castigation, mortification, religious austerity, devotion.' *Tapas* refers to an element of the spiritual path toward self-realization, through a variety of tension-eliminating practices ranging from asceticism to restraint through meditation.

126 Cf. Shelley, *Queen Mab*, II.236–37: 'I tell thee that those living things, / To whom the fragile blade of grass, / That springeth in the morn / And perisheth ere noon, / Is an unbounded world; / I tell thee that those viewless beings, / Whose mansion is the smallest particle / Of the impassive atmosphere, / Think, feel and live like man; / That their affections and antipathies, / Like his, produce the laws / Ruling their moral state.'

127 ஜய தர்ம ராஜாய *Jaya Tarma Rājāya,* Skt जय धर्म राजाय *Jaya Dharma Rājāya*, an invocation to Yama; ஜயயமாய *Jayayamāya* < जय यमाय *Jaya Yamāya*, an invocation to Yama; ஜய வைவஸ்வதாயா *Jaya Vaivasvatāyā* < जय वैवस्वत *Jaya Vaivasvata*, an invocation to Yama; ஜய ஸூர்ய தேஜஸ்வினே *Jaya Sūrya Tējasviṉē* < जय सूर्य तेजस्वीने *Jaya Sūrya Tējasviṉē,* an invocation to Surya, god of the Sun; ஜய மஹோக்ராய *Jaya Mahōkrāya* < जय महोग्राय *Jaya Mahogrāya*, an invocation to Surya; ஜய ஜய மஹாசாந்தாய *Jaya Jaya Mahācāntāya* < जय जय महाशान्ताय *Jaya Jaya Mahāśāntāya*, an invocation to Shiva.

128 Bal Gangadhar Tilak was a pioneer of the Indian independence movement, and before Gandhi, the most widely known Indian political leader. In April 1908, two Bengali youths, Prafulla Chaki and Khudiram Bose, threw a bomb at a carriage in Muzzafarpur (now in the state of Bihar), killing its occupants, the wife and daughter of Pringle Kennedy, a local barrister. The bombers' target had, however, been Douglas Kingsford, the district judge, who was travelling in a similar carriage just behind the one hit. For defending the assailants in his Marathi newspaper केसरी *Kesari* (lion), Tilak was arrested. Found guilty of sedition, he was sentenced to six years' imprisonment in Mandalay, Burma. In the same year, Bharatiyar, who was an ardent supporter of Tilak, wrote a song in his honour, the refrain of which is:

வாழ்க திலகன் நாமம் ! நாமம் ! வாழ்க ! வாழ்கவே !
vāḻka Tilakaṉ nāmam! nāmam! vāḻka! vāḻkavē!
வீழ்க கொடுங்கோன்மை ! வீழ்க ! வீழ்கவே!
vīḻka koṭuṅkōṉmai! vīḻka! vīḻkavē!

> Long live the name of Tilak. Long live, long live the good name.
> Down with autocracy! Down, down, may it fall!

129 மகா சக்தி *Makā Cakti*, Skt महाशक्ति *Mahāśakti*, an epithet of Shiva.

130 Ola leaves (ஓலை *ōlai*), that is leaves of the talipot palm (*Corypha umbraculifera*) were used in South India as

manuscript material before the widespread introduction of paper.

131 Bharatiyar uses the Sanskrit-derived compound கணிதசாஸ்திரம் *kaṇitacāstiram*, which can mean 'astrology' or 'astronomy' as well as 'mathematics'.

132 சாதுர் வர்ண்ணம் மயாஸ்ருஷ்டம் குணகர்ம விபாகச: *cātur varṇam mayāsruṣṭam kuṇakaram vipākacah*. This is a transliteration of Sanskrit of an extract from the Bhagavad Gita (श्रीमद्भगवद्गीता *Śrīmadbhagavadgītā*), Chapter 4, sloka 13: चातुर्वर्ण्यं मया सृष्टं गुणकर्मविभागश: *cāturvarṇyaṃ mayā sṛṣṭaṃ guṇakarmavibhāgaśaḥ*. The English translation here is from Lars Martin Fosse, *The Bhagavad Gita* (Woodstock, 2007, p. 42). See Swami Mukundananda (<www.holy-bhagavad-gita.org/chapter/4/verse/13>): 'The Vedas classify people into four categories of occupations, not according to their birth, but according to their natures. Such varieties of occupations exist in every society.... Vedic philosophy... states that the material energy is constituted of three *guṇas* (modes): *sattva guṇa* (mode of goodness), *rajo guṇa* (mode of passion), and *tamo guṇa* (mode of ignorance). The Brahmins are those who have a preponderance of the mode of goodness. They are predisposed toward teaching and worship. The Kshatriyas are those who have a preponderance of the mode of passion mixed with a smaller amount of the mode of goodness. They are inclined toward administration and management.

The Vaishyas are those who possess the mode of passion mixed with some mode of ignorance. Accordingly, they form the business and agricultural class. Then there are the Shudras, who are predominated by the mode of ignorance. They form the working class. This classification was neither meant to be according to birth, nor was it unchangeable. Shree Krishna explains in this verse that the classification of the *Varṇāśhram* [वर्णाश्रम् "caste stratification"] system was according to people's qualities and activities.' Bharatiyar wrote in an article entitled 'The crime of caste' (*The Commonwealth*, 6 [145], 6 October 1916), 'caste law is leagues away from the Gita theory... instead of the four Varnas, you have four thousand castes. ...But, alas, the ignorant masses or our country have been made to believe that this caste chaos is a special divine gift to our country and whoever transgresses it has to go to hell. It is this belief more than anything else that makes people insensible to the injurious results of caste.'

133 The Puranas (புராணம் *purāṇam*, Skt पुराण *purāṇa*) comprise a genre of ancient Indian literature covering a wide range of topics, particularly about legends and folklore, but also subjects such as astronomy, grammar, medicine, philosophy, and theology.

134 Itihasas (இதிகாசம் *itikācam*, here இதிஹாஸம் *itihāsam*, Skt इतिहास *itihiāsa*) are collections of ancient Sanskrit texts of important events in Hinduism, for example, the Mahabharata and the Ramayana.

135 Such is called अश्वस्तन *aśvastana* 'one who makes no provision for the morrow', considered a meritorious practice: see *Yajnavalka Smriti. Book I. The Âchâra Adhyâya*, tr. Śriśa Chandra Vidyârṇava (Allahabad, 1918, §5.128[a]).

136 கலியுகம் *kaliyukam*, Skt कलियुग *kaliyuga* 'Age of Kali', the last in the cycle of four *yugas*, or world ages, this one characterized by misery, corruption, conflict, social instability, and spiritual degeneration (Mahabharata, Book 3, §189). See Devendrakumar Patil, *Cultural History from the Vāyu Purāna* (Delhi, 1916, pp. 74–75): 'In this Yuga, the character of the people is dominated by vices, such as, violence, hatred, falsehood, etc. Dharma is on the decline and famine and pestilence take their toll....The people, impious and addicted to bad customs...do not study the Vedas nor do they perform sacrifices. The Kṣatriyas and the Vaiśyas become exterminated gradually, and the Śūdras and the low-born...are befriending the Brahmins in matters such as eating, drinking and merry-making. Society is topsy-turvy...The earth is barren of vegetation.'

137 The current cycle began 6,476,898 years ago. The present yuga is traditionally held to have begun in 3102 BC and will end in AD 428899, although other durations have been proposed.

138 கிருதயுகம் *kirutayukam*, Skt कृतयुग *kṛtayuga* 'Age of Truth', the first in the yuga cycle, preceded by Kaliyuga

of the previous cycle. Kritayuga lasts for 1,728,000 years. See Devendrakumar Patil, *Cultural history from the Vāyu Purāna* (Delhi, 1916, pp. 72–73): 'The people lived without malice towards each other and faced no mutual conflicts. There were no houses for them to reside [in] and they resorted to mountains and sea-shores for shelter. ...The animal kingdom did not exist, nor the vegetable world. The time was conducive to fulfilment of all desires and the climate was temperate. The people were ever young and...were all equal in matters of birth, beauty and of various virtues. ...The concept of varṇāśrama [caste stratification] ...did not exist then.' See S. Vijaya Bharati, *C. Subramania Bharati*. Second edn (New Delhi, 2014, p. 24): 'Bharati yearned for Krutha Yuga to become established at once in this world. ...He conceived Krutha Yuga in which the universe would be perfect and without evil. He pictured a joyous world free from sufferings, a world of enlightenment unmarred by ignorance, a world which rejected superstitions, a world of progress that had done away with corruption. Justice and wisdom lived together in this paradise of his conception; here unity and goodwill prevailed among men.'

139 For Bharatiyar's reference to the nature of a brahmin, see *Vajrasūchi-Upanishaḍ of Sāmaveḍa*, in K. Nārāyaṇ asvāmi Aiyar, *Thirty Minor Upanishaḍs* (Madras, 1914, pp. 111–12): 'Who indeed then is brāhmaṇa? Whoever he may be, he who has directly realised his Āṭmā and who

is directly cognizant, like the myrobalan in his palm, of his Āṭmā that is without a second, that is devoid of class and actions, that is free from the fault of faults of the six stains [fn. *hunger, thirst, grief, confusion, old age, and death*] and the six changes [fn. *Birth, existence etc.*], that is of the nature of truth, knowledge, bliss, and eternity, that is without any change in itself, that is the substratum of all the kalpas, that exists penetrating all things that pervades everything within and without as ākāś, that is of nature of undivided bliss, that cannot be reasoned about and that is known only by direct cognition. He who by the reason of having obtained his wishes is devoid of the faults of thirst after worldly objects and passions, who is the possessor of the qualifications beginning with śama [fn. *Sama, ḍama, uparaṭi, ṭiṭīkshā, samāḍhāna, and sraḍḍhā*], who is free from emotion, malice, thirst after worldly objects, desire, delusion, etc., whose mind is untouched by pride, egoism, etc., who possesses all these qualities and means – he only is the brāhmaṇa.'

140 சந்தியா தியானம் *cantiyā tiyāṉam*, Skt संध्याध्यानम् *saṃdhyādhyānam* 'evening meditation', that is prayers at twilight (= vespers, evensong).

141 Kanvar and Tapas meditate on the infinite, formless Brahman, beyond time and space; by contrast, Bharatiyar meditates on a symbol to invoke a deity, as an intermediary to understand Brahman. See Purushottam

Agrawal, 'Nirguṇa and Saguṇa', in *Brill's Encyclopedia of Hinduism Online*, <dx.doi.org/10.1163/2212-5019_BEH_COM_2050210> last accessed 15 February 2023.

142 In the Mahabharata, Maitreyi is described as unmarried, but she features in the Brihadaranyaka Upanishad debating metaphysical questions on the nature of eternity and temporality with her husband Yajnavalkya (possibly fl. eighth century BC), one of the earliest Hindu and yogic philosophers.

143 Traditionally, ascetics would wear clothes made of bark. In the Ramayana, Rama's stepmother, Kaikeyi, persuaded his father, King Dasaratha, to exile him, so that Bharata, her own son by Dasaratha, could become heir to the throne. In obedience, Rama accepted his banishment, and on his departure addressed Dasaratha (Ramayana, 2.37.4–5):

> O King, having renounced all pleasures to live on the products of the forest, what need have I for wealth, an army or other requisites?... Bring me garments of bark. I go to pass fourteen years in the forest, and need but a spade to dig for roots and fruit and a creel and basket.

From *The Ramayana of Valmiki*, tr. Hari Prasad Shastri (London, 1952, Vol. I).

144 Vyasa is traditionally credited with composing the Mahabharata, supposedly dictating the work from

memory to Ganesha, the elephant god, who acted as his scribe. The location of the battle was Kurukshetra, a region in the modern Indian state of Haryana. The conflict arose from a struggle between the scions of two related dynastic families, the Kauravas and the Pandavas (Vyasa features as grandfather of both), for the throne of Hastinapur, in the modern Indian state of Uttar Pradesh. Arjuna was a Pandava archer whose role in the confrontation has rendered him an important figure in Hindu scriptures, iconography, and mythology. He is the archetypal reluctant hero: although he was intrepid, before the battle he was overcome with doubt, and turned to Krishna, who served as his charioteer, for advice. Krishna reminded him that his hereditary duty (dharma) as a warrior was to fight for virtue, and refusing to do so would be cowardly. Arjuna is granted cosmic vision, allowing him sight of Krishna's true form, which is described as beyond human comprehension, encompassing the sun and moon, with all the deities merging into one. He begs Krishna to return to human form, as the divine manifestation is too overpowering to behold, and asks forgiveness for having failed to appreciate Krishna's divinity. With revitalized faith and renewed sense of dharma, Arjuna finds the courage to fight. Eventually, the Pandavas win the battle, and virtue prevails.

145 This is an allusion to a story in the *Devi Mahatmyam* (देवीमाहात्म्यम् *Devīmāhātmyam*), a Hindu devotional-

philosophical text of the fifth to seventh centuries AD, describing Shakti, manifesting as goddess Durga, leading the forces of good to victory over those of evil. Raktabija (Skt रक्त *rakta* 'blood' + बीज *bīja* 'seed'), an asura, or demon, had a favour from Brahma that whenever a drop of his blood fell on the ground, a duplicate Raktabija would spring up at that spot. To kill Raktabija, Durga created the warrior-goddess Kausiki from her own body. Kausiki took the form of Kali, who devoured the duplicate Raktabijas, and licked Raktabija's blood from his wounds before it could touch the ground. Thus was Raktabija's life energy gradually depleted, until he expired. See Manmatha Nath Dutt, *A Prose English Translation of Markandeya Puranam* (Calcutta, 1896, §lxxxviii).

146 Cf. the Greek myth of Heracles' labour to kill the nine-headed Lernaean hydra, or snake-like water monster. If one of its heads were cut off, two would grow back in its place. To accomplish his task, Heracles enlisted the help of his nephew Lolaus. As soon as Heracles cut off a head, Lolaus cauterized the neck stump with a flaming torch, to prevent any regrowth.

147 தமோகுணம் *tamōkuṇam*, Skt तमोगुण *tamoguṇa* 'The subtle quality of darkness or ignorance manifested in torpor, sleep, lust, anger, etc.' (*Tamil Lexicon*).

148 At the end of 'The cuckoo's song' (குயில் பாட்டு *kuyil pāṭṭu*) (1912), his daydream poem à la Samuel Coleridge's

Kubla Khan (London, 1816 [1797]), Bharatiyar has the poet embrace the cuckoo (*kuyil*), which immediately transforms into a beautiful young woman, whom he kisses. Here, he adapts some of the sentences from the end of Chapter Three and of this chapter of *Ñāṉaratam*:

பெண்ணவளைக் கண்டு
பெருங்களிகொண்டாங்ஙனே
peṇṇavaḷaik kaṇṭu peruṅkaḷikoṇṭāṅṅaṉē
நண்ணித் தழுவி நறுங்கள் ளிதழினையே
naṇṇit taḻuvi naṟuṅkaḷ ḷitaḻiṉaiyē
முத்தமிட்டு முத்தமிட்டு மோகப் பெருமயக்கில்
muttamiṭṭu muttamiṭṭu mōkap perumayakkil
சித்தம் மயங்கிச் சிலபோழ் திருந்த பின்னே,
cittam mayaṅkic cilapōḻ tirunta piṉṉē,
பக்கத் திருந்தமணிப் பாவையுடன் சோலையெலாம்
pakkat tiruntamaṇip pāvaiyuṭaṉ cōlaiyelām
ஒக்க மறைந்திடலும், ஓஹோ! எனக்கதறி
okka maṟaintiṭalum, ōhō! eṉakkataṟi
வீழ்ந்தேன். பிறகு விழிதிறந்து பார்க்கையிலே
vīḻntēṉ. piṟaku viḻitiṟantu pārkkaiyilē
சூழ்ந்திருக்கும் பண்டைச் சுவடி, எழுதுகோல்,
cūḻntirukkum paṇṭaic cuvaṭi, eḻutukōl,
பத்திரிகைக் கூட்டம், பழம்பாய் – வரிசை யெல்லாம்
pattirikaik kūṭṭam, paḻampāy – varicai yellām
ஒத்திருக்க 'நாம் வீட்டில் உள்ளோம்'
எனவுணர்ந்தேன்.
ottirukka nām vīṭṭil uḷḷōm eṉavuṇarntēṉ.

Seized by a supreme rapture I took her
and kissed her passionately on her lips.
In this loving swoon a few moments passed.
Suddenly garden and kuyil vanished.
I fell down, as everything blacked out.
Reviving at last, I saw around me
old manuscripts, pens, newspaper bundles,
the old mat – and I knew I was at home.

From 'Kuyil's song.' In Prema Nandakumar (Tr), *Poems of Subramania Bharati*. Second edn (New Delhi, 1982, p. 140).

ஞானரதம்

எழுதியவர்

சுப்பிரமணிய பாரதி

மொழிபெயர்ப்பாளர்

க்ரெகரி ஜேம்ஸ்

உள்ளடக்கம்

ஓம்,

ஸ்ரீமதி நிவேதிதா தேவிக்கு
ஸமர்ப்பணம் செய்யப்பட்டது.

முகவுரை.

புஸ்தகமெழுதினால் அதற்கு முகவுரை யெழுதித் தீரவேண்டு மென்ற ஸம்பிரதாயம் ஒன்றிருக்கிறது. உலகத்தில் எந்தவேலை செய்யப்போனாலும் 'ஸம்பிர தாயம்' என்ற தொல்லை யொன்று வந்து முன்னே நிற்கிறது. ஆனால், நான் இதை அதிகமாக நீட்டிப் படிப்பவர்களை ஆயாஸப்படுத்த உத்தேசமில்லை. ஒரே வார்த்தைமட்டிலும் இங்கு சொல்ல விரும்புகிறேன்.

அதாவது: இந்நூல் நானாக எழுதினதில்லை. எல்லாம் நடத்தும் பரமாத்மா ஞானதீர மிலலாத ஏழையேனைக் கொண்டு ஞானரதத்தில் ஏற்றினான். எத்தனையோ வினோதங்களில் இதுவு மொன்று. எனவே, இதிலுள்ள குற்றங் குறைகளுக்கு நான் பொறுப்பாளியில்லை.

இன்னுமொரு சிறிய செய்தி. இதில் ஒரு பகுதி பத்திரிகையில் வெளிபட்டபோது, எனக்கு மிகுந்த உற்சாக முண்டாகும்படி தூண்டிக் கடிதமெழுதிய எனது நணபர் மஹேசகுமார சர்மாவுக்கு பகிரங்கமாக

எனது நன்றியும் மதிப்பும் தெரிவிக்க விரும்புகிறேன். இவருடைய கல்வியையும், அறிவுத் தெளிவையும் ரஸிகத் தன்மையையும் தமிழ் நாட்டாருக்குப் பல முறை நன்கு திருஷ்டாந்தப்படுத்திக் காட்டியிருக்கிறார். ஆதலின் அதையெல்லாம் பற்றி விரிக்க எனக்கு விருப்பமில்லை. ஆனாலும், இப்படிப்பட்ட பண்டிதர்களைத் தமிழ்நாட்டார் போதியபடி ஆதரவு செய்து அவர்களை வேறு ஸாதாரணப்பிரவிருத்திகளில் மனம் செலுத்தாதபடி காத்துக்கொள்ளவில்லை யென்ற குறை என் மனதி லிருக்கிறது. இந்த ஸந்தர்ப்பத்தை யொட்டி அதனையும் வெளிப்படையாகச் சொல்லித் தீர்த்துவிட்டேன். வந்தேமாதரம்.

ஸௌம்ய ௵
தைமீ கரு-உ
புதுச்சேரி

சி. ஸுப்பிரமணிய பாரதி.

உ

ஞானரதம்.

பீடிகை,

பின் மாலைப்பொழுது. திருவல்லிக்கேணி, வீரராகவ முதலி தெருவில் கடற்பாரிசத்தை நோக்கியிருக்கும் ஓர் வீட்டு மேடையின் மீது சிரம பரிகாரத்தின் பொருட்டு ஓர் மஞ்சத்தின் மீது படுத்துக்கொண்டிருந்தேன். ஆனந்த கரமான கடற்காற்று நான் படுத்திருந்த முன்னறையிலே நான்கு பக்கங்களிலிருந்தும், கண்ணாடிச் சாளரங்களின் மூலமாகவும், புறக்கதவு நிலைகளின் மூலமாகவும், வந்து நிரம்பிய வண்ணமாக இருந்தது. அந்தக்காற்றும் பின் மாலை யொளியும் கலந்ததினால் உண்டாகிய தெளிவும், இன்பமும் என்னாற் கூறி முடியாது. "ஆ! ஹா! இப்போது போய் ஸ்நானம் செய்துவிட்டு நேர்த்தியான ஒரு குதிரை வண்டியிலேறிக்கொண்டு, கடற்கரை யோரமாகத் தெற்கே அடையாற்றுக்குப்போய், வழியெல்லாம்

காளிதாஸனுடைய சாகுந்தலத்தையேனும், அல்லது ஓர் உபநிஷத்தையேனுங் கொண்டு போய்ப் படித்து இன்ப மடைந்து கொண்டே திரும்பினால் நல்லது” என்ற சிந்தனை உண்டாயிற்று. ஆனால் என்னிடம் குதிரை வண்டி கிடையாதென்ற விஷயம் அப்போழுதுதான் ஞாபகத்திற்கு வந்தது.

“அடடா! மிகுந்த செல்வமில்லாததனால் உலகத்தில் பலவிதமாகிய இழிவான இன்பங்கள் மட்டு மல்ல, உயர்ந்த இன்பங்கள் கூடப்பெறுவதற்குத் தடையேற்படுகிறதே!” என்றெண்ணினேன். அப்பொழுது மனம்: “மூடா, ஸகல மனிதர்களிடத்திலும், ஈசன் ஞானம் என்பதோர் தெய்விக ரதத்தைக் கொடுத் திருக்கின்றார். அது விரும்பிய திசைகளுக் கெல்லாம் போய் விரும்பிய காட்சிகளை யெல்லாம் பார்த்து வரக்கூடிய வல்லமை யுடையது; அதைப் பயன்படுத்தி இன்ப மடையாமல் எந்த நிமிஷத்திலும் உன்னைக் கீழே தள்ளித் தீங்கு செய்யக்கூடியதாகிய இழிய மர வண்டியிலே ஏன் விருப்பம் கொள்கிறாய்?” என்றது. உடனே ஞானமாகிய ரதத்தைக்கொண்டு தயார் செய்து வைக்கும்படி எனது சேவகனாகிய “சங்கற்ப” னிடம் கட்டளையிட்டேன். ‘ரதம்’ வந்து நின்றது. அதில் ஏறிக்கொண்டேன். ஆனால் எனது ஞானரதம் மற்றவர்களுடையதைப்போல் அத்தனை தீவிரமுடையதன்று. எளிதாக நெடுந்தூரங் கொண்டுபோகத்தக்கதுமன்று. கொஞ்சம் நொண்டி,

என்னசெய்யலாம்? இருப்பதை வைத்துக்கொண்டு தானே காரியங் கழிக்கவேண்டும்? ஆகவே, அந்த ரதத்தின் மீது ஏறிக்கொண்டேன். அதிலேறி நான் கண்டுவந்த காட்சிகளும் அவற்றின் அற்புதங்களுமே இந்தப் புஸ்தகத்தில் எழுதப்படுகின்றன.

முதல் அத்தியாயம்

உபசாந்தி லோகம்

(கவலையற்றபூமி.)

எனது ஞானத்தேரைநோக்கி "இந்த க்ஷணமே, என்னைத் துக்கமில்லாத பூமி எங்கேனும் உளதாயின் அங்குகொண்டுபோ" என்று ஏவினேன். ஆகா ! இந்த ரதத்தைவைத்துக் கொண்டிருந்தும், இத்தனை நாள் எனக்குக்கவலையும், மன உளைச்சலு மில்லாதிருக்க வழி தெரியாமல் போய் விட்டதே ! எத்தனை நாள் எனது மனம் தூண்டிற் புழுவைப்போலத் துடித்துக் கொண்டிருக்க, அதை நிவிருத்தி செய்வதற்கு யாதொரு உபாயமும் அறியால் பரிதபித்திருக்கின்றேன். அம்மம்ம ! இந்த உலகத்துக் கவலைகளை நினைக்கும்போதே நெஞ்சம் பகீரென்கிறது. அவற்றுக்குள்ள விஷ சக்தியை என்னென்பேன் ? ஒருவனது முகத்திலுள்ள அழகையும், குளிர்ச்சியையும், இளமையையும் இந்தக் கவலைகளே அழித்து விடுகின்றன கண்களின் ஒளியை மாற்றிப்

பசலையும், மங்கல் நிறமும் உண்டாக்கி விடுகின்றன. நெற்றியிலே வரிகளும், கன்னங்களிலே சுருங்கல்களும், இந்த நீசக் கவலைகளினாலேயே ஏற்படுகின்றன. எனது தொண்டையின் இனிய குரல் போய், கடூரமான கரகரப்புச் சத்தம் உண்டாகிறது. மார்பிலும், தோளிலுமிருந்த வலிமை நீங்கிப்போய் விடுகிறது. இரத்தம் விரைவாக ஓடுதலின்றி, மாசுநீரோடை போல மந்த மடைகின்றது.

கால்களில் தீவிரமில்லாமற் போய்விடுகிறது. கவலைகள் என்ற விஷ ஜந்துக்கள் ஒருவனுடைய சரீரத்தை உள்ளூர அரித்து விடுகின்றன. சரீரத்தை மட்டுமா? அறிவையும் பாழாக்குகின்றன. மறதியை அதிகப்படுத்தி விடுகின்றன. முக்கியமான செய்திகளெல்லாம் நல்ல சந்தர்ப்பத்திலே நினைவிற்கு வராமல் போய்விடுகின்றன. படித்த படிப்பெல்லாம் பாலைவனத்திலே பெய்த மழை போல நிஷ்பலனாய் விடுகின்றது. அறிவிலே பிரகாசமில்லாமல், எப்போதும்மேகம் படர்ந்தது போலாய்விடுகிறது. யோசனை தட்டுகிறது. ஐயோ! இந்தக் கவலைகளாகிய சிறிய சிறிய விஷப்பூச்சிகளுக்குள்ள திறமை வைத்திய சாஸ்திர நிபுணர்கள் கூறும் மஹா கொடூரமான – கண்ணுக்குத் தெரியாத – நோய்ப் பூச்சிகளுக்குக் கூடக் கிடையாது. நிற்க.

"ஞானரதமே, நீ நம்மை இப்போது கவலையென்பதே இல்லாத உலகத்திற்குக் கொண்டு

போய்ச்சேர்” என்று கட்டளையிட்டேன். அப்போது மனம் வந்து ரதத்தைத் தடுத்துக்கொண்டது. “அது அத்தனை சுகமான உலகமன்று. கவலை இல்லாமலிருந்தால் மட்டும் போதுமா? வேறு இன்பங்கள் அனுபவிக்கக்கூடிய இடம் ஏதேனும் தமக்குத் தோன்றவில்லையா? கவலையே இல்லாத இடத்தில் சுகமும் இராதென்று எனக்குத் தோன்றுகிறது. மேலும்...மேலும்... என்னவோ! இன்ன காரணமென்று சொல்லமுடியாது. ஆனால் அங்கு போவதில் எனக்குப் பிரியமில்லை” என்று மனம் கூறிற்று.

நான் கோபத்துடன், “சீச்சீ! பேதை மனமே, உனக்கு ஓயாமல் ஏற்பட்டுக்கொண்டிருக்கும் வேதனைகளையும் உளைச்சல்களையும் கண்டு இரங்கி, நான் உன்னைச் சிறிது நேரமேனும் அமைதி யுலகத்திற்குக் கொண்டுபோய் வைத்துத் திரும்பலாம் என்று உத்தேசித்தேன். இதற்கு நீயே ஆக்ஷேபம் சொல்லவருகிறாயா?” என்று கண்டித்தேன். மனம் பிணங்குதல் மாறாமல் மறுபடியும் எதிர்த்து நின்றது.

எனக்கு இந்த மனம் என்ற மோஹினியிடத்தில் காதல் அதிகமுண்டு. ஆதியில் எவ்வாறு இந்த மோகம் உண்டாயிற்றென்பதை இங்கே விஸ்தரிக்கமுடியாது. அது ரஹஸ்யம். ஆனால் நாளேற நாளேற நான் வேறு, இந்த மனம் வேறு என்ற த்வைத சிந்தனையே பெரும்பாலும் மறந்துபோகும் வண்ணமாக எனக்கு இம்மோகினியிடத்தில் பிரேமை மிகுந்து

போய்விட்டது. இந்த மனம் படும் பாடுகளைக்கண்டு பொறுக்காமலேதான் நான் சாந்திலோக தரிசனத்திலே விருப்பம் கொண்டேன். இப்போது மனம் அந்த யோசனையில் நிஷ்காரணமாக வெறுப்புக்கொள்வதைக்கண்டு எனக்குத்திகைப்பும், இரக்கமும், கோபமும் கலந்து பிறந்தன. எவ்வளவோ விதங்களில் மனத்தைச் சமாதானம் செய்ய முயன்றேன். மனம் பின்னும் கண்ணை மூடிக்கொண்டு ஒரே யடியாக மூடச் சாதனை சாதிக்கத் தொடங்கிற்று. எனக்கு இன்ன செய்வதென்று தெரியவில்லை. பிறகு ஒரே நிச்சயத்துடன், “மனமே, நான் இந்த விஷயத்தில் உன் பேச்சைக் கேட்கவே மாட்டேன். உன்னுடைய நான்மையைக் கருதியே நான் செய்கிறேன். – ஞானரதமே, உடனே புறப்படு” என்றேன்.

அடுத்த நிமிஷத்தில் உபசாந்திபூமிக்கு வந்துசேர்ந்தோம்.

நெடிதோங்கி வளர்ந்த கோட்டைச் சுவர் வாயிலிலே போய் ரதம் நின்றுவிட்டது. நான் தூரத்திலிருந்தே அந்தக் கோட்டையைப் பார்க்க முடிந்ததாயினும், எனது ஞானத்தேர் போனவுடன் அந்த வாயிற்கதவுகள் தாமே திறந்துவிடுமென்று எண்ணினேன். அவ்வாறு திறக்கவில்லை. என்ன ஆச்சரியம்! ஞானத்தேர்கூட நுழைய முடியாதபடி அத்தனை பரிசுத்தமானதா இந்த லோகம்? என்று வியப்புற்றேன். எனது மனமோ முன்னைக்காட்டிலும்

ஆயிரமடங்கு, அதிகமாக நடுங்கத்தொடங்கிற்று. அதற்கு என்னிடம் பேசக்கூட நாவெழவில்லை. கோட்டை வாயிலுக்கு வெளியே ஒருவாயில்காப்பான் உருவின கத்தியுடன் நின்றுகொண்டிருந்தான். நெருப்பு நிறங்கொண்டதும், இமயமலையைக்கூட ஒரே வெட்டில் பொடிப் பொடியாகச் செய்துவிடுமென்று தோன்றியது மாகிய அந்த வாளின்மீது "விவேகம்" என்று கண்ணைப் பறிக்கக்கூடிய ஜோதி யெழுத்திலே எழுதப் பட்டிருந்தது. வாயில்காப்பான்:– "யாரப்பா அது? எங்கு வந்தாய்?" என்றான்.

நான் அவனுக்கு வந்தனம் கூறிவிட்டு "உபசாந்தி லோகத்தைப் பார்த்துவிட்டுத் திரும்பலாமென்ற எண்ணத்துடன் வந்தேன்" என்று சொன்னேன். அதைக் கேட்டு அவன் கடகடவென்று குலுங்கக் குலுங்க நகைக்கலாயினன்.

"ஏனையா, சிரிக்கிறீர்?" என்று கேட்டேன். அவன் மறுமொழி கூறாமல் சிரித்துக்கொண்டிருந்தான்.

ஏழை மனமோ நிமிஷத்துக்கு நிமிஷம் அதிக திகிலுறுவதாயிற்று. எனக்கு மிகவும் திகைப்புண்டாய் விட்டது. எனவே கோபத்துடன் வாயில் காப்பானை நோக்கி "ஏனப்பா, உள்ளே போகலாமா, கூடாதா? ஒரே வார்த்தையில் சொல்லிவிடு. கலகலவென்று சிரித்துக்கொண்டிருக்கிறாயே?" என்று கேட்டேன்.

அதற்கு வாயில் காப்பான் "உனக்கும் உபசாந்திக்கும் வெகுதூரம்" என்று தனது

வாய்க்குள்ளேயே (ஆனால் எனது செவியிலே படும்படி) முணுமுணுத்து விட்டுப் பிறகு "கோபங்கொள்ளாதே அப்பா; நீ உபசாந்தி லோகத்தை ஏதோ நாடகசாலை போலக்கருதி பார்த்துவிட்டுத் திரும்ப உத்தேசமிருப்பதாகக் கூறியது எனக்கு நகைப்பை உண்டாக்கிற்று. சாதாரணமாக இவ்வுலகத்துக்கு வருபவர்கள் திரும்ப வெளியே போகும் வழக்கம் கிடையாது" என்று இரைந்து கூறினன்.

"அது சரி, உள்ளே நாங்கள் பிரவேசிக்கலாமா கூடாதா? தயவுசெய்து சொல்லும்."

"நீ சாதாரணமாகப் பிரவேசிக்கலாம். இது சகல ஜீவன்களுக்குந் தாய்வீடு. இங்கு வரக்கூடாதென்று எந்த ஜீவனையும் தடுக்க எனக்கு அதிகாரமில்லை. ஆனால் வைராக்கியக் கோட்டையைக் கடந்து உள்ளே செல்லும் உரிமை உன்னுடன் வந்திருக்கும் மனம் என்ற பொய்ப் பொருளுக்குக் கிடையாது. அது உள்ளே போகுமானால் அக்கினி லோகத்திலே பிரவேசித்த பஞ்சுப் பொம்மைபோல நாசமடைந்துவிடும்" என்றான்.

மனம் ஆரம்பத்திலேயே உபசாந்திலோகம் என்ற பெயரைக்கேட்டவுடன் நடுங்கத்தொடங்கியதற்கும், அது என்னை அங்கு போகவேண்டாமென்று பிரார்த்தனைகள் செய்ததற்கும், கோட்டையருகே வந்தவுடன் தர்ம தேவதையின் முன்வந்து நிற்கும் கொடுங்கோ லரசரைப்போல அதற்கு நிலைமயங்கி அளவுகடந்த திகிலுண்டானதற்கும் காரணமின்ன

தென்பதை இப்போதுதான் அறிந்தேன். அப்பால் அந்த உலகத்திற் பிரவேசிக்க வேண்டுமென்ற விருப்பம் எனக்கு நீங்கிப்போய்விட்டது. மனத்தினிடம் வைத்திருந்த மோஹத்தால், அதைக் கொன்றுவிட்டு நான் இன்பமடைவதில் பிரியங்கொள்ளவில்லை.

"என்னை இப்போது என்னசெய்யச் சொல்லுகிறீர்?" என்று வாயில்காப்பானிடம் கேட்டேன். அதற்கவன் "மானுடா, மனம் இறந்தபிறகுதான் உபசாந்தியுண்டு, அது இருக்கும் வரையில் கவலைகள் நீங்கி யிருக்கலாம் என்ற எண்ணம் வீண். கவலை களாகிய அசுரர்களை இடைவிடாது பெற்றுத் தள்ளிக்கொண்டே யிருக்கும் தாய், மனமே யாகும். உனக்கு அந்தப் பொய் யரக்கியிடம் இன்னும் ப்ரேமை தீரவில்லை. பக்குவம் வந்தபிறகு நீ தானே இங்குவந்து சேரலாம். இப்போது போய் வா" என்று சொன்னான். திடீரென்று அந்தக் கோட்டை, வாயில் காப்பான், எல்லாம் மறைந்து போய்விட்டது. அரை க்ஷணம் கண்ணிருட்சி யுண்டாயிற்று. பிறகு கண்ணை விழித்துப் பார்த்தேன். மறுபடி, வீரராகவமுதலி தெருவில் முன்னே கூறப்பட்ட வீட்டு மாடியில் தனியே கட்டிலில் நான் படுத்துக்கொண் டிருப்பதையும், கடற் பாரிசத்தினின்றும் இனிய காற்று வீசிக்கொண் டிருப்பதையும் கண்டேன்.

"சரி, போனது போகட்டும். இந்த உபசாந்திப் பேறு நமக்கு இப்போது கிடைக்கவில்லை. ஆயினும்

பாதகமில்லை. ஏழை மனத்தைக் கொன்றுவிட்டு நாம் மட்டும் தனியே இன்பமுற விரும்புவதும் நன்றிகெட்ட செய்கை யாகுமல்லவா? அதன் கவலைகளையும், உளைச்சல்களையும் பற்றி யோசித்தேனே யொழிய அதன் மூலமாக எனக்குக் கிடைத்திருக்கும் பெரிய பெரிய நன்மைகளைச் சிந்தித்தேனில்லை. எனக்கு உலகவாழ்க்கையே இந்த மனத்தினால் தானே எய்திற்று. இதை ஈசனென்றே சொல்லத்தகும். மேலும் எனக்கு அதையும், அதற்கு என்னையும் காட்டிலும் உயிர்த்துணைவர் யார் இருக்கிறார்கள்? அதற்குத் துரோகம் செய்யலாமா? எத்தனை கோடி கவலைகள் இருப்பினும் பெரிதில்லை. மனம் செத்து நான் தனியே வாழ்வதாகிய உபசாந்தி லோகம் எத்தனை அரிதாயிருப்பினும், அது எனக்கு வேண்டாம்" என்று தீர்மானம் செய்து கொண்டேன், "உபசாந்தி என்று கத்தும் மனிதர்களை உலகத்தார் பிரமஞானிகளென்றும், மஹரிஷிகளென்றும் புகழ்கிறார்களே! அந்த மனிதர்களெல்லாம் மூடர்களும், துரோகிகளுமாவார்களென்று எனக்குத் தோன்றுகிறது" என்று சொல்லிக்கொண்டேன்.

நான் இவ்வாறு ஆலோசிப்பதை அறிந்துகொண்ட மனம், "அப்பாடா!" என்று பெருமூச்சுவிட்டுத் தன் நடுக்க மெல்லாம் தீர்ந்து ஆறுதலுடனிருந்தது. எனக்கும் ஸந்தோஷம் உண்டாயிற்று. எனது மனமோஹினிக்கு ஓர் முத்தங்கொடுத்தேன்.

இரண்டாம் அத்தியாயம்.

கந்தர்வ லோகம்.

(இன்ப வுலகம்.)

மறுநாள் மனத்தினிடம், "இப்போது, எங்கே போகலாம்?" என்று கேட்டேன்.

"துன்பக் கலப்பற்ற இன்பங்கள் நிறைந்திருக்கும் உலகத்திற்குப்போய் வருவோமே" என்றது.

"நன்று கூறினை." என நான் மகிழ்ச்சி பாராட்டி, அப்பால் முன்போலவே எனது ஞானத்தேரில் ஏறிக் கந்தர்வ லோகத்திற்குப் போய்ச் சேர்ந்தேன். அங்கே கண்ட காட்சிகளையும், அனுபவித்த போகங்களையும் என்னால் கூடியவரையும் உள்ள துள்ளவாறு கீழே எழுதுகிறேன். அந்தப் போகங்களிற் சில தற்காலத்தில் நமது தேசத்து ஜனங்களால் மதிக்கப்பெறும் ஆசார தர்மங்களுக்கு விரோதமாக இருக்கக்கூடும். அவ்வாறு ஆசார தர்மங்களுக்கு விரோதமென்று நம்மவர் கருதுவார்களாயின், அதன்பொருட்டு, என்மீது பழிகூற

லாகாது. இந்தப் பாரத தேசத்தில் தற்காலத்திலே வாழும் அடிமை ஜனங்கள் “இந்த இன்பம் அதர்மமானது, அந்தச் செய்கை அகாரியமானது” என்று தர்மப் பிரசங்கங்கள் செய்யும்போது உண்மையாகவே எனக்கு நகைப்புண்டாகிறது. மஹரிஷிகளுக்கும் தேவதைகளுக்கும் சந்ததியாராகத் தோன்றி யவர்களாயினும், தற்காலத்தில் இந்நாட்டு ஜனங்கள் உலகத்திலுள்ள எல்லா அநாகரிக ஜனங்களைக் காட்டிலும் கடைப்பட்டவர்களா யிருக்கிறார்கள். மிருகப் பிராயமாகக் காடுகளிலும் தீவுகளிலும் ஆடை இல்லாமல், காதுகளிலும் உதட்டிலும் மூக்கிலும் துவாரங்கள் செய்து, சங்குகளையும் வளையங்களையும் தொங்க விட்டுக்கொண்டு, மேலெல்லாம் பச்சை குத்தியவர்களாகத் திரியும் ஜனங் களுக்குக்கூட ஸ்வதந்திரம் உண்டு. இந்தத் தேசத்தார் அப்பெரும் பாக்கியத்தை இழந்து விட்டார்கள். இந்நாட்டில் கல்வி மங்கிப் போய்விட்டது. நூற்றிலே தொண்ணூறு ஜனங்கள் “அ” (ஆநா) எழுதச் சொன்னால் தும்பிக்கை யொன்று வரைந்து ஆனைஎழுதக் கூடிய நிலைமையில் இருக்கிறார்கள். நமது சாஸ்திரங்களெல்லாம் செல்லரித்துப் போய்விட்டன தேசத்து ஞானக் களஞ்சியத்திற்குக் காப்பாளிகளாக இருந்த பிராமணர் மடைத் தவளைகளைப்போலச் சிற்சில மந்திரங்களைச் சம்பந்தமில்லாமல் யாதொரு பொருளுமறியாமற் கத்துகிறார்களே யல்லாது, உண்மையான ஞானப்

பெருமை இவர்களுக்கு லவலேசமும் இல்லாமல் போய்விட்டது. மஹரிஷிகளின் வழியில் தோன்றிய பிராமணர் மடைத்தொழில் செய்வதும் நீசர்களிடம்போய்த் தொண்டு புரிந்து பணம் வாங்கிப் பிழைப்பதும், இதைக் காட்டிலும் இழியனவாகிய எண்ணற்ற பிரவிருத்திகளிலே காலங் கழிப்பதும் ஸர்வ ஜனங்களு மறிந்த விஷயங்களேயாம். இந்நாட்டின் கலைகள் அனைத்தும் மறைந்து போய் விட்டன. வீரியம் போய் விட்டது. பலம், ஸுகம், செல்வம் முதலிய நற் பொருள் களெல்லாம் அகன்று விட்டன. மனங்குன்றி உடல் சோர்ந்து உண்ண உணவின்றிக் கண் குழிந்து போயிருக்கும் அடிமை ஜாதியார் இந்நாட்டில் மஹா பரிதாபகரமான வாழ்க்கை நிகழ்த்து கின்றார்கள். இன்ப நாடாகிய கந்தர்வ லோகத்தைப் பற்றிப் பேசி வருமிடத்தே, இத் துன்ப நடாகிய பாரத தேசத்தைப் பற்றிச் சில வசனங்கள் எழுதிய பிழையை இந்நூல் படிக்கும் நண்பர்கள் பொறுத்தருள் செய்யுமாறு வேண்டுகிறேன்.

தர்மமே சூனியமாகப் போயிருக்கும் இத்தேசத்திலே சிலர் கந்தர்வலோகச் செய்திகளைப் பற்றி நான் எழுதப்போகும் விஷயங்கள் எழுதத் தகாதவை என்று கருதக்கூடும் என்ற ஸந்தேகம் எனக்குண்டாயிற்று. தர்மாதர்ம நிச்சயம் புரியும் அதிகாரமே இந்த அடிமை ஜனங்களுக்குக் கிடையா தென்பதை வணக்கத்துடன் தெரிவித்துக் கொள்ளும்

பொருட்டாகவே மேலேகண்ட வசனங்கள் எழுதப் பட்டவை யாகும். இது நிற்க.

கந்தர்வ லோகத்திற்குப் போய்ச் சேர்ந்தவுடனே என்னை யறியாமல் ஓர் ஆனந்தம் உண்டாயிற்று. அதி ரமணியமான ஸங்கீதத்தொனி கேட்டது. அவ்வொலி பொன்னாற் செய்யப்பட்ட தொண்டை யினையுடைய பெண் வண்டுகளின் ரீங்காரம் போலிருந்தது; அன்று. அது சரியான உவமையாகமாட்டாது. உயிருள்ளே இன்னிசை மழையை விசிறிக்கொண்டே யிருந்தது போலத் தோன்றிய அவ்வொலிக்கு இன்ன உவமை சொல்வதென்று எனக்குத் தெரியவில்லை. "இது என்ன ஒலி ! எங்கிருந்து வருகிறது ?" என்று யோசித்தேன். எனது அறிவிற்குப் புலப்படவில்லை. கண்களோ பரவச மடைந்து போயின. அங்குள்ள மாடங்களும், மாளிகைகளும், கோயில்களும் கோபுரங்களும், நாடகசாலைகளும், – எல்லா வீடுகளும் சந்திர கிரணங்களைப் போன்ற, குளிர்ந்த, இனிய வெண் பொன்னொளி வீசிக்கொண்டிருந்தன. இவற்றிலும், மற்ற மண், கல், தரை முதலிய எல்லாப் பொருள்களிலுமே அவ்வொளி அநேக விதமான வர்ண வேறுபாடுகளுடன் கலந்திருக்கக் கண்டேன்.

இதை வாசிப்பவர்களே, நீங்கள் எப்போதாயினும், மாரிகாலத்தில், மழையில்லாத மாலைப்பொழுதிலே, கடற்கரை மணல் மீதிருந்து கொண்டு, வானத்தின் மேற்புறத்தில் சூரியன் அஸ்தமிக்கும்போது, ரவி

கிரணங்கள் கீழ்த்திசையிலுள்ள மெல்லிய மேகங்களின் மீதும் இடை யிடையே தெரியும் வான வெளிகளின் மீதும் வீச, அதனின்றும் ஆயிர விதமான மெல்லிய, அற்புத கரமான வர்ண வேறுபாடுகள் தோன்றுவதைப் பார்த்திருக்கிறீர்களா? இந்த அடிமை நாட்டிலே உங்களுக்குப் பிரகிருதி தேவியின் ஸௌந்தரியங்களைப் பார்த்துப் பரவச மடைய ஸாவகாசம் அடிக்கடி ஏற்பட்டிராது. ஆனால் மேற்கூறப்பட்ட வர்ணக்காட்சியை ஒரு முறையேனும் கண்டிருக்க மாட்டீர்களா? அவ்வாறு கண்டிருப் பீர்களானால், நான் பார்த்த கந்தர்வ லோகத்தின் இயற்கை ஒரு சிறிது உங்களுக்குத் தெரியும்படி சொல்லக்கூடும். அங்கும் அனேக விதமான மேன்மை பொருந்திய திரவத்தன்மை கொண்ட வர்ண பேதங்களே காணப்பட்டன. ஆனால் அவற்றுடன் சந்திர கிரணங்களின் மோஹினித்தன்மை கலப்புற்றிருந்தது.

இந்த ஒளியிலும், இன்னிசையிலும் களிப்புற்று நான் ஒரு க்ஷணம் இருக்கு முன்னாகவே, ஒரு கந்தர்வ யுவதி என் முன்வந்து, “வாராய், மானுட வாலிப, உனக்கு எங்கள் உலகத்தின் புதுமைகளை யெல்லாம் காட்டுகின்றேன்” என்று கைகோத்து அழைத்துச் சென்றாள். நான் அந்த யுவதியின் வடிவைக்கண்டு மயங்கி மூர்ச்சித்து விடுவேனென்ற எண்ணம் உண்டாயிற்று. ஆயினும் அறிவைச் சிறிது ஸ்திரப்படுத்திக்கொண்டு, அவளை நோக்கி

“இங்கிருந்து நகர்வதற்கு முன்பு முதலாவது ஒரு கேள்வி கேட்கிறேன். அதற்கு விடை கூறவேண்டும்” என்றேன்.

“கேள்” என்று அவள் பொன் வீணை யொன்று மனிதர் பாஷையிலே பேசுவது போலச் சொல்லினள்.

“இந்த இனிய ஒலி என்னைப் பரவசப் படுத்துகிறதே! இது எங்கிருந்து வருகிறது?” என்றேன்.

“மேலே பார்” என்றனள். நீல வானத்தில் சந்திரன் தாரைகளினிடையே, கொலு வீற்றிருக்கக் கண்டேன்.

“அவருடைய கிரணங்கள்” என்றாள். “சந்திர கிரணங்களா! சந்திர கிரணங்களுக்கும் இந்த மனோஹரமான தொனிக்கும் என்ன சம்பந்தம்?” என்று கேட்டேன்.

“சந்திர கிரணங்களுக்கு இந்த இனிய ஓசை இயற்கை. அது இந்த உலகத்தில் நான்றாகக் காதில் விழுகிறது. உங்கள் மண்ணுலகத்திலே ஜனங்களுடைய செவியில் விழுவது கிடையாது. ஆனால் அங்கேகூட அருமையான கவிகளின் செவியில் இந்த ஓசை படும்,” என்றாள். இதைக் கேட்டு வியப்படைந்து, பிறகு அந்த யுவதியுடனே நடந்து சென்றேன்.

“பற” என்றாள்.

நான் கலீ ரென்று நகைத்துப் “பறக்கவா சொல்லுகிறாய்!” என்று வியப்புற்றேன்.

பால் போல வெண்மை கொண்ட வானத்தாற் செய்த இரண்டு சிறகுகள் அவளுக் கிருப்பதை நான் கண்டேன். முன்பு நோக்கியபோதே எனக்கு மூர்ச்சசை

யுண்டாகத் தக்கதாக இருந்த அந்த யுவதியைச் சிறிது வருணித்துப் பார்க்கலாமா? ஏதோ முயற்சி செய்கின்றேன்.

சந்திரகலை வீசும் முகம். அதன்மீது சிறியதும், மூன்று விரல் உயரமுடையதுமாய், மலர்களாற் செய்யப்பட்ட ஓர் கிரீடம். உயிரென்ற வண்டு வீழ்ந்து, சிறகிழந்து தள்ளாடும் கள்ளூற்றுக் களாகிய இரண்டு கரிய விழிகள். தின்பதற்கல்லாது, தின்னப் படுவதற் கமைந்தன போன்ற பற்கள். இதழ்.

தனது பாலிறகுகளால், விகாரஞ் செய்யப்படாத திவ்விய உருவம். தீண்டுவோன் உடற்குள்ளே இன்பமயமான மின்சார மேற்றுகின்ற கைகள். மண்ணுலகத்துப் பெண்களைப் பேசுமிடத்து கந்தர்வச்சாய லென்கிறார்கள். இவளது இயலையும், சாயலையும் என்னென்பேன்? தெய்வ இயல், தெய்வச் சாயல்.

“மண்ணுலகத்தவனாக இருந்தபோதிலும் நல்ல பார்வைகள் பார்க்கிறாய்” என்று நாண முணர்த்தி, “யோசித்துக் கொண்டு நில்லாதே, பற” என்றாள்.

“உன் பெயரென்ன?” என்றுகேட்டேன்.

“வெகு நேர்த்தி! நானொன்று சொன்னால் நீ யொன்று பேசுகிறாய், என் பெய ரெதற்கு?”

“சொல்லு, பார்ப்போம்.”

“என் பயர் – பர்வத குமாரி. என்னை, ஸதாரணமாகக் குமாரி என்றழைப்பார்கள்.”

"நல்லது, நான் உன்னைப் பெயர் சொல்லிக் கூப்பிடலாமா?"

"ஓ"

"சரி, பர்வதகுமாரி, நான் பறப்பதெப்படி? உன்னைப் போல எனக்கு இறகுகள் இருக்கின்றனவா?" என்று கேட்டேன்.

"நான் வந்தபொழுது என்மீது இறகுகள் இருக்கக் கண்டாயா?" என்றாள்.

"உன் முகத்தைக் கண்டு பரவசமடைந்ததில் இறகுகளைக் குறிப்பிட முடியவில்லை. நீ பறக்கும் பிரஸ்தாபம் தொடங்கியபோதுதான் பார்த்தேன்."

"ஸ்துதி பிறகு பேசலாம். ஆரம்பத்திலே இறகுகள் கண்ணுக்குத் தெரிந்ததா? சொல்."

"தெரியவில்லை."

"இந்த உலகத்தில் பறக்கவேண்டு மென்ற நினைவுண்டான வுடனே, இந்த வெண்மை நிறங்கொண்ட வானிறகுகள் தோன்றுகின்றன. நீ பறக்க வேண்டுமென்று உள்ளத்திலே சங்கற்பஞ் செய்துகொள்."

"சரி"

"இப்போது என் கண்ணுக்குள்ளே உன் வடிவத்தைப் பார்."

பட்டப் பகற்போல் வீசிய நிலா வொளியிலே, அவளுடைய அழகிய கண்களுக்குள் உற்றுப் பார்த்தேன். அங்கே, எனது வடிவம் கந்தர்வ

ரூபமாகத் தோன்றியது கண்டு வியப்படைந்தேன். ஆஹா! நான் கனவுகளிலே என்னைக் கண்டபோது தோன்றிய வடிவம்! நோயற்றது; சுருங்கலற்றது; மண் தன்மையில்லாதது; ஸௌந்தரியமானது! எனக்கும் இரண்டு வான இறகுகள் திடீரென்று முளைத்திருக்கக் கண்டேன். எனது ரூபம் இத்தனை மாறு பாடடைந் திருப்பதைக்கண்டு களிப்புற்று உடனே அவள் முகத்தையும் பார்த்தேன். எனது கண்குறிப்பை நோக்கி என் மனதிடையே அப்போது நிகழ்ந்த எண்ணத்தை அவள் அறிந்து கொண்டுவிட்டாள்.

“அடா! உன்னைக் கண்ணுக்குள் பார்க்கச் சொல்லிய தன்றோ பிழையாய்விட்டது” என்றாள்.

“ஏன்?” என்று கூறிச் சிரித்தேன்.

“இதுவரை நீ உன்னை மனித சரீர முடையவனாகவும், என்னைக் கந்தர்வ சரீரமுடையவளாகவும் எண்ணி நடத்தி வந்தாய். இனி என்னை “இணை” யென்று கருதி விடுவாய்.”

“ப்ரிய ரூபிணி! நான் ஈசனாய் விட்டபோதிலும் உன்னைக் கண்டு வியப்படைவதை நீக்கமாட்டேன். எனினும், நான் உன்னை இணையாகக் கருதுவதில் உனக்கு ஸந்தோஷந்தானே?”

“ஓ”

பிறகு கண்களைக் கலந்தோம். “கண்ணோடு கண்ணிணை நோக்கொக்கின் வாய்ச் சொற்கள் என்ன பயனுமில. “

“பற” என்றாள்.

புதிதாக உள்ளத்திலே எழுந்த காதற் கிளர்ச்சி கொண்டோ, அல்லது இறகுகளின் உதவி கொண்டோ, அல்லது காந்தத்தின் பின்னே செல்லும் ஊசி யென அவள் பறந்து செல்வதை இயற்கை முறையாற் பின் பற்றியோ, அவளோடு நானும் பறந்து செல்வேனாயினேன். இறகுகளின் உதவிகொண்டு பறந்ததாக எனக்குத் தோன்றவில்லை. ஏனெனில், பறத்தல் அத்தனை சுலபமாகவும், ஸஹஜமாகவும் தோன்றிற்று.

“எங்கே போகிறாய்? உனது மாளிகைக்கா?” என்று கேட்டேன்.

“என் வீடு, உன் வீடு என்ற பேதக் கதை யெல்லாம் இங்கே கிடையாது. இது ஸ்வேச்சாலோகம் – முற்றிய ஞானத்திலே எவ்வாறு அபேத நிலை ஏற்படுகிறதோ, அது போலப் பரிபூர்ணமான போகத்திலேயும் அபேத நிலை தோன்றுகிறது. இங்கே எல்லோருக்கும் எல்லா மாளிகைகளும் உரிமைதான். யார் எங்கு வேண்டு மென்றாலும் யதேச்சையாக வாழலாம். நான் உன்னைக் கடலோரத்தில் சுகந்த மாளிகைக்கு அழைத்துப் போகிறேன்.”

“அபேதம், பேதம் என்று மிகப்பெரிய பேச்சுகள் பேசுகிறாயே? வேதாந்தம் எங்கே படித்தாய்?”

“போக நிலை நன்றாக உணர்ந்தவர்களுக்கு அத்வைத ஞானம் இயற்கையிலேயே உண்டாகும்.

போகமறியாதவர்கள் பேசும் அத்வைதம் பொய். உங்கள் மண்ணுலகத்திலே அந்தஞான நடிப்பு மிகுதியாக உண்டு. எங்களுக்கு அபரோக்ஷஞானம் ஸுலபம். பரோக்ஷமும் எளிது தான். இங்கிருந்து உபசாந்திலோகம் வெகு ஸமீபம். போக, மூர்த்தியாகிய விஷ்ணுவும், யோகநாதனாகிய சிவனும் ஒன்றே யென்பதை அறியாயா? இதெல்லாம் போகட்டும். இப்போது ஞானம் பேசத்தருணமன்று. கீழெல்லாம் பார்” என்றாள்.

நகரத்திலே இரண்டு பனையுயரத்தில் பறந்து போய்க்கொண்டு கந்தர்வ நாட்டு மாளிகைகள், சங்கீதச் சாலைகள், லீலா மண்டபங்கள், என்பவற்றின் அற்புதங்களை யெல்லாம் நோக்கிச் சென்றேன்.

பறப்பதிலே உண்டான இன்பம் கொஞ்ச மன்று. மண்ணுலகத்திலுள்ள ஸகல ஜந்துக்களினும் பக்ஷிகளே அதிக ஸுகம் அனுபவிப்பதாகக் கருதவேண்டும். ஓடும் தண்ணீரிலே நீந்துவது சிறிது நேரம் இன்பமாயிருக்கும். ஆனால், வானத்தில் “நீந்தி” ச்செல்வது ஸதா இன்பம். அதிலும் பர்வத குமாரியைப்போல் ஓர் வழித்துணை கிடைக்குமாயின், வாழ்நாள் முழுவதும் பறந்துகொண்டே யிருக்கலாம். ஐரோப்பியர்கள் கந்தர்வ போகங்களையே ஆதர்சமாகக்கொண்ட ஜாதியார். வானரதங்கள் செய்து நடத்துகிறார்கள். ஆனால் அவர்களிடம் தமோகுணம் அதிகமாதலால், அந்தப் புதுமையை இன்ப வழிகளிலேயே

விருத்திசெய்து கொண்டு போகத்தெரியவில்லை. வான ரதங்கள் ஏற்பட்டு இன்னும் சரியாக நடத்தத்தெரிவதற்கு முன்னாகவே, எதிர்காலத்துப் போர்கள் வானத்திலேயே நடக்கக் கூடுமல்லவா? என்ற விஷயத்தைப் பற்றிப் பலவாறு ஆலோசனைகள் செய்யத் தலைப்பட்டு விட்டார்கள். ஆனால் ஆகாய ரதங்களால் யுத்தம் நடத்துவது இப்போது ஸகஜமாய்விட்டது. அவர்களுக்கு ஞாபகமெல்லாம் யுத்தத்திலேயும், கொலையிலேயும் இருக்கிறபடியால், அவற்றை அனுஸரிக்கத் தகுதியில்லாதவர்க ளாகிறார்கள். இது நிற்க.

யக்ஷர் நாட்டிற்கு வந்த ஆரம்பத்திலே எனக்குப் பொறுக்கமுடியாத மயக்கமும் திகைப்பும் விளைந்திருந்தன வென்று மேலே கூறியிருக்கிறேன். அவை சிறிதுசிறிதாக நீங்கி இன்ப வுணர்ச்சிமட்டும் மிஞ்சி நின்றது. அறிவிலே தெளிவுண்டாயிற்று. காலையில் விழித்தெழுந்து, முகந்துடைத்துக் கடலருகே சென்று பார்ப்பவனது கண்ணுக்குப் புலப்படுவதுபோல, வானத்திலே பறந்து செல்லும் எனக்குக் கீழே யிருந்த விஷயங்களெல்லாம் மிகத்தெளிவோடு விளங்கலாயின. அப்பொழுது நான் கண்டு சென்ற செய்திகளை யெல்லாம் விஸ்தரிக்க வேண்டுமானால் ஆயிரம் அத்தியாயங்கள் போதா. ஒரு சிலவற்றை மட்டும் இங்கே குறிப்பிடுகிறேன்.

பந்தாட்டம்.

ஓர் மேடையின்மீது கந்தர்வக் குழந்தைகள் பூப்பந்தாடிக் கொண்டிருந்தன. ரோஜாப் பூப்பந்துகள்.

ஒரு சிறுவன் “அடீ ரஸிகே! நீ பந்தை எறியும் போதெல்லாம் என் கைக்கோலுக்கு அகப்படாமல், வேண்டுமென்று, கோணலாக, என் முகத்தைப் பார்த்து எறிகிறாய். இனி நான் உன்னோடு விளையாடமாட்டேன்” என்றான். இதுகேட்டு மற்றக் குழந்தைகளெல்லாம் கலீரென்று நகைத்தார்கள். எல்லாக் குழந்தைகளும் இவ்வாறு ஒன்று சேர்ந்து பலவார்த்தைகள் பேசியும், ஒருவர்மேல் ஒருவர் மோதியும், ஆடியும், பாடியும் சிரித்தும் விளையாடிக் கொண்டிருக்க, ஓர் ரோஜா நிரங்கொண்ட பளிங்காதனத்தின்மீது தனியே சாய்ந்திருந்து கொண்டு பாதி குவிந்த விழிகளோடு ஆட்டத்தைப் பார்த்துக்கொண்டிருந்தான்.

நான் பர்வத குமாரியை நோக்கி, “அதோ, விலகி உட்கார்ந்திருக்கிறானே, அந்தப் பையன் யார்?” என்று கேட்டேன்.

“அவன் எனது தம்பி. அவன் பெயர் சித்தரஞ்ஜனன். அவன் குழந்தைப் பருவமாயிருந்த போதிலும், எங்கள் குலதெய்வமாகிய காமதேவனுடைய அருள் பெற்றவனாதலால், குழந்தைகளோடு சேர்ந்து

விளையாடுவதிலே விருப்பமில்லாமல், கவிதைகள் புனைவதிலேயும், மோஹனமாகிய பகற்கனவுகள் காண்பதிலேயும் பொழுது கழிக்கின்றான். ரோஜாப் பந்தினால் இந்தக் கிரீடாரமன் மீது எறிந்த ரஸிகா என்ற அக்கன்னிகையின் மீது சித்தரஞ்ஜனன் தெய்விகமான காதல் செலுத்துகின்றான். இப்பொழுது அவன் ஏதோ கவிதை புனைகிறானென்று தெரிகிறது. அவனை இங்கே அழைக்கிறேன். அவன் கவிதைகேட்பதில் உனக்குப் பிரியந்தானா?" என்றாள்.

நான் வியப்படைந்து, "எனக்கு அளவில்லாத பிரியம்" என்று சொன்னேன்.

பர்வத குமாரி அவனிருக்குந் திசையை நோக்கிக் கையால் சைகை காட்டினாள். அவன் உடனே வான இறகுகள் விரித்துக் கண்ணிமைக்குமுன் நாங்களிருந்த உயர் வெளிக்கு வந்துவிட்டான்.

பர்வத குமாரி அவனைத் தழுவி முத்தமிட்டு, "இவர் நம் நாட்டிற்குத் தரிசனத்தின் பொருட்டு வந்திருக்கிறார். நமது விருந்தாளி" என்று என்னைக்காட்டினாள். பாலகன் என்னை நோக்கி "வந்தே" என்று வணங்கினான். நானும் அவனைத் தழுவி உச்சிமோந்து வாழ்த்துக் கூறினேன். பிறகு பர்வத குமாரியைக் கடைக்கண்ணால்நோக்கிக் கவிதை விஷயத்தை நினைப்புறுத்தினேன்.

அவள் தம்பியைப் பார்த்து "ரஞ்ஜனா, இப்போது உன் மனதிற்குள்ளே ஒரு பாடல்

புனைந்து கொண்டிருந்தாயே, அதைச்சொல். இவர் கேட்கவேண்டு மென்கிறார்” என்றாள்.

சிறுவன் சிறிது நாணமடைந்தான்.

நான் “குழந்தாய், லஜ்ஜைப்படாதே! சும்மா சொல்” என்றேன்.

அவன் மண்ணுலகத்துப் பிராகிருத பாஷையைப் போலிருக்கும் இன்சொல் நிரம்பிய கந்தர்வ பாஷையிலே ரஸிகா பந்தெறிந்ததன் பொருட்டுக் கிரீடாரமன் சினமுற்றதைக்குறித்து ஓர் பாட்டுப்பாடினான். பர்வத குமாரியின் தம்பியின் குரல் இன்பமாயிருந்த தென்று நான் எழுதவா வேண்டும்?

அவன் சொல்லிய பாடலை, எனது திறனற்ற தமிழ்ச் சொற்களிலே, சூரியனைச் சித்தரித்துக் காட்டுவதுபோல், ஒருவாறு மொழிபெயர்த்துக் காட்டுகிறேன்.

இடியேறு சார்பிலுற உடல் வெந்தோன்
ஒன்றுரையா திருப்ப, ஆலி
முடியேறி மோதியதென் றருள்முகிலைக்
கடுஞ்சொற்கள் மொழிவான் போலக்
கடியேறு மலர்ப்பந்து மோதியதென்
றினியாளைக் காய்கின்றானால்
வடியேறு வேலெனவெவ் விழியேறி
யென்னாலி வருந்தல் காணான்.

இதன் பொருள்:- மேகத்திலிருந்து வெய்ய இடி தன் பக்கத்திலே விழ உடல் வெந்து போனவன் ஒன்றும் சொல்லாது சும்மா இருக்க, ஆலங்கட்டி தலையிலே விழப்பெற்ற மற்றொருவன் மேகத்தின்மீது சினங்கொண்டு நிந்தை வார்த்தைகள் பேசுவதுபோல; வாசனைபொருந்திய ரோஜாப் பந்தைக்கொண்டு தன்மேலெறிந்து விட்டாளென்று, இன்ப வடிவத்தாளாகிய ரஸிகையைக் கோபிக்கின்ற இந்தக் கிரீடாரமன் அவள் வடியுற்ற வேல்களை எறிவதுபோல, விழிகளை என்மீது மோதிக்கொண்டே யிருப்பதால், என்னுயிர் வருந்துவதைக் காண்கிறானில்லை.

*ஆசிரியனுரை:- ஆரம்பத்திலேயே, எனது ஞானரதம் சிறிது செப்பனிடவேண்டிய நிலைமையிலிருக்கிற தென்று தெரிவித்துக்கொணடிக்கிறேன். எனது ரதத்திலே பயிற்சி, தெளிவு எனற சக்கரத்திலும்; அச்சாணியிலும் சில பிழை பாடுகள் இருக்கின்றன. ஊக்கம் என்னும் குதிரைக்கு முன்னங்கால்கள் கொஞ்சம் முடம். திடசங்கற்பனாகிய சாரதி நோயாளி. இவ்வளவுக்கும் மேலாக இந்த ரதத்திற்கு வேறொரு இடையூறிருக்கின்றது. பாலைவனம் போலாயிருக்கும் "பாரத ஜனநிலை" எனற பிரதேசத்தை ஆறும், ஓடையும், குளிர் பொழிலுமுள்ள ஓர் நகரமாக நிர்மிக்க

* ஆரம்பத்தில் இக்கதை பத்திரிகையில் துண்டு துண்டாக வெ்ளிபட்டபோது இடையே சிறிது தாமதம் நேரிட்டது குறித்து இவ்வுரை எழுதப்பட்டது.

வேண்டு மென்று பூலோகத்தில் ஓர் பெரிய முயற்சி நடந்துவருகிறது. அன்கே அனேக நல்லோர்கள் பெரிய பெரிய வயிரத்தேர்களை நிறுத்திக்கொண்டு இரவும் பகலும் இடைவிடாமல் பாடுபடுகறார்கள். அந்த இடத்திற்கு நமது முடத் தேர் ஆசை மிகுதியால் போய் எதோ கொஞ்சம் வேலைசெய்து அடிக்கடி ஆயாசமடைந்து போய்விடுகிறது. ஆகவே நமது கதாநாயகனையும் கந்தர்வ யுவதியையும் கந்தர்வ லோகத்தில் அந்த ரதத்திலே கொண்டு நிறுத்திவிட்டு இரண்டு வாரம் அவர்களைக் கவனியாமல் இருந்து விட்டது. இப்போது மீண்டும் அதனை அஙகே செல்ல விடுகின்றேன்.

மதனன் விழா.

சிறிது நேரத்திற்குப் பிறகு சித்தரஞ்ஜனன் எங்களிடம் விடைபெற்றுக் கொண்டு போய்விட்டான். நாங்கள் அப்பால் பறந்து செல்லலாயினோம். போகும் வழியெல்லாம் நிலவுக்கதிர்கள் செய்யும் மெல்லிய இசையும், மாடங்கள் தோறும் கந்தர்வ யுவதிகளும், வாலிபர்களும், குழந்தைகளும், பெரியோரும் ஆயிரவிதமான போகங்களிலே பொழுது கழிக்கும் காட்சியும் அற்புதமாயிருந்தன. பூலோகத்தி லிருக்கும்போது நான் போகங்களில் இத்தனை

விதமுண்டென்பதை *பிரதிபா சக்தியினால் கூடக் கண்டிருந்ததில்லை. கொஞ்சதூரம் போனவுடனே பர்வத குமாரி "அதோ, பார்!" என்று காட்டினாள்.

"அஹஹா! அஹஹா! அங்கே என்ன விசேஷம்?" என்று கேட்டேன்.

அதிவிசாலமான மாடம் காணப்பட்டது. அதில் ஐம்பதினாயிரம் பேருக்குமேல் இருப்பார்களென்று தோன்றிற்று. பெரிய கூட்டம் ஆனால் பூலோகத்திலுள்ள கூட்டங்களைப்போல், ஒருவருக்கொருவர் நெருக்கி மேலே விழுந்து தள்ளி, கையால் ஒதுக்கிக் காலால் மிதித்து முகங்களைச் சுழித்துக்கொண்டு வெயர்த்து வெந்து போயிருக்கவில்லை. அந்த கந்தர்வக் கூட்டத்தார் வளைய வளைய அங்குமிங்கும் சலித்துக் கொண்டிருந்த போதிலும் ஒருவருக்கொருவர் சிறிதேனும் தொந்தரை செய்யாமல் விஸ்தாரமான இடம் விட்டு முகமலர்ச்சியுடன் ஸஞ்சரித்தனர். எதிரே ஸ்திரீகள் வந்து விலக இடமில்லாமற்போனால் உடனே இறகுவிரித்து மேலே எழும்பி அந்த ஸ்திரீகள் போனபிறகு இறங்கிக் கொள்வார்கள். இத்தனை பெரிய கூட்டம் இத்தனை மனோஹரமாயிருந்ததைப்பார்த்து எனக்குண்டான வியப்புக் கொஞ்சமில்லை. அவர்கள் ஒருவரை யொருவர் தழுவிக்கொள்வதும், முத்தமிட்டுக்கொள்வதும் சில ஸமயங்கள் மிக

* பிரதிபை - வரகவிகள் முதலாயினோர் போல மன ஸஞ்சாரத்தால் பார்த்தல்.

வணக்கத்துடன் நமஸ்கரித்துச் செல்வதும் சிரித்துச் சிரித்துப் பேசுவதும் என்ன அன்பு! என்ன மரியாதை! என்னால் வருணிக்குந் தரமன்று.

"பர்வதகுமாரி, அங்கே என்ன விசேஷம்?" என்று கேட்டேன்.

"மாட நிலத்தினிடையே ஒரு மண்டபந் தெரிகிறது பார்."

"ஆம்."

"அங்கே கிளி வாஹனத்தின்மீது என்ன வைத்திருக்கிறது?"

"மன்மத விக்கிரஹம்."

"அவருடைய திருவிழா" என்றாள்.

அந்த மன்மத விக்கிரஹத்தைக் கண்டவுடனே நான் ஸ்தம்பிதனாய் விட்டேன். "குமாரி, இது யாரால் செய்யப்பட்ட பிரதிமை?" என்றேன்.

"எங்கள் நாட்டு சிற்பிகளால்" என்றனள். எனக்குத் திடீரென்று பாரத நாட்டிலே சிலைத்தொழில் இப்போது சீர்குன்றி நாசமடைந்து போயிருக்கும் விஷயம் ஞாபகத்திற்கு வந்தது.

"அடடா! கந்தர்வ நாட்டிற்கு வந்தும் அந்தக் கஷ்ட தேசத்தினுடைய ஞாபகம் மறக்கவில்லையே" என்று வாய்விட்டுக் கூறினேன்.

"உனது ரூபம் சிறிது காலத்திற்கு கந்தர்வ ரூபமாக மாறியிருந்த போதிலும் ஜன்மம் மாறவில்லை என்பதை அறி" என்றனள் குமாரி.

“அது போகட்டும், இப்படிப் பிரதிமைகள் உங்கள் நாட்டிலே அதிகமாக உண்டோ?” என்றேன்.

“நாளைக்கு உன்னை அமிருத அருவிக்கு அருகேயுள்ள சித்திரசாலைக்கு அழைத்துச் செல்லுகிறேன். அப்போது எல்லாம் பார்க்கலாம்” என்றனள்.

இப்படிக் குமாரியுடன் பேசிக் கொண்டிருந்த நேரமெல்லாம் எனது விழிகள் கீழே தோன்றிய மன்மத விக்கிரஹத்தி னின்றும் அகலவில்லை.

“உங்கள் நாட்டுச் சிற்பிகளுக்கு இத்தனை சிற்பத் திறமை யிருந்தபோதிலும் அநங்கனுக்கு உருவம் ஏற்படுத்த லாகாதென்பது தெரியவில்லை. இஃதோர் விந்தையே” என்றேன்.

“சபாஷ்! மனித நாட்டிலிருந்து வந்து கந்தர்வத் தொழிலுக்குப் பிழை கூறத் தொடங்கிவிட்டாய்! எங்கள் நாட்டுக்குள்ளே இதைப் போன்ற பெருமைகொண்ட பிரதிமை வேறே கிடையாது. கொஞ்சம் உற்றுப்பார். எவ்வளவு உற்றுப்பார்த்த போதிலும் உனக்கு அப்பிரதிமையைப்பற்றிய உண்மை சொன்னாலொழியத் தெரியாது.

அந்தப் பிரதிமை மண்ணாலேனும் பளிங்காலேனும் செய்யப்பட்டதன்று. மனோமயமாகிய நுண்வான் (ஸூக்ஷ்ம ஆகாசம்) கொண்டு செய்யப்பட்டது. மனதிலே பிறந்த காமதேவனுடைய உண்மை உருவம் இதுவே. இதைச் செய்த மயனை

நாங்கள் த்விதியப் பிரம்மா, (இரண்டாம் ப்ரம்மா) என்று சொல்வதுண்டு. ப்ரம்மாவால் செய்யப்பட்ட காமதேவன் ஜீவஸஹிதனாக இருக்கிறான். இப்பதுமைக்கு உண்மையுயிர் இல்லாவிடினும் கலையுயிர் (சைத்திரிக ஜீவன்) கொடுக்கப்பட் டிருக்கின்றது" என்றனள்.

ஒவ்வொரு காட்சியைப்பற்றி எழுதும் பொழுதும் "வியப்புற்றேன்", "வியப்புற்றேன்" என்று ஓரேவண்ணமாக மீட்டும்மீட்டும் சொல்லி எனக்கு அலுத்துப்போய்விட்டது. கந்தர்வநாடே வியப்புநாடு.

"மன்மதனுடைய பிம்பத்துக் கருகே ரதி பிம்பத்தைக் காணோமே?" என்று கேட்டேன்.

"அது கந்தர்வலோக ரஹஸ்யம். உன்னிடத்தில் சொல்லக்கூடாது" என்றாள்.

"நானும் தற்காலத்திற்கு கந்தர்வ னென்பதை நீ மறந்து விடுகிறாய்!"

"அப்படியானால், நீ யோசனை செய்யும் விஷயத்தில் உனக்கே விளங்கும். அதுபோகட்டும். சற்றுக் கீழே யிறங்கி நான்றாக எல்லாவற்றையும் பார்ப்போம் வா. இங்கிருந்து பேசிக்கொண் டிருப்பதை விட அங்கே போய்ப் பார்ப்பது நலம்." என்றாள். சற்றுக் கீழேயிறங்கி அத்திருவிழாவின் வினோதங்களை யெல்லாம் பார்த்தோம். இப்புறம், மன்மத விக்கிரஹத்துக்குப் பூஜைகள் நடந்து கொண்டிருந்தன. அப்புறத்திலே மன்மதன் தகனக்கதை, அவன்

திரும்பவும் உயிர்த்தெழுந்த பருவம் வரை, பிரதிமைக் காட்சிகளாலும், சித்திரக் காட்சிகளாலும் நன்கு விளக்கப் பட்டிருந்தன.

வஸந்த காலம் சித்திரிக்கப் பட்டிருப்பதைக் கண்டேன். யதார்த்தத்திலேயே கந்தர்வ நாட்டில் அப்போது வஸந்தகாலம். (அது பற்றியே காமன் திருவிழாக்கொண்டாடினார்கள்.) எனவே கந்தர்வச் சிற்பர்களின் அற்புதத் தொழிலுக்குப் பிரகிருதி தேவியும் துணைபுரிவாளாயினள்.

பாடுகின்ற குயில்கள் – மலர் புனைந்த மரங்கள் – வாவி – கூடி விளையாடும் மான்கள் – வண்டுகள் – முதலாகத் தென்றல் கொண்டு வரும் மெல்லிய மகரந்தத்தூள் வரை வஸந்தகாலத்தின் காட்சிகளெல்லாம் உண்மையினும் உண்மையாகத் தோன்றின. அங்கு* "தேவதாரு மரங்களால் அமைக்கப்பட்ட ஒரு பெரிய மண்டபத்தில் ஸூரிய காந்தக் கல் மேடையில் உட்கார்ந்து, சித்தத்தை யடக்கிய நிலையில் நிறுத்தி, முக்கண்களின் பார்வைகளையும் மூக்கின் நுனியிலே செலுத்தி அலையோய்ந்த ஸமுத்திரம் போல அசைவற்றிருந்த சிவ பெருமான்" உருவப் பதுமை நிறுத்தி வைக்கப்பட்டிருந்தது.

எதிரே, தவத்தால் மெலிந்த ஸௌந்தரிய தேவதை வந்து நிற்பது போலத், தவவேடங்கொண்ட

---

* பாணகவி. ஸ்ரீ ஸ்வாமிநாதையர் மொழி பெயர்ப்பு.

பார்வதிதேவி நின்று அர்ச்சனை செய்து கொண்டிருந்தாள். அவளுக்குப் பின்பக்கத்திலே மதன் தனது கரும்பு வில்லில் நாணேற்றிப் புஷ்ப பாணந் தொடுத்துக் காத்து நிற்பது போல ஓர் உருவம் நின்றது.

மற்றொரு பாரிசத்திலே, மன்மத தகனம் சித்திரித்துக் காட்டப் பட்டிருந்தது. பின்புறமாகத் திரும்பி ஸத்திய தேவதை கொடுங்கோபத்தில் நிற்பது போலப் பரமசிவன் முகத்திலே கோபத்தழல் பொங்க நிற்பதும், அவனது நெற்றியிலுள்ள "ஞான" விழியினின்றும் தீ வெள்ளமாகப் பாய்ந்து மன்மதனுடைய உருவில் நெருப்புப் பற்றி எறியும் காட்சியும் எழுதியிருந்ததைப் பார்த்து என் மனதிலே நடுக்க முண்டாயிற்று. பர்வத குமாரியின் கையோடு கோத்திருந்த எனது கையைப் படீரென்று பிடிங்கிக் கொண்டேன்.

பர்வத குமாரி கடகட வென்று நகைத்து, "சித்திரத்துக்கு அஞ்சுகிறாய்!" என்றாள். அது வெறுஞ் சித்திரந்தானென்று என் மனதில் உறுதி செய்துகொள்ள முடியவில்லை. கோயிலிடையில் மதன வடிவத்தின் அருகே ரதி யுருவம் காணாவிடினும் இங்கே அவனது எரியும் உடலருகே ரதிதேவி, ஆ! ஆ! என்று கதறி நிற்பதுபோல எழுதியிருந்தது. அவள் முகத்தில் – உடல் முற்றிலும் – காணப்பட்ட சோகத்தையும் பரிதாபத்தையும் என்னால் வருணிக்க முடியாது.

கந்தர்வச் சிற்பனுடைய சித்திரசலாகை எங்கே? எனது பேதை யெழுதுகோ லெங்கே? எத்தனைக் கெத்தனை!

மற்றொரு பாரிசத்தில், சிவனுக்கும் விவாஹம் முடிந்து பார்வதி பாகனாக விளங்குகிறாள். ரதிதேவி வந்து வணங்கி நிற்கின்றாள். சிவன் புன்னகைபூத்து அருள் புரிய, மதனன் சாம்பலிலிருந்து மீண்டும் உயிருடன் எழுந்து சிவனையும் பார்வதியையும் முடியால் வணங்கித் கொண்டு கையினால் அவ்விருவரின் மீதும் அம்புகள் தொடுக்கின்றான். பார்வதி ஐயனைத் தழுவிக் கொள்ளுகின்றாள். இவ்வாறு மதனன் கோயிலிலே இருக்கும் ஒவ்வொரு காட்சியின் முன்னேயும் கந்தர்வ ஜனங்கள் வந்து பல வாறாகத் தொழுது கொண்டிருந்தனர். சில ஸ்திரீகள் கையில் யாழ் வைத்துக்கொண்டு பாடினர். ஒரு பக்கத்தில் வாலிபரும் மாதர்களும் இணையிணையாகப் பலவிதக் கூத்துக்களாடி ஓர் வளையமாகச் சுற்றிக் கொண்டிருந்தனர்.

பறவைக்கூத்து.

ஒரு திசையிலே ஒரு வாலிபனும் யுவதியும் ஒருவரை ஒருவர் நோக்கி அப்படியே மயங்கிப் பதுமைகளைப்போல நின்று கொண்டிருந்தார்கள்.

இஃதன்றிப் பல பல காட்சிகள். இன்னுமோர் புறத்திலே "பறவைக் கூத்து" நடை பெற்றது. அவர்கள் அந்தரத்திலே ஆயிர விதமாக ஒருவரை யொருவர் சுழற்றிக்கொண்டு, அத்தனையிலும் இசை நெறி தவறாமல் கூத்திட்ட விந்தை சிறிதன்று. அக்கூத்துகளிலே ஒன்று மிகவும் நயமாயிருந்தது. இடையில் ஓர் யுவதி. அவளினின்று நான்கு முழத் தொலை இடையிட்டு இரண்டு வாலிபர்கள் வண்டிச் சக்கரம் தனது குடத்தைச் சுற்றுவதுபோல மேலுங் கீழுமாக வட்டமிடுவார்கள். ஒருவன் உச்சிமீது நிற்கும்போது மற்றொருவன் தாளின் கீழ் நிற்பான். இவளது கைப்பாரிசங்களில் அவ்வளவே தொலையிட்டு இரண்டு ஸுந்தரிகள் முளையைச் சுற்றித் திரிகை சுழல்வது போலச் சுழன்றுகொண்டிருப்பார்கள். ஒருத்தி இடக்கைக்கு நேரே வரும்போது மற்றொருத்தி வலக்கைக்கு நேரே இருப்பாள்.

இங்ஙனம் சுற்றும்போது ஒவ்வொரு சுழற்சியிலும் இவ்விரண்டு சந்தி ஸ்தானங்கள் ஏற்படுமல்லவா? அப்போழுது அவர்கள் முத்த மிடுவதுபோல இதழ்த்தொனி செய்வது, இடையில் நிற்பவள் வாசிக்கும் புள்ளாங்குழல் கீதங்களுக்குத் தாளமாகும். இப்படி ஆயிரம் சேர்ந்து ஒரு பெரிய வளையம்! அரைநாழிகை கழிந்தவுடனே இந்தப் பாணி கழிந்து மற்றோர் பாணி.

"நேரமாய்விட்டது, நாம் கடற்கரைக்கு போகலாம்" என்றாள் பர்வத குமாரி. எனக்கு அந்தத் திருவிழாவை விட்டுப் பிரிந்து செல்ல மனமே யில்லை. ஆனால் பர்வத குமாரியின் சொல்லைத்தட்டயாருக்கேனும் மனம் வருமா?

கடற்கரை.

பறந்து பறந்து கடலுக்கருகே வந்து சேர்ந்தோம். நெருங்கி வரவே, உள்ளுயிரிலே புகுந்து இனிய சலனங்கள் தருவதும், காரமில்லாத தழதழத்த இயற்கையுடையதுமான மனோஹரத்தன்மை கொண்டதோர் ஸுகந்தம் புலப்பட்டது. குமாரி சொல்லியிருந்த ஸுகந்த மாளிகை ஸமீபித்து விட்டதென்பதை அறிந்து கொண்டேன். "இம்மாளிகைக்கு இத்தனை இனிய கந்தம் எப்படி ஏற்பட்டது?" என்று நான் கேட்க வாயெடுக்கு முன்பாகவே அவள் எனது உள்ளக்கருத்தைக் தெரிந்துகொண்டு பின்வருமாறு கூறலாயினள்:-

"கஸ்தூரிக் கற்களாலும், தேவ சந்தன மரத்தாலும் இம்மாளிகை ஆக்கப்பட் டிருக்கிறது. அன்றியும், இதைச் சூழ்ந்துள்ள பூங்கா வனத்திலே உங்கள் உலகத்தில் கண்டறியாத அதிஸுகந்த முடைய பலவித

மலர்ச்செடிகள் இருக்கின்றன” என்றாள்.

இங்ஙனம் பேசிக்கொண்டே, ஸுகந்த மாளிகையின் உச்சிமேடையில் போயிறங்கினோம். எங்களைப்போலவே இணையிணையாகப் பலர் அங்கே வந்திருந்து கடற்காட்சியை நோக்கிக் களித்துக் கொண்டிருப்பது கண்டேன். ஓர் ஓரத்திலே போடப்பட்டிருந்த இரண்டு ஆதனங்களில் போய் சிரமபரிஹாரமாகச் சாய்ந்து கொண்டோம். அவ்வாதனங்கள் இலவம் பஞ்சுபோன்ற யாதோ ஒரு பொருள் பொதிந்தனவாய், வெண்பட்டால் மறைக்கப்பட் டிருந்தன. அவற்றில் சாய்ந்தவுடனே, தாயின் மடியிலே சாய்ந்ததுபோல உள்ளத்திற்கு ஆறுதல் உண்டாயிற்று.

எதிரே கடல். சந்திரகிரணங்களால் ஜோதியுயிர் கொடுக்கப்பெற்ற அலைகள். வெள்ளை மலர்கள் புனைந்து, புஷ்பக் குன்றுகள் கிடப்பது போலத் தோன்றிய கப்பல்கள். தூரத்திலே, அன்னங்கள் மிதப்பதுபோல மிதந்த இன்பப்படகுகள். மேலே சந்திரன், வெள்ளிமேகங்கள், இம்மேகங்களிலே சில வலைகள் பரப்பி யிருப்பதுபோலத் தோன்றும். சில அலைகளடிப்பது போலிருக்கும். ஒன்று பூச் சிதறியது போலத் தோன்றும். கீழே மிதக்கும் படகுகளுக்கு வானக்கண்ணாடியிலே தோன்றும் சாயைகள் போலச் சில மிதந்து செல்லும். இனி, நக்ஷத்திரங்கள்! வானக்கடலிலே வெடித்தெழுந்த வயிரங்கள்!

சிதறுண்ட இன்பங்கள்! வானப் பொய் கையிலே மனமெனும் சிறிய வண்டுபோய் ஒளித்தேன் குடிப்பதற் கமைந்த எண்ணில்லாத மலர்கள். திசையென்ற அநந்தவஸ்து வுடன், ஈசனறிவு என்ற அநந்தவஸ்து தாக்கியபோது பொறித்தெழுந்த சுடர்ப்பொறிகள்.

படகுகளிலே இணையிணைபாக கந்தர்வ இளைஞர்களும், பெண்களும் சிலர் பாட்டிலும், சிலர் ஆட்டத்திலும், சிலர் வாத்தியங்கள் வாசிப்பதிலும், களிப்பவராகி, அலை முழக்கமாகிய பிராகிருதப் பேரிகைக்கு இவர்கள் பல விதங்களிலே அனுமோதஞ் செய்வாராயினர். சந்திர கிரணங்களும் இவற்றிடையே மாறாப் புதுமைகொண்ட பொன் வண்டொலி யிசைத்துக் கொண்டிருந்தன. கடற்காற்றோ பர்வத குமாரியின் நெற்றி மீதுள்ள குழற் சுருள்களுடன் விளையாடிக்கொண்டிருந்தது.

ஆ! உருவம் காந்தர்வமாக மாறிவிட்ட போதிலும், எனது ஜீவன் மானிட ஜீவனாதலால் இத்தனை இன்ப மிகுதியை என்னால் பொருக்க முடியவில்லை. புலங்கள் திகைத்துப் போய்விட்டன. அறிவுமயங்கிவிட்டது. இன்பமாகிய கடலின் அலைகளிலே எனதுயிர் சிறிய நுரைபோல எற்றுண்பதாயிற்று. இன்பமாகிய புயற்காற்றிலே எனதுயிர் சிறு துரும்புபோலச் சுழல்வதாயிற்று. என்ன ஸுகந்தம்? என்ன இசை! என்ன காட்சி! பர்வத குமாரியுடன் நான் ஏதேதோ, தொடர்பற்ற மொழிகள்

பேசுவேனாயினேன். இன்பக்கொடுங்கள் அறிவினை அமிழ்த்தி விடவே, நா, தனது கடிவாள மிழந்த காட்டுக் குதிரை போல கண்ட கண்ட இடங்களில் ஸஞ்சரிப்பதாயிற்று. இன்பம் தெவிட்டிப்போய் விட்ட தென்று நான் சொல்லவில்லை. நான் போக்தா (அனுபவிப்பவன்) ஆக இருந்தது போய் அது போக்தாவாகி என்னை விழுங்கித் தீர்த்துவிட்டது. பேசிக் கொண்டிருந்தபடியே கண்ணயர்ந்து விட்டேன்.

சிலபொழுது கழிந்ததின் பிறகு, விழிப்படைந்தேன். சூரியோதய காலம். கடலும் வானும் கூடித்தழுவிய இடத்தில், அவற்றின் கூட்டத்திலே தோன்றிய ஜோதிக் குழந்தைபோலப், பரிதிவட்டம் பிறந்தது. கிழக்குத் திசையில் வானமெங்கும் நெருப்புக் குழம்பு பறந்திருந்தது. தீப்பட்டெரியும் தீவுகள்போல மேகங்கள் காணப்பட்டன. மேகங்களுக்கு மனித புத்தியுண்டென்று நினைக்கிறேன். தமது இருளியற்கையை மாற்றித் தம்மை ஒளியுடையனவாகச் செய்யும் சூரியனை இவைகள் அமுக்கிக் கொன்றுவிடப் போகின்றன.

“பரஸ்பரம் அன்போடு வாழுங்கள்” – “அன்பே சிவம்” – என்ற பெருந் தர்மத்தைக்கூறி யூதஜாதியாரை ஒளிபெறச் செய்ய வேண்டுமென்று நாடிய கிறிஸ்து முனியை – தான் பிறந்ததால் யூதஜாதிக்கே ஓர் புகழும் மாண்புங் கொடுத்த கிறிஸ்து முனியை – யூதஜாதியார் பகைத்துக் கொல்லவில்லையா? அதாவது கொல்ல

முயன்றார்கள், அவர்களால் கொல்ல முடியவில்லை. கிறிஸ்து முனி இன்றுவரை உயிரோடிருக்கிறார். தர்மத்தின் பொருட்டாகவும், மக்கள் மீதுள்ள அன்பின் பொருட்டாகவும், உலகத்தாரின் தூற்றுதல், உலகத்தார் செய்யும் நிஷ்டூரம், என்ற சிலுவையில் ஏற்றுண்டு வருந்தும் ஒவ்வொரு மனிதனிடத்தேயும் கிறிஸ்துவே விளங்குகின்றார்.

எனக்கு அந்த மேகங்களைப் பார்க்கும்போது பாரிசேயர்கள், முதலிய யூதக் குருக்களின் நினைப்பு வந்தது. க்ஷணப்பொழுது. பின்பு அந்த ஜோதிக்கோளம் மேலெழுவதாயிற்று. வஜ்ராயுதங்கள் போலத் தோன்றிய தனது கிரணங்களால் அம்மேகங்களை உடைத்துச் சிதறி, எற்றி, அசைத்துக், குழப்பிப், புறட்டி, ஓட்டித் தொலைத்துவிட்டுப் பால சூரியன் மிகுந்த வெற்றிக் கோலத்துடன் கிரணங்களை உலகமுழுவதிலும் பரப்பி, விடுதலைபெற்ற ஓர் பேருண்மைபோல ஒளி வீசுவானாயினன். உலகம் மகிழ்ச்சி பெற்றது. கந்தர்வ மாதர்களெல்லாம் பூபாள ராகத்தில் காயத்ரி பாடித் துதித்தார்கள்.

அருவி.

“அருவிக்கு வா. எழுந்திரு, நீராடப்போவோம்” என்றனள், எனது உயிர்ப்படகிற்கு மீகானாக வந்து

முளைத்த இளையவள்.

அருவிக் கரைக்கு வந்துசேர்ந்தோம். அருவி உயர்ந்த குன்றுத் தலையிலிருந்து இரண்டு படிகளாக இடை நிலத்திலுள்ள பொய்கையில் வீழ்ந்து, அங்கிருந்து மறுபடி தரையில் விழுகின்றது. நீரருவிக்குப் பல புலவர்கள் மாலை முதலியவற்றை உவமையாகச் சொல்லியிருக்கிறார்கள். அது எனக்கு ஸம்மதமில்லை. வானும், கடலும், இராமாயணமும் தமக்குத் தாமே நிகர் என்று பெரியோர் சொல்லி யிருப்பதுபோலவே, அருவியையும் உவமையற்றதாகக் கொள்ள வேண்டும். நாங்கள் வருவதற்கு முன்னாகவே அங்கு பலர் வந்து ஸ்நாநம் செய்துகொண்டிருந்தார்கள். அவர்கள் ஸ்நாநம்செய்த வினோதங்களைப் பார்க்கும்போது அற்புதமாயிருந்தது. இப்பொழுது மண்ணுலகத்திலிருந்து திரும்ப எழுதும்போது உள்ளபடி யெழுதச் சிறிது கூசுகின்றது. மண்ணுலகத்திலே சிலர் எழுத்திலும் பேச்சிலும் மஹா சுத்தர்கள். நினைப்பிலும், நடையிலும் – ? கீழே விழுந்த அருவி சிறிய ஆறாக ஓடுகின்றது. அந்த ஆற்றில் வழியெங்கும் சிறு சிறு பாறைகள். ஒவ்வொரு பாறையிலும் ஒவ்வோரினை பார்க்கலாம். பாறை மீதிருந்து சிவ்வென்று பறந்து வந்து அருவியை வலம் செய்து இடையே நின்று கொண்டிருந்து விட்டு மறுபடி தத்தம் பாறைக்குப் போய்விடுவார்கள். "தூய நெஞ்சுடையவர்களுக்கு எல்லா விஷயங்களும் தூய்மை கொண்டனவாகவே தோன்றும்." கந்தர்வ நாட்டில்

எவர் மனதிலும் விகற்பம் கிடையாது. ஆகையால் ஆடை முதலிய விஷயங்களில் அவர்கள் அதிக நாணம் பாராட்டுவதில்லை. – ஆ! என்ன ஸௌந்தர்யம்! –

அருவியில் ஸ்நாநம் செய்து முடிந்தபிறகு பக்கத்திலுள்ள ஓர் ஆலயத்திற் சென்று அனேகர் தத்தம் இஷ்ட தெய்வங்களுக்குப் பலவகைகளிலே பூஜை புரிந்தார்கள். சித்திர வித்தையிலே, ஒப்பற்று விளங்கும் கந்தர்வ நாட்டார் தமது கோயில்களிலே யாதொரு பிரதிமைகளும் இல்லாதனவாகச் சில கோயில்கள் வைத்திருக்கிறார்கள். அக்கோயில்களின் சிகரத்திலே "ஓம்" என்று ஒளியெழுத்தில் எழுதப்பட்டிருக்கிறது. உற்சாகக் கொண்டாட்டங்களும், வேடிக்கைகளும், பிரதானமாகக் கொண்ட ஆலயங்களிலேதான் பிரதிமைகள் வைத்திருக்கிறார்கள். மனப்பூர்வமாக ஆத்மசுத்தி தேட விரும்பும் இடங்களில் பிரதிமைகள் வைப்பதில்லை. அவரவர்கள் தத்தம் இஷ்ட தெய்வங்களைத் தியான ரூபமாக வணங்குகின்றார்கள். "போகத்திற்கும் யோகத்திற்கும் ஸம்பந்தமுண்டு. கந்தர்வ லோகத்திலிருந்து சாந்தி லோகம் வெகு ஸமீபம்" என்று குமாரி சொல்லியதின் பொருள் எனக்குச் சிறிது சிறிதாக விளங்குவதாயிற்று. ஸௌந்தரியத்தை தாகத்துடன் தேடுவோர்களுக்கு ஸத்தியமும் அகப்பட்டுவிடும். "உண்மையே வனப்பு, வனப்பே உண்மை" என்று ஓர் ஞானி சொல்லியிருக்கிறார். அந்த ஆலயத்துக்குள்ளே நானும்

குமாரியும் பிரவேசித்தோம். "குமாரி! இஷ்டதேவதா பூஜைக்குரியது, இவ்வாலய மென்கிறாய். உனக்கு இஷ்டதெய்வம் எது? நீ எதை வணங்கப்போகிறாய்?" என்று கேட்டேன். குமாரி:– "எனக்கு இஷ்ட தெய்வம் மதனன். நான் அவனைத் தியானம் செய்வேன், நீ உனக்கு விருப்பமான தெய்வத்தை வரித்துக்கொள்" என்றாள்.

"எனக்கு இஷ்ட தெய்வம் நீயே. நான் உன்னையே தியானம் செய்யப்போகிறேன்" என்று நான் சொன்னேன்.

"நன்று! நன்று!" என்று கூறிச் சிரித்தாள். பிறகு "தோழா, மனங்கொண்டது தெய்வம். நீ எந்த வடிவத்திலே தெய்வத்தை வணங்குகிறாயோ, தெய்வம் உனக்கு அந்த வடிவமாக வந்து அருள் செய்கின்றது. தெய்வ மென்பது யாது? தெய்வ மென்பது ஆதர்சம். தெய்வ மென்பது சித்த லக்ஷ்யம். தெய்வ மென்பது உண்மை. தெய்வ மென்பது வனப்பு" – என்றாள்.

ஆம். "உலகத்திலே மனிதனாகப் பிறந்தால் இராமனைப் போல ஒழுகவேண்டும். அதிற் சிறந்தது வேறெதுமில்லை" என்று சொல்பவனுக்கு இராமன் தெய்வம். தன்னை மறந்து, தனதின்பம் கருதாமல், ஸௌந்தரிய வெள்ளத்திலே தனது உயிரை யிழந்து பர்வத குமாரியை நான் தெய்வமாகக் கொள்ளும் பக்ஷத்தில் எனக்கு அதுவே மோக்ஷஸாதனம்.

காளிதாஸன் தாஸி வீட்டில் செய்த பூஜையைப்பற்றி நம்மவர் சொல்லும் பொய்க் கதையிலே கூட உண்மை யிருக்கின்றது.

ஆலயத்துள்ளே ஓர் தனியிடத்தில், கீழ்த்திசை நோக்கிப் பத்மாஸனமிட்டு உட்கார்ந்து கொண்டு கண்ணிலே பரவசவெறி மிதக்க, "ஓம் நம: ப்ரம்மணே" என்று சொல்லிச்சொல்லி ஜபித்தாள். நானும் – விளையாட்டென்று, யதார்த்தமாகவே – அவளெதிரில்பத்மாஸனத்திலிருந்து கொண்டு, திரிகரணங்களையும் அவள்மீது செலுத்தி "ஓம் நம: குமாரியை" என்று யோகத்திலே அமர்ந்து விட்டேன். யோகந்தெளிந்து எழுந்து நின்றோம். பர்வத குமாரி "புறப்படு" என்று சைகை காட்டினாள். காலை ஞாயிற்றின் பால கிரணங்களை தாகந் தீரக்குடித்துக் கொண்டு பறக்கலாயினோம். பறந்து சித்திரசாலைக்கு வந்து சேர்ந்தோம்.

ஆஹா ! எத்தனை பெரிய முயற்சியிலே தலையிட்டு விட்டேன் ! சாதாரணமாகக் கல்கத்தாவிலுள்ள காட்சிச்சாலையை வர்ணிக்க வேண்டுமென்றால் அதற்கென்று ஓர் நூலெழுதவேண்டும். கந்தர்வ நாட்டுச் சித்திரசாலையிலுள்ள காட்சிகளை நான் எப்படி எழுதிக் காட்டுவது ?

"சித்திரசாலைக்குப் போவோம் வா. நேற்றெல்லாம் இயற்கை நலம் பார்த்தாய் விட்டது.

இன்று காலை அருவி பார்த்தோம். இனி உங்கள் நாட்டுச் செயற்கை நலங்களைக் காணவேண்டு மென்ற விருப்பம் எனக்குண்டாகிறது. இந்த வானமோ மிகப்பெரியது, அதி ஸுந்தரமானது. அதோ தூரத்திலே தெரியும் குன்றும் அதன் முடியிலே வானமும் சேர்ந்து நிற்குமிடத்தில், எத்தனை அழகாயிருக்கிறது. பார்? ஓகோ! – இதை யெல்லாம் நின்று பார்த்துக் கொண்டே யிருந்தால் இப்படியே பொழுது போய்விடும். சித்திரைசாலைக்குப் போகலாம்" என்றேன். பர்வத குமாரி கல்லென்று நகைத்தாள். அவள் விழிக்கடைகளிலே குறும்புக் குணம் தோன்றியது. "குமாரி! இப்படி யெல்லாம் சிரித்தால் பிறகு நீ எனக்கு இஷ்ட தேவதையில்லை. உன்னை முத்தமிடுவேன், பார்த்துக் கொள்" என்றேன்.

பர்வதகுமாரி முன்னிலும் இருமடங்கு நகைத்தாள். நானும் அவளைப் பயமுறுத்தியபடியே தண்டனை செய்தேன். அவள் சினந்தோன்றிய விழிகளோடு பார்த்தாள். "நான் தான் முதலிலேயே எச்சரித்தேனே. நீ ஏன் இரண்டாம் முறை சிரித்தாய்?" என்று வணக்கத்தோடு சொன்னேன்.

"நான் அதன் பொருட்டுக் கோபிக்கவில்லை. கந்தர்வ நாட்டு யுவதிகளை உண்மையான பக்தர்கள் இவ்வித தண்டனை செய்யும்போது கன்னத்தைத் தீண்டுவதில்லை. நீ "க-க" என்று குழறிவிட்டாள். நான் கந்தர்வ விதிப்படியே அந்த அற்புதக் குற்றவாளியின்

இதழிலே தண்டனை நிறைவேற்றினேன்.

கலீரென்று நகைத்து, "மூடத்தோழா! இதுதான் சித்திரசாலை" என்றாள்.

ஸ்தம்பிதனாகிவிட்டேன்.

"குமாரி, பரிஹாஸம் செய்கிறாய். இதுவா சித்திரசாலை!"

"ஆம், இது எங்கள் சித்திரசாலையிலே பூர்வத்தில் ரமாநாதர் என்பவரால் அமைக்கப்பட்ட வனக்காட்சி. இதை வனமென்று நீ நினைத்தது பெரியதில்லை. எங்கள் உலகத்தார்களே இது இயற்கைவன மென்றும், செயற்கை வனமென்றும் தெரியாமல் அடிக்கடி ஏமாந்து போவதுண்டு" என்றாள்.

அப்பால் பிரதிமைகள் வைத்திருக்கும் மண்டபத்திற்குப் போனோம். ஒரு பக்கத்தில் ஜீவராசிகளின் வடிவங்கள் காணப்பட்டன. கண்ணுக்குத் தெரியாமல் பூதக்கண்ணாடியால் பார்ப்பதற்குரிய சிற்றுயிர்களைத் தவிர மற்றப்படி அனேக மாக எல்லா ஜந்துக்களின் உருவங்களும் அங்கே யிருப்பதுகண்டேன். எனக்கு ஜந்து நூலில் தக்க பயிற்சியும், அபிருசியும் இல்லை யாதலால், அக் காட்சியின் ரஸங்களைப் போதியபடி அனுபவிக்க முடியவில்லை. மற்றொரு புறத்திலே, கந்தர்வப்பிரதிமைகள் வகுப்புற்றிருந்தன. அங்கு, மிகுந்த ஆவலுடன் போனேன். பெண்ணிடத்தேனும், ஆணிடத்தேனும் ஸுந்தரமான

வடிவம்காணப்படுமாயின், அதைப்போன்ற இனிய காட்சிகள் உலகத்திலே பலில்லை. அசேதனப் பொருள்களிலே கூடச் சிறந்த அழகு தோன்று மிடத்துக் கையெடுத்துக் கும்பிடத் தக்கதாக இருக்கின்றது. அவ்வாறிருக்க, ஓர் ஸ்திரீ அல்லது புருஷனுடைய முகத்திலே சைதன்ய ஒளியுடன் கலந்து அழகு தோன்றுமாயின், அது மிகவும் கவர்ச்சியுடையதாகு மென்பது சொல்லி யாகவேண்டுமோ? மனுஷ்ய வடிவம் ஸௌந்தரியமா யிருப்பதைக் காண்பதில் எனக்கெப்போதுமே அளவிறந்த தாகமுண்டு. ஆனால் பூலோகத்தில் பரிபூரண ஸௌந்தரியமுடைய ஸ்திரீ புருஷர்கள் இல்லை. மனதினிடத்தே சுத்தமும் சாந்தியும் இல்லாதபடியால் பூமண்டலத்து மனிதர்கள் பொதுவாகப் பார்ப்பதற்கு விகாரமாயிருக்கிறார்களள. ஏனெனில், உள்ள நிலை உடலிலே தோன்றி விடுகிறதாதலின். அதிலும் நான் பிறந்த நாட்டிலே பஞ்சத்தாலும், நோயினாலும், அவற்றின் மூலமாகிய அடிமை நிலையாலும் ஆண்களும் பெண்களும் கண்ணால் பார்ப்பதற்குக் கூசும்படி அத்தனை குரூபிகளா யிருக்கிறார்கள். இது பாரத நாட்டிலே தற்காலத்தில் விதியா யிருக்கின்றது. இதற்கு விலக்குகள் உண்டென்பது சொல்லாதே அமையும். வல்லோர் தீட்டிய சித்திரங்களும், வல்லோர் செய்த பதுமைகளுமே பாரதவாஸிகள் ஸௌந்தரியக் காட்சியை இழந்துவிடாமல் காக்கின்றன.

நமது புராதனக்கவிஞர் முதலாயினோரும் தமக்கு இவ்விஷயத்தில் துணை செய்கிறார்கள். இத்தருணத்தில் நமது நாட்டுச் சித்திரத் தொழிலை நாம் பாதுகாக்காமலிருப்போமானால், இன்னும் இரண்டு மூன்று தலை முறைகளுக்கப்பால் பாரதநாட்டில் எவருக்கும் கண்தெரியாமலே போய் விடும். நிற்க., சித்திரசாலையிலே கந்தர்வ வடிவங்களைப் பார்த்தபோது எனக்கு முன்பு மதன விக்கிரஹத்தைக் கண்டவுடன் பிறந்த பரவசநிலை பிறக்கவில்லை. ஏனென்றால் கந்தர்வ நாட்டில் தெய்வப் பிரதிமைகளைத் தவிர, மற்றப் பிரதிமைகள், அந்நாட்டுச் சிற்பிகளின் தொழில் வன்மையைக் காட்டுகின்றனவே யல்லாது, அவர்களுடைய உள்ளத் தேட்டத்தை விளக்குந் தகைமை யுடையன அல்ல. எப்படியெனில், பூலோகத்திலே யவன (கிரீஸ்) தேசத்துப் பிரதிமைகள் மிகக் கீர்த்தி கொண்டவை. இப்பிர திமைகளைச் செய்த சிற்பிகள் குறைவுபட்ட மனித வடிவங்களையே பார்த்தவர்களானும், தமது உள்ளத் தேட்டத்தால் பரிபூர்ண ஸௌந்தரியத்தைக் கண்டுபிடித்து அதைக் கல்லிலே ஸ்தாபித்திருக்கிறார்கள். இத்தன்மை கொண்ட மேலோரை நாம் நல்ல தொழிலாளிகளென்பது மட்டுமே யன்றி வரபுமான்களென்றும், அருட்காட்சி பெற்றோரென்றும்சொல்லுகிறோம்.

கந்தர்வலோகத்திலோ ஒவ்வொருவரும் ஒவ்வொரு விதத்திலே பரிபூர்ண ஸௌந்தரிய முடையவர்களா யிருப்பதால், சிற்பிகளுக்குப் பிரதிபா சக்தியை உபயோகப்படுத்த இடமில்லாமற் போய்விடுகின்றது. நான் அங்கே கண்ட பிரதிமைகள் அளவற்ற வனப்போடு விளங்கின வென்பது மெய்யேயாகும். ஆனால் அவற்றையொத்த வனப்புடையவர்களாகவே அந்நாட்டு ஸ்திரீ புமான்களும் விளங்குகின்றார்கள்.

என் பக்கத்திலே யிருந்த ஜீவப் பிரதிமையாகிய பிரிய குமாரியை விட அழகான பிரதிமை யொன்றகப்படுமா என்று தேடித்தேடிப் பார்த்தேன், கிடைக்கவில்லை.

உணவுக்குப் புறப்பட்டோம். ஐம்புலன்களுக்கும் தெவிட்டாத நல்லின்பம் கொடுக்கும் உலகமாதலால் அங்கு நாப்புலனுக்குச் சிறந்ததோர் விருந்து கிடைக்குமென்றெண்ணி நான் மகிழ்ச்சியோடு சென்றேன். ஓர் பூஞ்சோலைக்கு வந்து சேர்ந்தோம். அங்கு ஓர் குளிர்ந்த லதா மண்டபத்தில் இருந்துக் கொண்டு குமாரி “ரஞ்ஜனா, ரஞ்ஜனா” என்று கூவினாள். சிறிது தூரத்திலிருந்து குமாரியின் தம்பியாகிய சித்தரஞ்ஜனன் வந்தான். “எனக்கும் நமது – நமது – விருந்தாளியாகிய இவருக்கும் உணவு கொண்டு வந்துகொடு” என்றாள். ஒரு விதமாக நகைத்துக் கொண்டு இளைஞன் சென்றான். சில நிமிஷங்களுக்கப்பால் அவனும் அவனுடைய நண்பன்

ஒருவனும் கையில் பொற்றட்டுகள் ஏந்திக்கொண்டு வந்து அவற்றை எங்கள் பீடங்களுக்கு முன்னே போடப்பட்டிருந்த பளிங்கு மேஜையின் மீது வைத்தார்கள். அவ்வுணவு யாதாயிருக்கலாமென்று ஆவலுடன் பார்த்தேன். கனிகள், கனிகள், கனிகள். கனிகளைத் தவிர வேறொன்றுமில்லை. எனது உள்ளக்குறிப்பை எப்போதும் அறிய வல்லவளாயிருந்த குமாரி பின்வருமாறு கூறலாயினள்.

"தோழா, உங்கள் உலகத்தாரைப் போல நாங்கள் உணவிலே மிகுந்த நாட்டம்வைத்துப் பல்வகைகொண்ட சுவைகளைத் தேடுவதில்லை. ஐம்புலன்களிலே நாப்புலன் மற்ற நான்கிற்கும் விரோதி. உண வின்பத்திலே பிரிய முடையவர்கள் செவி, கண் என்ற தெய்வப்புலன்களின் பரமஸுகங்களை நான்கு தேர்ந்துண்பதற்கு வலியிழந்து போய்விடுவார்கள். வெறுமே உயிர் நிற்பதற்கு மட்டிலும் நாங்கள் உண்பதல்லாமல், உணவிலே இன்பங்தேடுவதில்லை. ஆயினும் இக்கனிகளின் சுவை ஸாமான்யமான தன்று. தின்றுபார். பிறகு தெரியும்" என்றாள். சுவையிலும் பயனிலும் மிகுந்த அக்கனிகளைத் தின்று பசிதீர்த்துக் கொண்டோம். பிறகு மதுக்கிண்ணங்களை சித்தரஞ்ஜனன் எங்கள் முன்பு கொண்டுவைத்தான்.

சித்தரஞ்ஜனன் கொண்டு வைத்த கிண்ணங்களை நான் கையால் தொடவில்லை.

பர்வத குமாரி திரும்பிப்பார்த்தாள்.

“எனக்கு வழக்கமில்லை” என்றேன்.

“இது மண்ணுலகமில்லை” என்றாள்.

“உங்கள் நாட்டுக் காற்றும், ஒளியும், குளிர்ச்சியும், காட்சிகளும் துணைக்கு நீயும் – இத்தனை வகைகள் போதாதா? இத்துடன் மதுவேறு குடித்தா அறிவு மயங்க வேண்டும்?” என்று பலவாறு பேசிக் குமாரியின் வற்புறுத்தலினால் மதுக்கிண்ண மொன்றை வெறுங் கிண்ணமாக்கினேன். இன்பக்களிநிலை பிறந்தது.

இன்பம் ஒரு ஜ்வரம். ஜ்வரத்திலே உஷ்ணம் ஓர் வரை கடந்துவிட்டால் பிறகு குளிர்ச்சி தோன்றி ஜந்நி பிறந்து விடுவது போலவே, இன்பத்தின் முடிமீது துன்பமிருக்கின்றது. மேலே பலவாறாக வகுக்கப்பட்ட இன்பங்களும், பிறவும் கண்டேன். நாட்கள் பல கழிந்தன. இப்போது அந்த நாட்களை நினைத்துப் பார்க்கும்போது ஒருவாறு அத்தனை நாட்களும் ஒருகணம் போலவும், மற்றொரு வகையிலே அந்நாட்களின் ஒவ்வொரு கணமும் ஒவ்வொரு இன்ப யுகம்போலவும் புலப்படுகின்றது. நாட்கள் பல கழிந்தன. குமாரியும் எனது உயிர்த்தோழியாய் விட்டாள். நான் எக்காலத்தும் கனவிலே கூடக் கண்டிராத உள்ளக் கிளர்ச்சியும், சோர்வு, நோய், மனத்தளர்ச்சி, மனத்துயர் என்பற்றின் முழுமறதியும் ஏற்பட்டன. எனினும் மனது திருப்தி பெறவில்லை. ஏதோ ஒன்று குறைவா யிருப்பது போலவே தோன்றியது. நாளடைவில் கந்தர்வ நாட்டின்பங்கள் கூடக் கைத்துப்போகவில்லை. ஆனால்

ஸாதாரணமாய்ப் போய்விட்டன. ஆரம்பத்திலிருந்த பரவச நிலைக்கிடமில்லை. கடல், நிலா, முதலிய இயற்கை யழகுகளிலே எப்போது லயித்தாலும் பரவசந்தோன்று மெனினும், கள்ளமனம் அவற்றில் நிலைத்திருக்க வன்மையில தாகி நின்றது. ஆ! குமாரியினிடத்திலே கூட மனம் தொடக்கத்திலே கொண்ட பற்றை நெகிழ்ந்து விட்டது.

ஒருநாட் காலையில் நான் தனியே உட்கார்ந்துகொண்டு பின்வருமாறு யோசிக்கலாயினேன்: "ஆஹா! இன்பக் களஞ்சியமாகிய இந்நாட்டிற்கு வந்துங் கூட நமது மனதிற்குத் திருப்தி விளையவில்லையே. இந்த கந்தர்வ நாட்டிலுள்ளவர்கள் ஒருநாளைப் போலவே அனுதினம் செய்ததைச் திரும்பச் செய்துகொண்டு மகிழ்ந்த முகத்துடனே ஸுகத்தில் வாழ்கிறார்கள். இவர்களுக்கு இதில் அதிருப்தி ஏற்பட்டதாகத் தோன்றவில்லை. நமக்கு மட்டிலுந்தான் எம்மருந்துக்கும் தீராத மனநோய் பிறந்திருக்கிறது. இதென்ன ஆச்சரியம்!"

நான் இங்ஙனம் சிந்தனை செய்து கொண்டிருக்கையில் குமாரி எங்கிருந்தோ பறந்துவந்து என்னருகே தழுவி வீற்றிருந்தாள். பின், வழக்கம் போலவே எனது உள்ளக் கருத்தை எளிதில் தெரிந்து கொண்டவளாகி எனக்குச் சில அரிய உண்மைகள் கூறுவாளாயினள்.

"தோழா! எங்கள் உலகத்தார் செய்கைகளிலே

புதுமை யில்லையென்று நீ வியப்படைகிறாய். மண்ணுலகத்தார் வாழ்க்கையை மறந்துவிட்டாயா? அதில் ஏதேனும் புதுமை யுண்டா? மனித மிருகங்களிலே பாக்கியம் பெற்ற சில மிருகங்கள் வாலிபத்திலேயே இறந்து விடுகின்றன. சில எண்பது தொண்ணூறு நூறு வருஷங்கள் வரை வாழ்கின்றன. எட்டா மாதத்திலே தின்னத் தொடங்கிய சோற்றை எண்பதாம் ஆண்டிற்கூட ஸாதாரணமாகக் கருதுகிறா னில்லை. மானுடா, உங்கள் உலகத்திலே வாழ்வோர் சோற்றுக்கும், ஆடைக்குமாகப் பொய் பேசுகிறார்கள். வஞ்சனை செய்கிறார்கள். நடிக்கிறார்கள். ஏமாற்றுகிறார்கள். திருடுகிறார்கள். ஹிம்ஸைகள் செய்கிறார்கள். கொலை புரிகிறார்கள். உடலை விற்கிறார்கள். அறிவை விற்கிறார்கள். அடிமைகளாகி ஆத்மாவை விற்கிறார்கள். மானுடா, உங்கள் உலகத்திலே ஏழைகளாயிருப்போர் பெரும்பாலும் மானமற்ற அடிமைகள். அவர்கள் அற்ப ஸுகத்தின் பொருட்டு எதுவேண்டுமாயினும் செய்வார்கள். செல்வரா யிருப்போரில் பெரும்பாலார் திருடர்கள். உங்கள் உலகத்திலே எளியோரா யிருப்போர் வெறுத்தற்குரிய நீச குணமுடையார். வலியோரா யிருப்போர் காலால் மிதித்து நசுக்குதற்குரிய தீக்குண முடையார். அவர்களெல்லாம் செய்ததைச் செய்ததைத் திரும்பச் செய்யாமல் வேறென்ன செய்கிறார்கள்? உண்டும், உறங்கியும், நடித்தும் சாகிறார்கள். எங்கள்

உலகத்திலே மரணமில்லை, பொய்யில்லை. மேலும் தீய நடிப்பு, நீசப்பாசாங்கு, வேஷம் போடுதல், ஒன்று நினைத்து வேறொன்று பேசுதல், இந்த மஹா பாதகக் குணமில்லை. இவற்றால் விளையக்கூடிய துன்பங்கள் அனைத்துமில்லை. ஆயினும், உனக்கு எங்கள் வாழ்க்கையிலே திருப்தியுண்டாகாம லிருப்பது ஓர் குற்றமன்று. ஏனென்றால், மானுட ஜன்மம் எவ்வளவு இழிவுகளுடைய தாயினும் ஒரு முக்கியமான விஷயத்திலே எங்கள் பிறப்பைக் காட்டிலும் சிறந்தது. ஆத்மத் தேட்டத்திற்கு மனிதப் பிறவி மிகவும் ஸௌகரியமானதாக அமைக்கப்பட் டிருக்கின்றது. "திருப்தி எதிலும் ஏற்படாதிருத்தல்" இந்த ஒரு குணமே மனிதப் பிறவிக்குக் காப்பாகவும், அதன் பெருஞ் சிறப்பாகவும் விளங்குகின்றது. மாயா ஸம்பந்தமான எந்த நிலையிலும் மனிதன் ஸ்திரமின்மை கண்டு அதிருப்தி யடைகின்றான். உங்களிலே பெரும் பான்மையோர் அறிவைப் பலவாறு குழப்பிக் கொண்டு உண்மை நினைப்பேயின்றிப் புழுக்கள் போல மடிவது மெய்யே யாயினும், ஒரு சிலர் பரமநிலை கண்டு விடுகிறார்கள். தேவர்கள் கூட மோக்ஷ மடைய வேண்டு மாயின் மனித ஜன்மமெடுத்துத் தீர வேண்டுமென்று நீ கேள்விப்பட் டிருக்கலாம். அது மெய்யே. உங்கள் உலகத்துச் சங்கரன், சுகன், ஜனகன், கிருஷ்ணன், புத்தன், இயேசு முதலியவர்களைப் போன்ற

அற்புதப் பெரியோர் எங்கள் நாட்டிலே தோன்றுவது சாத்தியமில்லை. மாயை விலங்கு; அதில் எங்களுக்குப் பொன்விலங்கு பூட்டியிருப்பதால் வெறுப்புண்டாவது எளிதன்று. உங்களுக்கு கோரமான தளைகள் போட்டிருப்பதால் மேலோர் எளிதாக வெறுப்படைந்து விடுகிறார்கள். ஓரிரண்டு மஹான்கள் அத்தளைகளை அறத்தேதொலைத்து விடுகிறார்கள். ஸ்திரீயாகிய நான் முத்தமிடுவதற்கும், பாட்டுக் கேட்பதற்குமே தகுதியென்று உனக்கு அடிக்கடி தோன்றவும் இப்படி ஓர் பெருந் துறவிபோல வார்த்தைகள் சொல்வதைக் கேட்டு நீ இப்பொழுது உன் மனத்திலுள்ளே பெருவியப் படைகின்றாய். எங்கள் நாட்டினருக்கு அறிவுத் தெளிவு ஸஹஜமாகையால் இந்த விஷயங்கள் எங்களுக்கு ஸுலபமாகப் புத்தியில் பட்டு விடும். ஆனால் அனுபவத்திற்கு வருவது கஷ்டம். அதற்கு மானுட ஜன்மம் வேண்டும்” என்றாள். எனக்கு இவள் இப்படி யெல்லாம் பேசுவதுகூட வியப்பாகத் தோன்றவில்லை. இவ்வளவு பேசுவதுடன் என் மன மாறுபாடுகளை யெல்லாம் நிமிஷந்தோறும் அறிந்து விடும் இந்தக் கிராதகி பேச்சு முடிந்தவுடன் ஒன்று மறியாத மான் கன்று போல விழிப்பதுதான் வியப்பாயிருந்தது.

“கள்ளி, கள்ளி” என்று முணுமுணுத்தேன். “ஒரு தரம் சிக்ஷை விதித்துவிடு’’ என்று கெஞ்சினள்;

அதாவது பழைய இதழ்ச்சிக்ஷ, ''நீ என் காதலியன்று, நீ பெரிய ரிஷிக்கிழவர்” என்றேன். “எல்லாம் ஒன்று போலவேதான்! போ” எள்றாள்.

அப்பால் இதழோடு இதழ் பொருந்திப் பல நிமிஷங்கள் உயிர் கலந்திருந்தோம்.

மூன்றாம் அத்தியாயம்

ஸத்ய லோகம்.

அடுத்த நாள் ஸத்தியலோகம் சென்றேன். அங்கே மாசற்ற சூரியப் பிரகாசம்போன்ற ஒளியொன்று பிரகாசித்துக் கொண்டிருப்பதைக் கண்டேன். ஆனால் வானத்தில் சூரியனில்லை. அவ்வுலகத்தின் கண் மத்தியபாகத்தில் ஓர் திவ்ய வடிவம் உட்கார்ந்து கொண்டிருந்தது. அதின் முகத்திலிருந்தே கிரணங்கள் பொங்கி வெளிப்பட்டன. அக்கிரணங்களின் ஒளியே வானத்திலுஞ் சென்று மோதுவது கண்டேன். பலபல திசைகளிலே என் ரதத்தைத் திருப்பிவிட்டேன். அந்நாட்டு ஜனங்களெல்லாம் அவரவர்கள் பாட்டில் மிகுந்த முயற்சியுடையவர்கள் போலப் போகிறார்கள். சிற்சில ஜனங்கள் வெயர்க்க வெயர்க்கக் கஷ்டத்துடன் நடந்து செல்கிறார்கள். சிலர் என்போல

ரதங்களில் ஊர்ந்து செல்கிறார்கள். வேறு சிலர் சிறகு புடைத்துக்கொண்டு அதிவேகமாய்ப் பறக்கிறார்கள். சிலர் மலர்ந்த முகத்துடன் போகிறார்கள். சிலர் மிகக் களைப்படைந்தவர்போலக் காணப்படுகிறார்கள். சிலர் திடீர் திடீரென்று வந்து தோன்றி அவ்வொளி பொறுக்கமாட்டாமல் கண்ணைக் கையால் மூடிக்கொண்டு அவ்வப்பொழுதே மறைந்து விடுகிறார்கள். இங்ஙனம் மறைந்து செல்வோர் என்போலப் புதிதாகப் பார்க்க வந்தவர்களென்றும், இங்கிருக்க முடியாமல் ஓடி வேறு வேறுலகங்களுக்குப் போகிறார்களென்றும் தெரிந்துகொண்டேன்.

சிலர் தேவர்களைப் போலிருந்தனர். அவர்களே மலர்ந்த முகத்துடன் உல்லாஸமாகவும் வேகமாகவும் சுற்றித்திரியும் கூட்டத்தார். என்போன்ற மனிதஉருவ முடையோர்களிலேயே பலர் களைப்புக்காட்டினர். (கந்தர்வ லோகத்திற்கு வந்தவுடன் எனக்கு உருவமாறுபாடு தோன்றியதுபோல இங்கே உண்டாகவில்லை.) ஓடிப்போனவர்களும் மனிதவர்க்கத்தினரேயாம். பருத்த தொந்தியுடன் கையில் பொற்காப்புப் போட்டுக்கொண்டு ஒருவன் வந்தான். அவன் ஓவென்றலறிக்கொண்டு ஓடிப்போய் விட்டான். ஒருவன் மனைவி மக்களுடன் வந்துசேர்ந்தான். “இங்கேன் காணும் கூட்டிக்கொண்டு வந்தீர் இங்கே கடைத்தெருவா, கிடைத்தெருவா, கோயிலா, குளமா, வேடிக்கையா, விளையாட்டா ஒரு

மண்ணையுங் காணவில்லை. அவனவன் பைத்தியம் பிடித்ததுபோல ஓடிக்கொண்டு திரிகிறான். நான், குழந்தைகளையுங் கொண்டு இங்கே ஒரு க்ஷணம் கூட இருக்க மாட்டேன். ஊருக்குப் போகலாம் வாரும்" என்று பொதிமாட்டைப் போலிருந்த அந்த ஸ்திரீ கத்தினாள். அந்த மனிதன் – "இருடி, இரு. இந்த ஒரு கிரணத்தை மட்டிலும் பார்த்துவிட்டு வருகிறேன், அவஸரப்படாதே" என்றான். "கிரணமுமாச்சு மரணமுமாச்சு, புறப்படும், புறப்படும்" என்று அவள் ஏதேதோ கூச்சலிட்டாள். அவன் மனமில்லாவிடினும் அவள் செய்யும் தொல்லையை எதிர்க்கத் திறனற்றவனாய் மறைந்து விட்டான். இன்னுமொருவன் ஏட்டு மூட்டைகளை ஒரு வண்டியில் சுமத்திக்கொண்டு அங்கு வந்து சேர்ந்தான். மற்றவர்களெல்லாம் என்னிடம் பேசாமலிருக்க இவன் மட்டிலும், என்னருகே வந்து, "ஏனையா ஏடுகளெல்லாம் மிக விசேஷமானவை. ஏதேனும் உமக்கு வேண்டியதைப் பரிசோதனை செய்து பார்த்து விலைக்கெளளுடுத்துக் கொள்கிறீரா?" என்று கேட்டான். அவன் பேசிக்கொண்டிருக்கும்போதே பின்னே நின்ற வண்டியில் நெருப்புப் பிடித்து ஏடுகள் சாம்பாவது கண்டு, நான், "அதோ, பாரையா?" என்றேன். அந்த மனிதன் வயிற்றிலும், வாயிலும் அடித்துக்கொண்டு ஸத்யலோகத்தை நிந்தனை செய்துகொண்டே போய்விட்டான்.

இன்னும் எத்தனையோ ஜனங்கள் – மனவுறுதியில்லாதோர், சித்தத்தைப் புலன் வழியிலே சிதறவிட்டோர், ஸத்தியத்தில் மெய்யன்பில்லாது போலியன்பு பாராட்டும் வேஷதாரிகள், இவர்களனைவரும் வந்து வந்து மறைந்து விட்டார்கள். இது நிற்க., மேற்கூறப்பட்ட ஒரு மனிதனைத் தவிர வேறெவருமே, என்னிடம் வார்த்தையாட வில்லை யென்று சொல்லி யிருக்கிறேன். கல்விப்பயிற்சிக்குத் துணைவேண்டு மென்று பெரியார் சொல்லுகிறார்கள். அது மெய்யே. ஆனால் உண்மைத் தேட்டத் (ஸத்திய பரிசோதைத்) திற்குத் தனித்தனியே போக வேண்டுமென்று இப்பொழுதுதான் கண்டேன். உண்மை தேடப்போகும்பொழுது துணை கூட்டிக்கொண்டு போகலாகாது. உண்மையைக் கண்டு மீண்ட பின்பு அதைப் பிறருக்குக் கூறலாம், கூறுதல் கடமை. ஆனால் ஆரம்பத்தில் தன்னந்தனியாகச் செல்லவேண்டும். இன்னொருவனைத் துணையாக அழைத்துச் செல்வாயாயின், அவனுக்கும் உனக்கும் விவாதங்கள் உண்டாகும். "மாறுபடு தர்க்கம் தொடுப்" பதனால் அறிவிலே கலக்க முண்டாகு மல்லாது, தெளிவேற்படாது. அறிவுத் தெளிவிலேதான் உண்மை தோன்றும். மேலும் இன்னொருவனோடு சேர்ந்து உண்மை தேடப் போவாயானால் அவன் ஒரு பாதையில் இழுப்பான், நீ மற்றொரு பாதையிலே இழுப்பாய். இரண்டிலொன்று யதார்த்தவழியாக

இருக்கும். ஆனால் உங்களுக்குள் விவாதம் தீரும் பொருட்டு, நீங்கள் பெரும்பாலும் என்ன செய்வீர்களென்றால், “அப்பா நீ சொல்லியதும் வேண்டாம். நான் சொல்லியதும் வேண்டாம். இரண்டுக்கும் நடுவாக ஒருவழியிலே போவோம்” என்று பொது உடன்பாடு செய்து கொள்வீர்கள்.

இந்தப்பொது உடம்பாடு செய்தாலொழிய இருவருக்கும் திருப்தி யேற்படாது. இந்தப்பொது உடம்பாட்டுப்பாதை உங்களைக் கழுத்துவரை சேறுள்ள குழிகளிலும், ஏரிகளிலும், மடுக்களிலும், முள்ளிலும், கல்லிலும் பொதி மணலிலுங்கொண்டு இறங்கச் செய்யும். ஆரம்பத்திலே உங்களுக்கு இயற்கையாகக் காணப்படும். இரண்டு பாதைகளில், யதார்த்தப் பாதையை நீக்கிப் பொய்ப் பாதையிலே போனபோதிலும், ஒருவேளை நல்லது. இறுதி வரையில்போய், அங்கே தேடிய உண்மையில்லா திருத்தல் கண்டு, மறுபடி மீண்டு நல்ல மார்க்கத்திலே புகலாம். நீங்கள் அப்படிச் செய்யமாட்டீர்கள். உடன்பாட்டுப் பாதையொன்றுகொண்டு அதிலேதான் போவீர்கள். அந்தவழி சூனியத்திலேதான் கொண்டுவிடும். ஞானிகளுடைய “ஸமரஸம்” பிழையென்று நான் கூறியதாகக் கொள்ளவேண்டாம். ஸாமாநியர்கள் செய்துகொள்ளும் “ஒப்பு” அதாவது உடம்பாடு எப்போதும் பிழை என்பதையே வற்புறுத்திச் சொல்லுகிறேம். எனவே ஸத்தியலோக யாத்திரை

செய்வோர் யாரும் வீண் ஸம்பாஷணையிலே காலங் கழிப்பதில்லை யென்பதை அறிந்துகொண்டேன். ஆதலால், நானும் பிறர்களைத் தொந்தரவு செய்யலாகாதென்று சும்மா இருந்துவிட்டேன்.

கிரண பரிசோதனையிலே எனக்குப் புத்தி செல்லவில்லை. மத்யபாகத்திலே யிருந்த திவ்ய வடிவத்தினருகே நேராகப்போய் விடவேண்டுமென்று எனக்குத் தோன்றியது. அப்போது உயர ஓர் தொனி பிறந்தது. அதிலே கவனம் செலுத்தினேன். அது சொல்லிற்று – “நடுவே யிருக்கும் உருவமே பிரமன். அது ஸத்யஸ்வரூபம். திடீரென்று அதனருகே பாய்ந்துவிடுதல் யாராலும் முடியாது. ஒரு கிரணத்தைப் பற்றிக்கொண்டு, அதன் வழியே அணுவணுவாக நகர்ந்து செல்லவேண்டும். ஒரே பாய்ச்சலாகப்பாய முயற்சி செய்து நீ வீணே ரதத்தை உடைத்துக் கொள்ள வேண்டாம்.”

எனக்குச்சோம்பர் அதிகம். கிரணங்களோ நெடியவை. இவற்றின் வழியாய் மெல்ல மெல்லப் புழு ஊர்வதுபோல ஊர்ந்து செல்ல எனக்கு மனம் இணங்கவில்லை.

“நன்று. இப்பிரமன் விஷயத்தைப் பின்பு பார்த்துக் கொள்ளுகிறேன். இப்போது இந்நாட்டைச் சுற்றி ஓரமாக ஓர் வளையமிட்டு வருகின்றேன்” என்றெண்ணித் தேரைப் பிரதக்ஷிணமாகச் செலுத்தினேன்.

சிறிது தொலைவு கடந்தவுடனே வேறு வர்ணங்கொண்ட ஒளி கண்டேன். அவ்விடத்தினின்று எங்கே பார்த்தாலும் அந்தப் புதியவர்ணமே காணப்பட்டது. "இதென்ன விந்தை!" என்று பிரமிப்படைந்து அப்பால் சென்றேன். போகப் போகப் புதிய புதிய வர்ணங்கள் தோன்றிக் கொண்டிருந்தன.

உண்மை பல வர்ணங்களுடையது என்று தெளிந்துகொண்டேன். நெடுநேரத்தின் பிறகு வடக்குக் கோட்டை வாயிலருகே வந்து சேர்ந்தேன். அங்கிருந்து பார்க்கும்போது மறுபடியும் பிரமனுடைய தெய்விக வடிவம் என் கண்ணுக்கு நேரே எதிர்க்கெதிராக விளங்கிற்று. இதென்ன செய்தி! யென்று யோசனை செய்தேன். முகம் முன்பு தோன்றியது போலவேதா னிருக்கிறதா என்று கூர்ந்து பார்த்தேன். அப்போது ஒரு புதிய அற்புதங் கண்டேன். நான் எவ்வளவுக்குக் கூர்மையாகப் பார்க்கிறேனோ அவ்வளவு அத்திருமுகத்தின் ஒளி அதிகரித்து வரலாயிற்று. சிறிது பொழுதுக் கப்பால் என் கண்கள் கூசத் தொடங்கிவிட்டன. அதினின்றும் கண்களை மீட்டுக்கொண்டேன்.

மறுபடியும் முன் கேட்டது போன்ற ஓர் தொனி பிறந்தது:-

"மானிடா! உண்மை தொடக்கத்தில் தெளிவாகத் தெரிவதுபோலத் தோன்றும். கொஞ்சம் கவனம்செலுத்துவாயானால் கண் கூசத்

தொடங்கிவிடும். நீ தளர்ச்சி பெறாமல் ஓர் கிரணத்தைப் பற்றிக்கொண்டு நெருங்கி நெருங்கிப் போவாயாயின் பிறகு கண் வருத்தம் தீர்ந்துவிடும். இறுதியில் நீ அருகே வந்த பிறகு உண்மை உள்ளங்கை நெல்லிக்கனிபோல்த் தெற்றெனத் தெளிந்து புலப்படும்.” இதைக் கேட்டவுடனே, எனக்கு ஓர் கிரணத்தைத் தான் பற்றிச் செல்லலாமா என்ற விருப்பம் நிகழ்ந்தது. மறுபடியும் எனது சோம்பர்க்குணம் மனதிலே பிரதானமாய் விட்டது. “ஐயோ! இந்தச் சோம்பர் என்ற பாவி! மண்ணுலகத்துப் பெருமையையும், பொருளையும் நான் விரும்பிய காலத்தில் இதுதான் வந்து குறுக்கிட்டது. இப்பொழுது விதிவசத்தால், அவ்வித விருப்பங்களெல்லாம் அகன்றுவிட்டன. எனவே, ஸத்யலோகத்திற்கு உண்மைத் தேட்டத்தால் வந்து நிற்கும் போதும் அத்தீய சோம்பர் வந்து கெடுக்கின்றது” என்று பலவாறு வருத்தமடைந்தேன். “அழுதாற் பயனென்ன, நொந்தாற் பயனென்ன? ஒன்றும் ஆவதில்லை.”

முன்னர்ச் செய்தது பின்னை விளையும். அவரவர் செய்கைகளின் பயனையே அவரவர் நுகர்தற்குரியர். தர்மதேவதையின் ஆட்சிக்குட்பட்ட இஜ்ஜகத்தில் தத்தம் செய்கைப் பயனுக்குமேல், ஓரணுக்கூடவேனும் அன்றி அதற்கு ஓரணுக்குறையவேனும் உயிர்கள் பெறவொண்ணாது. எனது இயற்கையிலே சோம்பரை வளர்த்துவிட்டேன். இப்போது அதன்

பயனை நுகர்கின்றேன். மண்ணுலகத்துப் பொருளும் பெருமையும், மிக இழிவுடையன வாயினும், அவற்றைக்கூடச் சோம்பரால் துறந்திருப்பவன் நற்கதியடையமாட்டான். உழைத்துத்தேடி அவற்றின் இயற்கையை அனுபவித்துப் பார்த்துப் பின்பு துறக்கவேண்டும். “பாடுபட்டுத்தேடிப் பணத்தை” அடைபவனைக் கவி நிந்தனை செய்யவில்லை! அதைப் போற்றுதற்குரியதோர் பெருமை யுடைய தென்றெண்ணிப் “புதைத்து” வைப்பவனையே நிந்தைசெய்கின்றார். அதை நன்கு செலவிடுகிறானா அல்லது துர்வினியோகம் செய்கிறானா என்பதைப் பற்றி இங்கு விவகாரமில்லை. அது வேறு விஷயம். அதைத்தேடிக் கண்டு அனுபவித்துணர்ந்த பிறகுங்கூட அதன் சிறுமையை அறிந்து வெறுத்துத் தள்ளிவிடாமல், அதில் மேன்மேலும் ஆசைகொண்டு ஆதரிப்பவனே, “கேடுகெட்ட பாவி” யாவானென்று கவி சொல்லுகிறார்.

ஆம். மண்ணுலகத்துப் புலைப்பொருளைக் கூடச் சோம்பரால் பிரிந்திருப்பவன் புகழ்ச்சிக் குரியவனாகமாட்டான். இடைவிடாத உழைப்பினாலேதான் அண்ட பஹிரண்டங்கள் இயங்குகின்றன. தமோகுணம் நாசத்துக்கு முற்குறி. சோம்பர் அழிவுக்குக் காரணம். யமபடர்கள் மூதேவியின் மக்கள். நிற்க. சிறிது நேரம் ஆலோசனை செய்துகொண்டிருந்து விட்டு “இந்த மூடத்திகைப்புக்கும், சித்த

சலனத்திற்கும், சோம்பருக்கும் இடந்தரலாகாது. இனி நமது வாழ்நாளை ஸத்யநாட்டத்திலேதான் செலவிடவேண்டும்” என்று நிச்சயம் செய்துகொண்டேன். அப்போது மனம் சொல்வதாயிற்று:– “கந்தர்வ லோகத்திலே யிருந்த ஸுகம் இங்கேயுண்டா? ஆஹா! அதிலே நாம் சலிப்படைந்தது பிசகென்று இப்பொழுதுதான் தெரிகிறது. மீண்டும் அங்கே போகலாம் வா, உனக்கு அந்நாட்டு இசையும், வானும், நீரும், ஒளியும், மலரும், மாதரும் தந்த இன்பங்களைக் காட்டிலும் அதிகமாகவா இந்தக்கிரண மூர்கின்ற ஆமைத்தொழிலிலே கிடைக்கப் போகின்றது?” இது கேட்டு, ஒருக்ஷணம் மறுபடி சலனமடைந்தேன். பின் பூர்வ கர்மப் பயனால் எனக்கு என்று மறியாத தைரியம் பிறந்தது.

“மனமே! உன்னை அறிந்து விட்டேன். எனது நன்மைக்கெல்லாம் நீ கேடு சூழ்வாய். எனக்கு வருந்தீமைகளுக்கெல்லாம் நீ உபகாரம் செய்வாய். இதோ உன்னைக்கொன்று விடுகிறேன். பார்” என்று, அதன் கழுத்திலே கைபோட்டு விட்டேன். மனம் கோ கோ வென்றலறிற்று. அப்போது மறுபடியும் ஆகாசத்திலிருந்து பின்வரும் வாக்குப் பிறந்தது:– “மானிடா, வீண் முயற்சிசெய்யாதே. மனதை உன்னால் கொல்ல முடியாது. மனங் கடந்த நிலையிலே நீ தாகத்துடன் பாயும்போது அது தானாகவே மடிந்து சூனியமாகிவிடும். அதற்கு உனக்குப் பக்குவம் வரவில்லை. அதுவரை

நீ எதுசெய்தாலும் மனம் சாகாது. மேலும் நீ உனது யாத்திரையை வினோதார்த்தமாகத்தொடங்கினாய். வேடிக்கை பார்க்கவந்தவனுக்கு ஸத்தியம் புலப்படாது. கந்தர்வ நாட்டிலே போய் இன்பங் கண்டதுபோல இங்கும் உண்மையை எளிதில் கண்டுவிடலாமென்ற பேதமை யெண்ணத்தை விட்டுவிடு. நீ பாக்கியவானாதலால், உனது தேர் நீ முன் கண்ட வேறு பலரின் தேர்களைப் போல, இங்கிருந்து துரத்துண்ணாமல், இங்கே நிற்பதற்கும், ஸஞ்சரிப்பதற்கும் வலிமையுடையதா யிருக்கிறது.

மேலும், பூ, புவ, ஸ்வ, மஹ, ஜன, தப என்றாறுலகமும் கடந்துவந்த ஜீவன்களே ஸத்யலோகத்தில் தரித்து நிற்க முடியும். நீ வரபுருஷனாதலால் உனக்கு அத்தனை கஷ்டம் வேண்டுவதில்லை. நீ ஒருமுறை தர்மலோகத்திற்குப்போய், அங்கே உள்ள அனுபவங்களை அறிந்துவா. அப்பால் உனக்கு இப்போது நேர்ந்துள்ள உண்மை நாட்டம் பயன்பெறும். தர்மலோகத்திலே மனம் இறந்து போகாவிடினும், நீ விதிக்கும் கட்டுப்பாடுகளுக்கெல்லாம் அடங்கி உனக்குத் தொண்டுபுரியும். பின் இங்கு வந்தாயானால், மேல் நடக்கும் செய்திகளை நீயே அனுபவத்தில் தெரிந்துகொள்வாய். போய் வா'' என்றது.

கண்கள் சுழன்றன. சிறிதுநேரம் மயக்கமுண்டாயிற்று. பின் மயக்கம் தெளிந்தது.

கண்ணை விழித்துப் பார்த்தேன். மறுபடி மண்ணுலகத்திலே, திருவல்லிக்கேணி வீரராகவமுதலித் தெருவில், கிழக்கு முகமுள்ள வீட்டு மேன்மாடத்தில்,………… நானும் என் பக்கத்திலே சில வர்த்தமானப் பத்திரிகைகள், எழுதுகோல், வெற்றிலை, பாக்கு முதலிய என்னுடைய பரிவாரங்களும் இருப்பது கண்டேன்!

நாலாம் அத்தியாயம்

மண்ணுலகம்.

எனக்குத் தலைநோவு பலமாயிருந்தது. படுக்கையை விட்டிறங்கிக் கிழக்கே இரண்டு மூன்று சந்துகளுக்கப்பால், ஏதோ பெயர் மறந்துபோன தெருவில், நான் கூலி கொடுத்து வாஸம் செய்து கொண்டிருந்த வீட்டிற்கு வந்து சேர்ந்தேன். அந்த வீட்டைக் கொஞ்சம் வர்ணிக்கலாமா? கந்தர்வ நாட்டைப் பற்றிக் கேட்டீர்களே! இந்த மண்ணுலகத்தில் நமக்குள்ள ஸௌகரியங்களைப் பற்றிச் சிறிது கேளுங்கள்.

நானிருந்த வீட்டிற்கு முன்பக்கத்திலே ஓர் கூடமும் அதைச்சுற்றி இரண்டு மூன்று அறைகளும் உண்டு. மேற்கே பார்த்த வீடு. அந்தக் கூடத்திற்குத் தென்புறத்திலே ஒரு முற்றம். இது முன் பகுதி. பின் பகுதியிலே சில அறைகள். ஒரு முற்றம். மேல்மெத்தை.

அதில் இரண்டறைகள். இவ்விரண்டு பகுதிகளுக்குப் பொதுவாகத் தென்பாரிசத்திலே கொல்லைப் புறத்தில் ஓர் கிணறும் தண்ணீர்க் குழாயும் உண்டு. பின் பகுதியில் நான், என் சிறிய தாயார், மனைவி, மைத்துனிப் பெண், தம்பி, எனது குழந்தை ஆகிய அறுவரும் வசிப்பது. முன் பகுதியில் ஒரு ராயர் பெரிய குடும்பத்தோடிருந்தார். அவருக்குப் பகல் முழுதும் உழைத்துக் கொண்டிருக்கும் படியாகத் தபால் கச்சேரியிலோ, எங்கேயோ, ஓர் உத்தியோகம். உடம்பிலே கோபிமண் முத்திரைகள் எத்தனையோ, அத்தனை குழந்தைகள். அவர் மனைவி மறுபடியும் கர்ப்பம். அந்த முற்றத்திலேயே ஒரு பசுமாடு. இத்துடன் ஒட்டுக்குடியாக அவருடைய பந்துககள் சிலர் வஸித்தார்கள்.

நான் இருந்த பகுதியிலேனும் மேன்மாடமென்று ஒன்றிருந்தபடியால், கொஞ்சம் காற்றுவரும். ராயர் கூட்டத்தாருக்கு அது கூடக் கிடையாது. இரவிலே கொசுக்களின் தொல்லை பொறுக்கமுடியாது. எனக்குத் தூக்கமே வராது. ராயருக்குக் காச நோயாதலால் அவர் இருமிக் கொண்டே யிருக்கிற சப்தம் ஓயாமல் கேட்கும். அவருடைய குழந்தைகள் ஒன்றுமாற்றி மற்றொன்று அழுது கொண்டே யிருக்கும். கர்ப்பிணியாகிய அவர் மனைவி இடையிடையே விழித்துக் குழந்தைகளையோ, அல்லது கடவுளையோ அல்லது ராயரைத்தானோ, யாரையோ கன்னட பாஷையிலே திட்டிவிட்டு மறுபடியும் உறங்கி விடுவாள்.

ராயர் வீட்டு விஷயங்கள் இவ்வாறிருக்க நமது

வீட்டுச் சம்பிரமங்கள் இதைக்காட்டிலும் விசேஷம்.

கதையை இடையிலே விட்டுவிட்டேனே.

வீரராகவ முதலி தெருவிலிருந்து வீட்டிற்கு வந்தேனா? வரும் வழியிலே "ஜட்கா" வண்டிகள், "துரை"கள் போகும் "கோச்சு"கள், புழுதி, இரைச்சல், துர் நாற்றம், இவற்றை யெல்லாம் கடந்து, முன் பகுதியிலே, பசுமாடு, ராயர் வீட்டம்மாள், குழந்தைக் கூட்டங்கள் முதலிய விபத்துகளுக்கெல்லாம் தப்பிப் பின் புறத்திலே "மெத்தை"க்கு வந்து சேர்ந்தேன். அங்கே, எனது படுக்கை, படிப்பு, எழுத்து, பகலில் ஸிநேகிதர்கள் வந்தால் அவர்களுடன் ஸல்லாபம் முதலிய நாலாயிர விஷயங்களுக் குபயோகப்படுத்தப்பட்ட அறையின் வெளிப்புறத்தில் வந்து உட்கார்ந்துகொண்டு, என் மனைவியைக் கூப்பிட்டேன். அவள் வந்து ஏனென்றாள். "தலைநோவு பொறுக்க முடியவில்லை. கொஞ்சம் மிளகு அரைத்துக்கொண்டு வா" என்றேன். "ஆமாம்; இரண்டு நாளைக்கொருமுறை இதொரு பொய்த் தலைவலி வந்துவிடும், என்னை வேலை யேவுகிறதற்காக அதெல்லாம் ஸரிதான், பால்காரி வந்து மத்யானம், பணம் கேட்டுவிட்டுப் போனாள். ராயர்வீட்டம்மாள் குடிக்கூலிக்கு ஞாபகப்படுத்தச் சொன்னாள். ராயர் நேற்றே சொன்னாராம். இந்த மாதம் குழந்தைக்குக் காப்புவாங்க ரூபாய் தருவதாகச் சொல்லி யிருந்தீர்கள். என்னைத்தான் ஏமாற்றுகிறது வழக்கமாகவே போய்விட்டது. இன்னும், அது,

இது” என்று ஆயிரங்கணக்கு சொன்னாள். அன்று மாலை அவள் சொல்லிய கணக்குகளை எல்லாம் தீர்க்கவேண்டுமானால் குறைந்த பக்ஷம் மூன்றுலக்ஷம் ரூபாய் வேண்டுமென்று என்புத்திக்குப் புலப்பட்டது. கடைசியாக “தெருவிலே போகிற நாய்களுக்கெல்லாம் பணத்தை வாரி யிறைக்கிறது? வீட்டுச் செலவைப்பற்றிக் கேட்டால் முகத்தைச் சுளிக்கிறது? இப்படிச் செய்துகொண்டே வந்தால், அப்புறம் என்ன கிடைக்கும்? மண் தான் கிடைக்கும்” என்று ஆசீர்வாதம் பண்ணிப் பிரசங்கத்தை முடித்தாள்.

“தலைநோவு தீர்ந்து போய்விட்டது. நீ தயவுசெய்து கீழே போகலாம்” என்று வணக்கத்துடன் தெரியப்படுத்திக் கொண்டேன்.

“ஆமாம்! ஊர்க்காரரர் கூடவெல்லாம் ஓயாமல் பேசித் தொண்டைத் தண்ணீரை வற்ற வைத்துக்கொண்டிருக்கலாம். நான் ஒரு வார்த்தை பேசவந்தால் உடனே கோபம் வந்துவிடும்” என்றாள். அவள் மனதில் என்னை ஸமாதானப் படுத்துவதாக ஞாபகம். அப்பால் பல தினங்கள் கழிந்த பின்புதான் நான் தர்மலோக யாத்திரை செய்வதாகத் தீர்மானம் செய்து வைத்திருந்தேன். இடையே நிகழ்ந்த சிற்சில ஸம்பவங்களும், காலதேச வர்ணனைகளுமே இங்கே எழுதப்படும். மண்ணுலகம் மிகப்பெரிது. அதில் என் அனுபவ முழுவதையும் எழுதவேண்டுமானால் மஹா பாரதத்தைப் போலப் பதினெட்டு மடங்கு புஸ்தகமாகும்.

இங்கு ஓரிரண்டு “மாதிரி ஸீன்”, களே குறிப்பிடப்படும்.

உ0-ம்தேதி. குழந்தைக்குக் காய்ச்சல். மனைவிக்குக் காதுவலி. எனக்குப் பித்தக் கிறுகிறுப்பு.

உக-ம்தேதி – தம்பிக்குப் பாடசாலைச் சம்பளம் கொடுக்கவேண்டிய கடைசி நாள். நான் காரியஸ்தலத்திலிருந்து பணம் கொண்டு வைக்க மறந்து விட்டேன். அவன் அதுபற்றிப் பாடசாலைக்குப் போவதையே நிறுத்தி விட்டான். நான் சுதேசிய விஷயத்தில் ஊக்கத்துடன் பாடுபடுவதன் பொருட்டாக, என்னை எப்போதும் கவனித்து வரும்படியாக ராஜாங்கத்தாரால் அனுப்பப்பட்ட ஒற்றர்கள் எனது தம்பியிடம் செய்த ஸம்பாஷணையில் “உம்முடைய அண்ணனது ஸிநேகிதரான இன்னாரை ராஜாங்கத்தார் பிடிக்கப்போகிறார்கள்” என்ற மங்கள ஸமாசாரம் சொல்லி விட்டுப் போனதாகத் தம்பி வந்து சொன்னான்.

உஉ-ம்தேதி. – மனைவிக்கும் சிறிய தாயாருக்கும் மனஸ்தாபம் வந்துவிட்டது. ஒருவரை யொருவர் மாற்றி என்னிடம் பிழைகூறத் தலைப்பட்டார்கள். என் ஜீவதர்மமாகிய “சுதேசியம்” தப்பு முயற்சியென்றும், வீணென்றும், அதில் நான் தலையிட்டதி லிருந்தும், குடும்பத்துக்குப் பற்பல கேடுகளுண்டாகு மென்றும் சிறுதாயார் ஸன்மார்க்க போதனைசெய்தாள். என்மூக்கில் அடிக்கடி ஒருவித ஊறுதல் உண்டாவதுபோலத் தோன்றிற்று. அது ஓர் பொல்லாத

நோயா யிருக்குமோ வென்ற மூடத்தனமான கவலை கொண்டேன். அக் கவலையிலிருந்து மனதை அடிக்கடி திருப்பியும், மனம் மீட்டும் மீட்டும் அதில் போய் விழுந்தது.

உங-ம் தேதி – வெற்றிலையில் சுண்ணாம்பு அதிகமாகச் சேர்ந்து விட்டபடியால், வாயெல்லாம் புண்ணாய்ப் போய்விட்டது வாய்க்குள் ஜலம் விடுவதற்குக் கூடத் தகுதியில்லை. எனக்கு ஸாதாரணமாகவே உழைப்பு அதிகமாதலால், அத்துடன் சோறும் விழுங்கமுடியாமற் போகவே, சோர்வும் முகக் கடுகடுப்பும் அதிகப்பட்டன. இத்யாதி .... இத்யாதி.

நாள் தவறினாலும், இந்தக் கணக்குத்தவறுவதில்லை. சிச்சீ! இந்த மண்ணுலகம் ஓரிடமா? இதில் மனிதன் வஸிக்கலாமா? ஆமைகளும் ஓநாய்களும் வாழலாம். இது துன்பக் களம். இது சிறுமைக் களஞ்சியம். இது நரகம். இதில் வெறுப்படையாத மனிதர்களின் முகத்திலேகூட விழிக்கலாகாது.

வீட்டு வியாபாரங்களையும் எனது சொந்த வர்த்தமானங்களையும் குறித்துச் சில திருஷ்டாந்தங்கள் காண்பித்தேன். இனி வெளி வியாபாரங்கள், எனது மித்திரர், அயலார் முதலியவர்களின் செய்திகள் ஸம்பந்தமாகச் சில திருஷ்டாந்தங்கள் காண்பிக்கிறேன். திருவல்லிக்கேணியிலே (“செ...........ஸங்கம்”) என்பதாக ஓர் தேசபக்தர் சபை உண்டு. அதில் தேசபக்தர்கள் தான் கிடையாது. நானும் சிற்சில

ஐயங்கார்களுமே சேர்ந்து "காரியங்கள்" – ஒரு காரியமும் நடக்கவில்லை – நடத்தினோம். நாங்கள் தேசபக்தர்கள் இல்லை யென்று, அந்தச்சவை ஒன்று மில்லாமற் போனதிலிருந்தே, நன்கு விளங்கும்.

நான் சோம்பருக்குத் தொண்டன். எனது நண்பர்களெல்லாம் புளியஞ் சோற்றுக்குத் தொண்டர்கள். சிலர் மட்டிலும் பணத்தொண்டர். "காலணா"வின் அடியார்க்கும் அடியார்.

ஆனால், எங்களிலே ஒவ்வொருவனும் பேசுவதைக் கேட்டால் கைகால் நடுங்கும்படியாக இருக்கும். பணத் தொண்டரடிப்பொடி யாழ்வார் எங்களெல்லோரைக் காட்டிலும் வாய்ப்பேச்சில் வீரர். ஒருவன் வானத்தை வில்லாக வளைக்கலாமென்பான். மற்றொருவன் மணலைக் கயிறாகத் திரிக்கலாமென்பான் ஒருவன் "நாம் இந்த ரேட்டில் (இந்தவிதமாகவே) வேலைசெய்து கொண்டுவந்தால் ஆங்கிலேயரின் வர்த்தகப்பெருமை ஆறுமாதத்தில் காற்றாய்ப் போய்விடும்" என்பான். மற்றொருவன் "சியாம்ஜி கிருஷ்ணவர்மா ஸ்வராஜ்யம் கிடைக்கப் பத்துவருஷமாகுமென்று கணக்குப் போட்டிருக்கிறார். ஆறு வருஷத்தில் கிடைத்து விடுமென்று எனக்குத் தோன்றுகிறது" என்பான். தவளை யுருவங்கொண்ட மூன்றாமொருவன் – "ஆறுமாதமென்று சொல்லடா" என்று திருத்திக் கொடுப்பான்.

ப............ஆழ்வார் எங்களிலே முக்கியஸ்தர், அவர் இதை எல்லாம் கேட்டுப் பரமானந்த மடைந்து

கொண்டிருப்பார். ஆனால் ஒரு தேவதை அவரிடம் வந்து, "உங்களுக்கு நான் ஸ்வராஜ்யம் நாளை ஸூர்யோ தயத்திற்கு முன்புஸம்பாதித்துக்கொடுக்கிறேன். நீ உன் வீட்டிலிருந்து அதற்காக ஒரு வராகன் எடுத்துக்கொண்டுவா" என்று சொல்லுமாயின், அந்த ஆழ்வார், "தேவதையே உனக்கு வந்தனம் செய்கிறேன். ஓம் சக்த்யைநம: ஓம் பராயை நம: இத்யாதி ....; அம்பிகே, இந்த உபகாரத்துக்கு நாங்கள் உனக்கு எவ்வாறு நன்றி செலுத்தப் போகிறோம்? எங்கள் உடல், பொருள், ஆவி மூன்றும் உன்னுடையதே யாகும், ஆனால் ஒரு வராகன் கேட்ட விஷயத்தைப்பற்றி நான் ஒரு வார்த்தை வணக்கத்துடன் தெரிவித்துக் கொள்ளுகிறேன் அதைக் கேள். நீ சொல்லுகிற காரியமோ பொதுக்காரியம். அதற்குப் பொதுஜனங்கள் பணம் சேர்த்துக் கொடுப்பதே பொருத்த முடையதாகும். நான் ஒருவன் மட்டிலும் கையிலிருந்து பணம் செலவிடுதல் பொருத்தமன்று. இவ்விஷயத்தைப்பற்றி நாங்கள் அடுத்தவாரம் கூடப்போகிற "மீட்டிங்கில்" பேசித் தீர்மானம் செய்கிறோம். அதன் பிறகு நீ பெருங்கருணையுடன் எழுந்தருள வேண்டும். இப்போது போய்வருக. வந்தேமாதரம்" என்று மறுமொழி சொல்லியனுப்பி விடுவார்.

ஐயோ! என்ன உலகமடா இந்த மண்ணுலகம்! ஒழியாத ஏமாற்று, ஒழியாத வஞ்சனை, ஒழியாத கவலை? ஸாரமில்லை, ஸத்துக் கிடையாது; உள்ளூரப் பூச்சி யரித்துக் குழலாயிருக்கும் வாழ்க்கை,

ஒவ்வொருவனும் மற்றவன் மீது பழிகூறுகின்றான். ஒவ்வொருவனும் தன்னிஷ்டப்படி விட்டுவிட்டால் எல்லாம் நேராக நடக்குமென்ற நம்பிக்கையுடனே தா னிருக்கிறான். ஆனால் "நான் ஒருவன் சரியாக இருந்தால் போதுமா? மற்றவர்களை நம்புவதற்கிடமில்லையே" என்று நினைக்கிறான். பிறரை நம்புவதற்கிடமில்லை யென்றெண்ணி ஏமாற்றுகிறான். ஐயோ, மூடா! நீ ஏமாற்றுவதனால், முன்னைக்காட்டிலும் பரஸ்பர நம்பிக்கை அதிகரித்து விடுமென்றா நினைக்கிறாய்? மனித ஜாதிக்குத் தீராத நோய் ஒன்று பிடித்திருக்கிறது. மாறாத சாபம். இறங்காத விஷம். இதன் பெயர் பணம். மனித ஜாதியைக் கவர்ந்திருக்கும் தெய்விகமாகிய அன்பென்னும் வலையை அறுத்தெரியும் நீசத் தன்மைகொண்ட எலியொன்றிருக்கிறது – இதன் பெயர் பணம்.

இப்பேய்க்கு வணங்கும்படி அவனைத் தூண்டி விடுவது விருப்பம், அதாவது, ருசி நீங்கிய விருப்பம் (ருசி ஸஹிதமான விருப்பமுடையோர் கந்தவர்கள்.) அறிவற்றவிருப்பம். (அறிவு ஸத்யலோகர் கருவி.)

இன்னும் எத்தனையோ காட்சிகள் மண்ணுலகத்திலிருந்து எடுத்துக் காட்ட வேண்டுமென்ற விருப்பம் எனக்கிருந்தது. ஆனால் "பயனற்ற" இவ்வுலகத்தைப்பற்றி அதிகமாக விஸ்தரிப்பது பயனுடைய கார்யமாகாதென்பது கருதி இத்துடன் நிறுத்தி விடுகின்றேன்.

ஐந்தாம் அத்தியாயம்

தர்மலோகம்.

சில தினங்களின் பிறகு, ஒருநாள் ஞான ரதத்தில் ஊர்ந்து தர்மலோகத்திற்குப் போனேன். கந்தர்வலோகத்திற்குப் போனவுடன் தேரிலிருந்து இறங்கி யதேச்சையாகத் திரிந்ததுபோல, இங்கும் ஸஞ்சரிக்கலாமென்று கருதித் தேரைவிட்டிறங்கினேன். அப்போது தெளிந்த வதனமும், அகன்ற, அடங்கிய விழிகளும், கருமையாகச் சுருள்கள் அமைந்த தாடியும், வலக்கையிலே ஒரு சுவடியும் கொண்ட ஒருவாலிபன் என் முன்னேவந்து, "தேரை விட்டிறங்க வேண்டாம். அதிலேயே இரு; நானும் ஏறிக்கொள்ளுகிறேன். உன்னுடன் வந்து உனக்கு இந்நாட்டின் விஷயங்களைக் காண்பிக்கவேண்டு மென்று எனக்குத் தர்மதேவதையின் கட்டளை" என்றான்.

நான் அவனைக் கண்டவுடனே அவனிடம் எனக்கு ஒருவிதமான அச்சமும் மதிப்பும் ஜனித்தன.

அவனைப் போன்ற துணைவன் இருந்தால் பல அரிய விஷயங்கள் தெரிவதுடன், நற்கதியும் பெறலாமென்று எனக்கு எக்காரணத்தாலோ மிக நிச்சயமாகத் தோன்றியது. அந்த வாலிபன் தேர்மீது வந்து ஏறிக்கொண்டான். மறுபடியும் அவனை ஒருமுறை ஏற இறங்கப் பார்த்தேன். ஆ! ஹா! என்ன அற்புதவடிவம்! அவன் தேகத்திலே ஒரு சுருங்கல் கிடையாது. ஒரு கோணல் இல்லை. தத்தம் இயற்கையளவுக்குச் சிறிதும் மாறுபடாமல் கணித தேவதையால் அமைக்கப்பட்டன போன்று விளங்கின. உடல் முழுதும் ஒரு சோபை காணப்பட்டது. அது கந்தர்வலோகத்தவரிடம் காணப்பெற்ற மயக்குந் தன்மை கொண்ட "லாஹிரி"-ப்பிரகாசமன்று. இயற்கையின் திகழ்ச்சி பிரகிருதியிலே, மலர், செடி, முதலிய – தத்தம் கடைமைகளை நேர்மையுறச் செலுத்தும் – பொருள்களிலே ஓர்விதமான திகழ்ச்சி தெரியவில்லையா? அவ்வகைப்பட்டது. ஸாஷ்டாங்கமாக அவன் பாதத்தில் விழுந்து வணங்கினேன். அவன் "தர்மம் சர" (அறத்தை ஒழுகு) என்று ஆசீர்வாதம் செய்தான்.

பின்பு, – "மகனே, என்பெயர் தபஸ். நான் இந்நாட்டில் வழி காட்டும் தொழில் உடையவன். அவரவர்கள் எவ்வெத் தருமங்களைக் காண விரும்புகிறார்களோ அவற்றவற்றைக்

காட்டுவேன். திமிங்கலமுதல் அமீபாப் பூச்சிவரை ஒவ்வோருயிர்க்கும் அததற்குரிய தருமங்கள் உண்டு. மகா ஸூர்யர்கள் முதலாக அணுக்கள்வரை ஒவ்வொரு வஸ்துவுக்குரிய தர்மங்களுண்டு. மேலும் ஒன்றிற்கே காலதேச வர்த்தமானங்களுக்குத் தக்கபடி தருமங்கள் மாறுபடுகின்றன. அவற்றையெல்லாம் ஒவ்வொன்றாகப் பார்த்துக்கொண்டு வரவேண்டுமானால் பதினாயிரம் வருஷங்களாகும். ஆதலால், நீ எந்த தர்மங்களை முக்கியமாக அறிய விருப்பமுளதென்று குறிப்பிடுவாயோ நான் அவற்றைமட்டும் உனக்குக்கொண்டு காட்டுவேன். வேறுபல விஷயங்களையும் நீ பொதுப்படையாகப் பார்த்துக்கொண்டு போகலாம்" என்று கூறினான். அதற்கு நான், "முனிவரே, நான் பிராமண தருமத்தையும், க்ஷத்திரிய தருமத்தையும் அறிய விரும்புகிறேன்" என்றேன்.

"நல்லது என்னுடன் வா. பிரதமத்திலே அறக்கடவுளின் ஆலயத்தில்போய் வழிபாடு செய்துவிட்டு வரலாம்" என்றான். இருவரும் உடன் சென்றோம்.

இடைவழியில் என்னபொருள்கள் உள்ளதென்பதைப் பார்க்கக்கூட முடியாதபடி, கண்மூடித் திறக்கு முன்பாகத்தூய வெண்மை நிறங்கொண்ட ஸ்படிகத்தால் மிக விசாலமாகப்

கட்டப்பட்ட ஓர் ஆலயத்தி னருகே வந்து சேர்ந்தோம் பின்புறத்திலிருந்திறங்கித் தபோமுனி முன்செல்ல, நான் இவரைத்துடர்ந்து அவ்வாலயத்துக்குள்ளே இருவரும் புகுந்தோம். “ஜய தர்மராஜாய. ஜய யமாய. ஜய வைவஸ்வ தாயா. ஜய ஸூர்யதேஜஸ்வினே. ஜய மஹோக்ராய. ஜயமஹா சாந்தாய” என்ற ஒலிகள் கேட்டன. என் மனம் திடுக்கிட்டது. கைகால்கள் நடுங்கின. உடம்பெல்லாம் வெயர்த்து விட்டது. பதரிப்போய், “முனிவரே எங்கே அழைத்துச் செல்லுகிறீர்?” என்று கேட்டேன். “யம ஸன்னிதானத்துக்கு” என்றார். “ஏன்? ஐயோ! எதற்கு?” என்று அலறினேன். முனிவர் என்பக்கமாகத் திரும்பி என் மெய்யைத்தடவித் தமது விசாலமான அருள் விழிகளின் பார்வையை எனது கண்களிலே செலுத்தி “அஞ்சாதே அறத்துக்கு அஞ்சலாமா?” என்றனர். எனது பொறுத்தலரிய பயந் தெளிந்து விடும்போல் இருந்தது. அதற்குள் மூர்ச்சை போட்டு விழுந்துவிட்டேன். அப்போது சில கனவுகள் கண்டேன். ஆ! என்ன தீய கனவுகள்: பெரிய பெரிய புழுக்கள் வந்து என்னை விழுங்குவதுபோலிருந்தது. ஐயோ! என்ன பாதகம் செய்தோ நரகத்தில் வந்து விழுந்து விட்டேன். நரகத்தில் நெருப்பால் சுடுவார்கள், அங்கத்தை யெல்லாம் வெட்டி வெட்டிச் சித்திரவதை செய்வார்கள், என்று சொன்னார்களே. அப்படியெல்லாம்

செய்தாலும் கூட நான் பொறுத்திருப்பேனே, பொறுக்கமுடியாத அசுசிகொண்ட உயிர்களுக்கும், பொருள்களுக்குமிடையே என்னைப்போட்டு ஹிம்சை செய்கிறார்களே! ஈசா, அசுத்தமான எண்ணங்கள் எண்ணியதற்கும், அசுத்தமான வஸ்துக்களை விரும்பிய தற்கும் இதுவா தண்டனை! ஐயோ! அந்த நாளில் தெரியாமல் போய் விட்டதே. உற்றார், நண்பர்கள், அயலார், எல்லோரும் அசுத்த சிந்தைகளில் ஆழ்ந்திருந்தபடியால், அவர்களுடைய ஸஹவாஸத்தா லல்லவோ, நானும் கெட்டுப்போய்விட்டேன். எனக்குத் தெரியாதே, எனக்குத் தெரியாதே என்று கூவினேன். அதோ, அதோ, அதோ பார். எனக்குத் தெரிந்தவர்களாக எத்தனையோ பேர் வந்து நான் படும்பாடுகளையே அனுபவித்துக்கொண்டு கிடக்கிறார்கள். சிலர் என்னைக் கண்டு வெட்கமடைகிறார்கள் ஓர் பிரமாண்டமான சங்குப் பூச்சியின் கொம்புகளின் கீழ் முகத்தை மறைத்துக் கொள்கிறார்கள். சிலர் என்னைக் கண்டு அழுகிறார்கள். அப்பப்பா! நத்தை, நண்டு, பாச்சை, பல்லி – எல்லாம் பெரிய பெரிய ஆகிருதி – இவற்றினிடையேயும், இவற்றைக் காட்டிலும் அசுத்த வஸ்துக்களினிடையேயும், நான் கண்ட அனுபவங்களை இங்கே எழுதவும் கூச்சமுண்டாகிறது. மானிடர்களே! அசுத்த எண்ணங்களை நீக்குங்கள். அன்பினால் சொல்லுகிறேன். அசுசியான சிந்தனைகள்

வேண்டாம். ஈசா, அனலிலே போடும், என்னை அனலிலே போடும். எனக்கு இந்த நிலை போதும், போதும். இனிப் பாவம் செய்யமாட்டேன் என்று கூறி விம்மி விம்மி அழுதேன்.

பின் பார்க்கிறேன். என்னை மற்றோரிடத்தில் போட்டிருந்தார்கள். என் பேரிலெல்லாம் நோய்கள் தோன்றி இருந்தன. கரிய குஷ்டம், யானைக்கால், பக்கவாதம், க்ஷயம், குன்மம்; ஒன்றா? இரண்டா? (உடலிலே பிரியங் கொண்டு, அதன் போஷணைக்காக அதர்மங்கள் செய்யும் மூடர்களே, உங்களை எச்சரிக்கின்றேன். ஐயோ! ஏன் கெடுகிறீர்கள்?)

சிறிது நேரம் கழிந்தது. நெருப்புக்களிலேயே என்னைச் சில பிசாசுகள் கொண்டு தள்ளின. ஆரம்பத்தில் அனல் வந்தாலும் பெரிதில்லை என்று எண்ணிய நான் அனற்குழியைக் கண்டவுடன், கால்களால் உதைத்தும், பல்லாற்கடித்தும், கையால் மோதியும் அந்தப் பிசாசுகளிடமிருந்து திமிறிக்கொள்ள முயன்றேன். ஐயோ! அவைகளுக்குத் தான் என்ன பலமடா? என்னை ஒவ்வொரு குழிகளாக முறையே போட்டுப் போட்டு எடுத்தன. மேல் தபிக்கிறதே, அங்கங்களெல்லாம் வேகின்றனவே. ஐயோ, வெட்டி வெட்டி ஆட்டிறைச்சையைத் தொங்கவிடுவதுபோல் எனது கைகளையும், கால்களையும் தொங்கவிடுகிறார்களே, என் முண்டத்தைத்

தீப்பாறைகளில் மோதுகிறார்களே, என்னை எவரும் காப்பவர்களில்லையா? காப்பவர்களில்லையா? தபோமுனியே, வந்து ரக்ஷிக்கமாட்டாயா? என்று கதறினேன். மூர்ச்சை தெளிந்து கண்களை விழித்துப்பார்த்தேன். தபோமுனி என்முகத்தை நீரால் துடைத்து, என்னைத் தூக்கி நிறுத்திக்கொண்டு தனது அருள் விழிகளிலே நீர் பொழிய "மகனே, இனி நீ ஸுகம் பெறுவாய். பிராப்த கருமங்கள் அனுபவித்தாலொழியத் தீரமாட்டா. நீ கண்ட கனவுகளை எல்லாம் மறந்துவிடு. முன்சென்ற துன்பத்திற்கு இப்போது நினைத்து வருந்துதல் பேதமை. இனி, நல்லற வழியிலே நான் உன்னைக் கொண்டு சேர்க்கின்றேன். ஜய தர்மராஜாய என்று சொல்" என்றார்.

"ஜய தர்மராஜாய" என்று வாழ்த்தினேன்.

பின்பு பல வளைவுப்பாதைகளின் வழியே சுற்றிச் சுற்றி என்னைக்கொண்டு போய், முனிவன் தர்மராஜாவின் ஸபையிலே கொண்டு சேர்த்தான். பளிங்குத்தளம், பளிங்குச் சுவர்கள், பளிங்குத் தூண்கள், வயிரச் சிங்காதனம். அதன் கீழே பொன்னால் செய்யப்பட்ட பாம்பு, புலி இவற்றின் உருவங்கள் நசுங்கிக் கிடந்தன. ஸபாமண்டபத்திற்கு மேல் விதானம் கிடையாது. ஆகாயமே கூரை. ஸூரிய கிரணங்கள் நேரே தர்மராஜாவின் முடிமீது வந்து விழுகின்றன. அவருடைய ரத்தின மகுடத்தை ஜாஜ்வல்யமாகச்

செய்கின்றன. ஸூர்ய குமாரனாதலால், அவனையும், அவன் ஸபையிலுள்ளோரையும் ஸூர்ய கிரணங்கள் சுடவில்லை யென்று தெரிந்து கொண்டேன். நெருப்பை நெருப்புச்சுடுமா? தர்மராஜாவின் மகுடத்துக்கு நேரே உயர ஓர் அக்கினிவாள் இடைவானிலே பொறிகள் பறக்குமாறு தக தக வென்று ஒளி வீசி நிற்கின்றது. இது தர்மத்துக்கு ரக்ஷணை. தர்மத்தைப் பிறர் துன்பப் படுத்த வந்தால் அவர் தலையிலும், தர்மம்தானே சிறிது தவறுமாயின் அதன் தலையிலும் இவ்வாள் விழுந்து நாசப்படுத்திவிடுமென்பதை அறிந்தேன்.

தர்மராஜாவின் முகத்தைப் பார்த்தேன். பால கங்காதர திலகரின் முகத்துச்சாயல் கொஞ்சம் தென்பட்டது. இலேசான சாயல், ஆனால், தர்மராஜா தாமே காலமாதலால், காலத்தினால் மனிதர் முகத்தில் ஏற்படுத்தப்படும் சிதைவுகள் அவருடைய திவ்விய வதனத்தில் காணப்படவில்லை. பொன் வர்ணமுடையதும், வயிர ஸாரங்கொண்டது மாகிய ஒரு அற்புத உலகத்திலே வார்த்து, அதனுள்ளே மஹா சக்தி கொண்ட உயிர்த் திகழ்ச்சி செலுத்தப் பட்டிருக்கிறது போல விளங்கிற்று. இத்தனைக்கும் மேலே அருட்ஜோதி கூத்தாடுகின்றது. தர்மம் இரக்கமில்லாததென்று நான் பல ஸமயங்களில் நினைத்திருக்கிறேன். சிங்காதனத்தைப்போலவே நெஞ்சமும் வயிரத்தால் செய்யப்பட்டதாக

இருக்கலாமென்று நினைத்தேன். அது பிழை. தர்மம் பக்ஷபாதமற்றது. குருட்டன்பில்லாதது. ஆனால் அருளும் விவேகமும் கலந்து வார்க்கப்பட்ட விக்கிரகம் தர்மம்.

*

தபோமுனி என்னைக்கொண்டு தர்மராஜாவின் திருமுன்னே நிறுத்தினார். தருமன் முகமலர்ந்து “வருக” என்று சொல்லி “ஓம்” என்று ஆசீர்வதித்தான். அவன் வாய் திறக்குமுன்பாகவே நான் அவன் தாளில் வீழ்ந்து ஸாஷ்டாங்கமாக வணங்கி அவன் பாத விரல்களைக் கண்ணீரால் நனைத்துவிட்டு எழுந்து நின்றேன்.

தர்மன் என்னை நோக்கி “உனது பாவங்களெல்லாம் நீங்கிப்போயின. உன் குறைகளெல்லாம் தீர்ந்து நீ பரிபூர்ணம் பெறும் மார்க்கத்திலே செல்வதற்குத் தகுதியுடையவனாய் விட்டாய். இனி இந்திரிய விருத்திகளிலே உன் மனம் செல்லமாட்டாது. அற்பப்பொருள்களிலே ஆசை வைக்கமாட்டாய். ஆணவத்திலே அடங்கி நிற்க மாட்டாய். மனம் உன் வசப்பட்டு நீ சொன்னபடி யெல்லாம் கேட்கும். தபோமுனி நீ விரும்பியதை யெல்லாம் காட்டுவான். உனக்கு மங்கள முண்டாகுக!” என்றான். அவனை மறுபடியும் வணங்கி விடை பெற்றுக்கொண்டேன்.

*

அடர்ந்ததோர் காட்டிற்கு என்னை முனி அழைத்துச்சென்றான். அதனருகே ஏறக்குறைய இருபது சிறிய கூரை வீடுகளுள்ள ஒரு கிராமம். ஒவ்வொரு கூரை வீட்டையும் சூழ்ந்து ஒரு தோட்டம். வீடுகள் நெருக்கமாகச் சேர்ந்திருக்கவில்லை. விஸ்தாரமான இடைகள்விட்டுக் கட்டப்பட்டிருந்தன. வனப்பு, சுத்தம், வணங்குதற்குரிய எளிமை என்னும் இம்மூன்றிற்கும் ஒவ்வொரு வீடும் இலக்கியமாக விளங்கிற்று. அசுசியான தோற்றமேனும், நாற்றமேனும், அங்கு தேடித் தேடிப் பார்த்தாலும் கிடையாது. அவ்வனத்திலும் அதி சுத்தமாயிருந்த வீட்டிற்குள் நானும் முனிவனும் சென்றோம். அங்கே ஒரு பிராமணன் விசாலமான தோள்களும், ஞானச் சுடர் விடும் முகமும், பரந்த கண்களும், வெளுத்து நீண்ட தாடியும் உடையவனாக வீற்றிருந்தான்.

அவனுக்கெதிரே ஐந்தாறு சிஷ்யர்கள் சுவடிகள் கையிலே வைத்துக்கொண்டு பாடங் கேட்டுக் கொண்டிருந்தார்கள். நானும் தபோமுனியும் போனவுடன் எங்களுக்கு வழக்கப்படி உபசாரங்கள் கூறி உட்காரவைத்து விட்டு, மாணாக்கர்களை நோக்கி:–

“மக்களே, இன்றைக்குப்பாடம் போதும். போய்வாருங்கள்” என்றான். நான் “பாடம் நடத்துங்கள். நாங்கள் இடையூறாக வந்ததைக் கருதவேண்டாம்” என்றேன்.

அதற்குப் பிராமணர் “அதனால் பாதகமில்லை. ஏற்கெனவே பாடத்தை முடிக்கும் நேரமாய்விட்டது. அதற்கேற்ப நீங்களும் வந்துசேர்ந்தீர்கள். உங்கள் வரவினால் பாடத்திற்கு விக்கினமில்லை. இந்த உலகத்தில் அவரவர் தர்மஸேவைக்கு விக்கினங்கள் ஏற்படமாட்டா” என்று கூறினான்.

தபோமுனி அந்த உபாத்தியாயரை நோக்கி, “கண்வாசாரியாரே, இவர்கள் என்ன பாடம் படித்துக்கொண்டிருந்தார்கள்?” என்று கேட்டான். அதற்குக் கண்வர் “இவர்கள் கணிதசாஸ்திரம் படிக்கிறார்கள்” என்றார்.

தபோமுனி:– “முன் நான் வரும்போது சிற்ப சாஸ்திரம் சொல்லிக்கொடுத்துக் கொண்டிருந்தீர்களே?”

கண்வர்:– “ஆம், அவர்கள் தொழிலாளிகள். இப்போது இருந்தவர்கள் பிரம, க்ஷத்திரிய என்னும் இரண்டு வகுப்புகளைச் சேர்ந்தவர்கள்.”

“ஸர்வ சாஸ்திரங்களின் கடல்” என்று நான் வாய்க்குள்ளே சொல்லிக் கொண்டேன்.

அதுகேட்ட கண்வர்:– “அப்படி யொன்றுமில்லை. எனக்கு வேதாந்த சாஸ்திரம், தர்ம சாஸ்திரம் இவற்றைத் தவிரச் சிற்பம், கணிதம் என்ற இரண்டுதான் தெரியும். வந்துகேட்கும் மாணாக்கர்களுக்கு தெரிந்ததைச் சொல்லிக் கொடுக்கிறேன். அது எனது தர்மம்.”

இவ்வளவு நேரத்தின்பிறகு கண்வாசாரியாரிடம் என்னைச் சுட்டிக்காட்டி, "இவருக்குப் பிராமண தர்மத்தைக் காட்டவேண்டு மென்பதாக தங்களிடம் அழைத்துவந்திருக்கிறேன்."

கண்வர் புன்னகைசெய்து "ஆஹா! ஸர்வதர்மங்களுக்கும் தாமே மூலஸ்தானமா யிருக்கும்போது, என்னை ஒரு பொருளாகக்கருதி வந்தது வியப்பே. தமது கட்டளைக்கிணங்கி அவர் கேட்பதெல்லாம் கூறும் கடமையைச் சிரமேற்கொண்டிருக்கிறேன்" என்றனர். எனக்குத் தொடக்க முதலாகவே இருந்த ஆவலை எவ்வாறு அடக்கி வைத்துக்கொண்டிருந்தேன். இப்போது அவர்சொல்லைக் கேட்டு மகிழ்ச்சியடைந்தவனாய், அவ்வாசாரியனிடம் நியாயஸ்தலத்திலே சாக்ஷியிடம் கேட்பது போல் – ஆனால் வணக்கம், பக்தி, சிரத்தை, இவற்றுடன் – கேள்விகள் சோனாமாரியாகப்பொழிந்தேன். அவரும் சலிப்பில்லாமல், ஐயந்திரிபற மறுமொழிகள் சுருங்கச்சொல்லி விளங்க வைத்துக் கொண்டு வந்தார்.

சில கேள்விகளையும் உத்தரங்களையும் இங்கே குறிப்பிடுகின்றேன்:–

கேள்வி:– "ஸ்வாமி, ஒருவன் பிறக்கும் போதே பிராமணனாகப் பிறக்கிறானா? அல்லது பயிற்சியால் பிராமணனாகிறானா?"

உத்:– "பிறக்கும்போது மனிதர்களெல்லாம் மிருகங்களாகப் பிறக்கிறார்கள். பயிற்சியினாலும் குண கர்மங்களினாலும் வெவ்வேறு வர்ணத்தின ராகின்றார்கள். "சாதுர் வர்ண்ம் மயாஸ்ருஷ்டம் குணகர்ம விபாகச:" என்று பகவான் சொல்லியிருக்கிறார்."

கேள்:– "ஸ்வாமி, இந்த விதி அனுபவத்திலிருக்கிறதா?"

உத்:– "ஆம், எனது பிதா க்ஷத்திரியர்; நான் பிராமணன்; என் மக்கள் பன்னிரண்டுபேரில் ஒருவனை மட்டுமே பிராமண காரியங்களுக்குச் தெரிந்தெடுத்திருக்கிறேன். மற்றவர்களையெல்லாம் பிரம்ம, க்ஷத்திரிய, வைசிய என்ற மூன்று வர்ணங்களின் காரியங்களுக்கு அவரவர்களின் தகுதி, ஸ்வபாவம் முதலியவற்றைக் கருதி உரியவாறு பயிலும்படி செய்திருக்கிறேன்."

கேள்:– "மண்ணுலகத்திலே பாரத தேசத்தில் தான் வர்ணா சிரமபேதங்கள் இருக்கின்றன. அங்கே தாம் சொல் வதுபோல நடக்கவில்லையே?"

உத்:– "பாரத தேசத்தில்தான் வர்ணா சிரமபேதங்களிருப்பதாகச் சொல்வது பிழை. ஸகலதேசங்களிலும் உண்டு. ஆனால் பாரத தேசத்தில் தான் வர்ணாசிரமநெறி சீர்கெட்டுப் போயிருக்கின்றது. பூர்வத்திலே பாரததேசத்தில் வர்ணாசிரமநெறி

நான் சொல்வது போலத்தான் இருந்தது. அதற்கு அந்நாட்டிலுள்ள வேதங்கள், உபநிஷத்துக்கள், புராணங்கள், இதிஹாஸங்கள் முதலிய ஸகல நூல்களும் ஸாக்ஷி. இப்போது பாரத நாட்டைத் தவிர மற்றெல்லா நாடுகளிலும் பகவான் சொல்லிய முறைதான் நடைபெற்று வருகிறது – பாரதநாட்டில் அம்முறை தவறி விட்டது.

அது பற்றியே, அந்நாட்டினர், வறுமை, நோய், அடிமைத்தனம் என்ற இழிவுகளிலே வீழ்ந்திருக்கிறார்கள்.”

கேள்:– “பிராமண தர்மங்களை எனக்குப்போதனை செய்யவேண்டும்.”

உத்:– “ஸங்கிரஹமாகச் சொல்லுகிறேன். பிராமண வர்ணத்தார் ஒரு ஜன ஸமூஹத்தின் அறிவுச் செல்வத்திற்குக் காவலாளிகள்; அறிவுப் பயிருக்கு உழவர்கள். அவரவர் தத்தம்மால் இயன்ற சாஸ்திரங்களைப் படித்து வைத்துக்கொண்டு அவற்றை வெள்வேறு வர்ணத்தாருக்கு உரிமை நோக்கிக் கற்பிக்கவேண்டும். அவ்வாறு கற்பிப்பதற்குத் தமது உணவுமட்டிற்கு மேற்பட்ட எவ்விதமான கிரயமும் வாங்கலாகது. எவன் வீட்டில் மறுநாள் ஆஹாரத்திற்கு இன்றே நெல் சேர்த்து வைக்கப்பட்டிருக்கிறதோ அவன் பிராமணன் ஆகமாட்டான்” என்று யாக்ஞவல்கியர் சொல்கிறார்.

ஜனங்களுக்கு ஏற்படக்கூடிய துன்பங்களுக்கெல்லாம் அறிவின்மையே காரணமாதலாலும் அந்த அறிவின்மை ஏற்படாமல் பாதுகாப்பதே பிராமணன் கடமை யாதலாலும், பிராமணர்களே பொறுப்பாளிகளாவார்கள். ஜனங்களுக்குள் சூத்திர தர்மம் குறைந்துபோனால், அப்போதுபிராமணர் சூத்திர தர்ம போதனையே முதல் தொழிலாகக்கொண்டு நாட்டில் உண்மையான சூத்திரர்களை அதிகப்படுத்தவேண்டும். வைசிய தர்மம் குறைந்தால் அறிவு வகுப்பினர் தாம் வைசியநூல் கற்பதும் கற்பிப்பதுமே கடமையாக முதற்கொண்டு, கையில் அகப்பட்டவர்களை யெல்லாம் மெய்யான வைசியராக்கிவிடுவார்கள். க்ஷத்திரிய தர்மத்திற்கும், பிராமண தர்மத்திற்கும் ஊனம் வர இடங்கொடுக்கவே கூடாது. க்ஷத்திரிய பிராமண தர்மங்களுக்கு ஊனம் நேரிடுமாயின் ஜன ஸமூஹ முழுவதுமே க்ஷீணமடைந்து போய்விடும்.

அப்படி ஏதேனும் மஹாவிபத்து நேரிடக்கூடிய தருணத்தில், அவரவர், தத்தம் தர்மங்களைமட்டுமே கருதி நிற்போம், மற்றவர் தர்மங்களை நாமேன் கருதவேண்டும், என்று சும்மா இருத்தல் கூடாது. வீடு தீப்பற்றியெரியும்போது, தகப்பன் தனது காரியஸ்தலத்திற்கும், மகன்

பள்ளிக்கூடத்திற்கும், பெண்கள் பூஞ்சோலைக்கும், தாய் கோயிலுக்கும், வேலைக்காரன் காய்கிழங்குகள் வாங்கும் பொருட்டுக் கடைக்கும், பரிசாரகன் சமையலுக்காகத் தண்ணீருக்கும், உல்லாஸமாக புறப்பட்டுக்கொண்டிருக்கலாமா? நெருப்பை அவிக்க முயலவேண்டியது எல்லோருக்கும் கடமை. காரியஸ்தலத்திற்குப் போவதைப் பற்றிப் பிறகு பார்த்துக்கொள்ளலாம்; கோயில்களையும், பள்ளிக்கூடங்களையும் கள்வன் கொண்டுபோய் விடமாட்டான்; மறுநாள் கவனித்துக் கொள்ளலாம். விளையாட்டுக்குப் பூக் கொய்து வருதல் பெரிதன்று; காய்கிழங்குகள் பெரிதில்லை; சமையல் பெரிதில்லை; வீட்டிலே பற்றியிருக்கும் நெருப்பை அவிப்பதுதான் பெரிது – அதற்குத்தான் எல்லோரும் பாடுபடவேண்டும். கலியிலே வர்ண வேறுபாடுகள் பொய்; வெறும் ஏமாற்று. பாரத நாட்டைப்பறறி நீர் கேட்டீர். பாரதநாட்டில் இப்போது கலியுகம். ஆனால், இன்னும் இரண்டு மூன்று தலைமுறைகளில் கலியுகம் நீங்கிக் கிருதயுகம் பிறக்கப் போகின்றது. அப்போது அந்த நாட்டிலே உண்மையான வர்ணாசிரம பேதங்கள் ஏற்பட்டு விளங்கும். இப்போதிருக்கும் வஞ்சனைப்பேதங்கள் நீங்கிவிடும்.

பாரமார்த்திகத்திலே பிரம்மஞான முடையவனே பிராமணன் என்றபெயருக்குத் தகுதியுடையவ

னாவான். 'வஜ்ரஸூசிகை' என்ற உபநிஷத்திலே இதை நேர்த்தியாக எடுத்து விளக்கியிருக்கின்றார். ஆனாலும், வியவஹாரத்திலே, உலகத்தாருக்கு அறிவுப்பயிற்சி கொடுக்கும் வகுப்பினர் பிராமணராவார்கள். ஸகலவிதமான நூல்களிலும் பயிற்சி கொண்டிருந்தால், அதனை உலகத்தாருக்குப் போதனை செய்து, உலகத்துத் தொழில்களெல்லாம் இனிது நடப்பதற்கு ஆதரவாயிருத்தல், லௌகிகப் பெருமைகளிலே, ஆசையில்லாமை இவையே சுருங்கச்சொல்லு மிடத்து பிராமண தர்மத்தின் ஸாராம்சங்களாகும்" என்று முடித்தார்.

பேசிமுடிந்தவுடன் திடீரென்று எழுந்து வெளியே போனார். உடனே திரும்பி எங்களிடம் வந்து ஸந்தியாத் தியானத்திற்கு நேரமாய் விட்டதென்று தெரிவித்தார். மூவரும் எழுந்து, கிராமத்துக்கு வெளியே சிறிது தூரத்துக்கப்பால் மாச்சோலையை யடுத்துள்ள ஆற்றங்கரைக்குச் சென்றோம். ஸூர்ய கோளம் மேற்றிசை வானத்திலே பாதி மறைந்திருந்தது. மேகங்கள் எல்லாம் நெருப்புத் தீவுகள்போலத்தோன்றின, பிரகிருதி தேவி அற்புதமான அழகுடன் விளங்கினள். அத்தருணத்தில் ஸ்நாநம் முடித்து தனித்தனியாகத் தூரத்தில் உட்கார்ந்து கொண்டு முனிவர்கள் இருவரும் பிரமத்தியானத்திலே அமர்ந்திருந்தார். நான் "ஓம்" என்று ஜெபித்து சாந்தி தேவியை வரிக்கலாயினேன்.

*

ஜபதபங்கள் முடித்துக்கொண்டு மறுபடியும் கண்வ முனிவரின் வீட்டிற்கு வந்தோம். அங்கு நானும் தபோ முனிவரும் அவரிடம் விடைபெற்றுக்கொள்ள விரும்பிச் சில வார்த்தைகள் சொன்னோம். அதற்குக் கண்வர், “இராப்பொழுதாய் விட்டது. தாம் இருவரும் இன்றிரவை எனது சிறு குடியிலேயே கழித்துக்கொண்டு போக வேண்டும்” என்றார்.

எனக்கு உடனே, “மறுநாள் காலை ஆஹாரத்திற்கு வீட்டிலே நெல் வைத்திருப்பவன் பிராமணனாகமாட்டான்” என்று சொல்லிய வசனம் ஞாபகத்திற்கு வந்தது. ஆதலால், அவர் மிகவும் எளியவராயிருப்பாரென்பது கருதி “வேண்டியதில்லை. நாங்கள் சென்று வருகிறோம், தயவுசெய்து மன்னிக்கவேண்டும்” என்றேன்.

கண்வமுனிக்கு எனது ஹிருதயம் தெரிந்து விட்டது.

“ஸஹோதரா, தர்மமுள்ள இடத்தில் வறுமை கிடையாது. நீர் அதைப்பற்றி யோசிக்க வேண்டாம். தயவுசெய்து இவ்விரவு தங்கியே போகவேண்டும்.”

எனக்கு வெட்கம் பொறுக்க முடியவில்லை. தலைகுனிந்துவிட்டேன். முனிவர்கள் இருவரும் புன்னகை செய்தார்கள். பின்பு இராப்பொழுதை அங்கேயே கழிப்பதாகத் தீர்மானம் செய்துகொண்டோம்.

கண்வர் வீட்டு நடையிலே ஓர் பாயின்மீது உட்கார்ந்திருந்தபோது, கந்தர்வ லோகத்தில் ஸுகந்த மாளிகையின் மாடத்திலே பர்வத குமாரியுடன் பஞ்சணைமீது உட்கார்ந்திருந்த பொழுதைக் காட்டிலும், என் மனதில் அதிக சாந்தி ஏற்பட்டு விளங்கிற்று. கண்வரும் தபோமுனிவரும் வேதாந்த விசாரணை செய்யத் தொடங்கினார்கள். தபோ முனிவர் விவஹாரத்தின் நடுவிலே சில அருமையான விஷயங்கள் சொல்லினர். அப்போது கண்வருடைய பத்தினியும் வந்து உட்கார்ந்துகொண்டு சிரவணம் செய்தாள்.

கண்வருடைய பத்தினியைநோக்கும்போது, வேதங்களிலே படித்திருக்கும் மைத்ரேயி முதலிய ஸ்திரீகளின் சித்திரம் மனவிழியிலே எழுந்தது. கற்பு, தெளிவு, அடக்கம், அறிவு, தயை, என்ற குணங்கள் அனைத்தும் அந்த தேவியைச் சூழ்ந்து விளையாடிக்கொண்டிருந்தன. முனிவர்களின் ஜீவகளை ஸம்பாஷணை ரஸத்தால் இயக்கத்தில் விளக்குவதும், தேவியின் ஜீவகளை அடக்கத்தில் ஒளிர்வதும், ஒப்புநோக்கும்போது மிக நான்றாயிருந்தது. சிறிது நேரத்திற் கப்பால் கண்வரின் குமாரன் வந்து தாயின் பக்கத்திலே உட்கார்ந்தான். ஆ! இந்த வாலிபனைத் தவவேடத்திலே கண்டபோது என் மனம் பொறுக்கவில்லை. இவனை ராஜகுமாரனாக அமுத விழிகொண்டமாதர்களோடு கொஞ்சிக்

கொண்டிருக்கப் பார்க்கவேண்டும். இவனை ஸேனாதிபதியாக வாலிப வீரர்கள் சேர்ந்திருக்கும் ஸைன்ய முகத்திலே பார்க்கவேண்டும். கிரக கணங்களை அழைத்துக்கொண்டு பாலஸூரியன் முன்வருவதைப் போலிருக்கும்.

இவனுக்கா மரவுரி? இவனுக்கா வெறும் தானியமும், காய் கனிகளும் சேர்ந்த உணவு! இவனுக்கா சுனைநீர்ப்பானம்? இவனுக்கா இடைவிடாத ஏட்டுக்கவலை? கடபட விவஹாரம்? முனிவர் பன்னிரண்டு குமாரர்களிலே தவத்திற்கென்று இவனைத் தெரிந்தெடுத்தது பிழையென்று என் சிந்தைக்குப் புலப்பட்டது. நான் இப்படி யோசனை செய்து கொண்டிருக்கும் போதே முனிவர்களின் வேதாந்தத் தர்க்கம் முடிந்துவிட்டது. தபோமுனி என் சிந்தையை விழியால் நேருக்கு நேராகப் பார்த்தவர் போன்று, இத்தனை ராஜலக்ஷணம் வாய்ந்த குமாரனைத் தாம் பிராமண தர்மத்திற்கு எடுத்துக்கொண்டு, மற்றப் பிள்ளைகளை யெல்லாம் வெளியே அனுப்பிவிட்டமைக்கு முகாந்தரம் தெரிவிக்கவேண்டும். என்று கண்வரிடம் கேட்டார்.

கண்வர் மகனை நோக்கிக் "குழந்தாய், இன்றைக்கு ஜ்யோதிஷத்திலே (அதாவது, வானத்து கிரக நக்ஷத்திரங்களை அளக்கும் கணித நூல். எருமை மாடு கெட்டுப்போனால், வழிசொல்லப்

படிக்கும் பல நூலன்று) தரிசனாப்பியாஸம் (பார்த்துப் பழகல்) செய்ய வேண்டிய தினமாயிற்றே. நீ தனியே போயிருந்து நக்ஷத்திர ஸ்தானங்களை ஸரியாகத்தெரிந்துகொண்டுவா” என்று சொல்லி அனுப்பிவிட்டார்.

மகனைப்பற்றி புகழ்ச்சியாகச் சில வார்த்தைகள் சொல்ல நேரிடுமாதலால், அவற்றை அவன் காதில் விழும்படி செய்ய முனிவருக்கு விருப்பமில்லை. குமாரன் வெளியே சென்றான். பின்பு முனிவர் பின்வருமாறு சொல்லலாயினர்:–

“அதர்மத்தைக் கொல்வதைக் காட்டிலும், அஞ்ஞானத்தைக் கொல்வதற்கு அதிக வீரத்தன்மை வேண்டும். ஜனங்களுக்கு சரீர ஸம்பந்தமான இன்மைகளைத் தவிர்த்து ரக்ஷிப்பது சூத்திர, வைசியர்கள் கடமை. தர்மத்தை க்ஷத்திரியன் ரக்ஷிக்கிறான். நான் முன்பு சொல்லியபடி, ஞானத்தைப்பிராமணன் ஸம்ரக்ஷணை செய்கிறான். பிராமணனுக்கு அளவற்ற வீர்யம் வேண்டும். அளவற்ற தேஜஸ் வேண்டும். அளவற்ற திடமும் பாராக்கிரமமும் வேண்டும். அஞ்ஞானத்தின் படைகள் எண்ணற்றன. அஞ்ஞான ஊற்று வற்ற வற்றத் தொலையாது. அஞ்ஞான விருக்ஷத்தின் வேர் ஆதிசேஷன் முடிவரையிலே உண்டு. அப்படைகளை வெல்வதும், அவ்வூற்றை வற்றடிப்பதும், அந்த மரத்தை வேரறுப்பதும், ஸாமான்யமான காரியமன்று.

மஹாபாரதப் போரிலே, பார்த்தனைவிடக் கிருஷ்ணனுக்கு வேலை அதிகம். கிருஷ்ணனுக்கு எவ்வளவு வேலையுண்டோ, அவ்வளவு வேலை வேத வியாஸருக்கு முண்டு."

நானாவிதமான விஷயங்களைப் பற்றி ஸம்பாஷணை செய்துவிட்டு, இலேசான ஆஹாரமுண்டு பின் நித்திரைக்குப் போய்விட்டோம். மறுநாள் காலையில் எழுந்து தபோ முனிவரும் நானும் நித்யானுஷ்டானங்கள் முடித்துக் கொண்டு, ஸத்ய ராமன் என்ற க்ஷத்ரிய வீரனுடைய மாளிகைக்குச் சென்றோம். தபோ முனிவர் வரவைக் கேட்டவுடனே, ஸத்திய ராமன் எதிர் கொண்டு வந்து, உபசாரங்கள் பேசி ஓர் மண்டபத்திற்கு அழைத்துப் போய், எங்களை ஆஸனங்களிலே அமர்வித்துத் தானும் வீற்றிருந்தான். முனிவர் மெல்ல என் கதையைத் தொடங்கினார்.

ஸத்திய ராமன் தனது வீரத்தோள்கள் குலுங்க நகைத்துப் பின் "நான் காவலாளி, எனக்குச் சாதுரியமாகவும், தெளிவாகவும் ஒரு விஷயத்தை யெடுத்து உபதேசிக்கும் திறமை கிடையாது. மேலும், தர்ம ராஜனுடைய ஸேனைத் தலைவர்களில் என்னிலும் க்ஷத்திரிய குணங்களிலே சிறந்தோர் பலர் இருக்கின்றார்கள். அவர்களை யெல்லாம் விட்டுத் தர்ம திருஷ்டாந்தமாக அடியேனைத் தெரிந்து கொண்டதை, நான் பாக்கியமாகக் கருதுகின்றேனாயினும்,எனது

தகுதியின்மையைப் பற்றிய உணர்ச்சி என் மனதிலிருந்து மாறவில்லை” என்றான்.

பின்பு, என்னை நோக்கித் “தாம் கேள்விகள் கேட்டால் என்னால் இயன்றமட்டும் மறுமொழிகள் சொல்ல ஸந்தேக நிவர்த்தி செய்யக் காத்திருக்கிறேன்” என்று கூறினான்.

“ஓர் க்ஷத்திரியனுக்குரிய கடமைகளிலே, முதற்பட்டதும், மற்ற கடமைகளுக்கெல்லாம் ஆதாரமுமாகிய மூலதர்மம் யாது? அதை எனக்குத் தெளிவுறக் கூறவேண்டும்” என்றேன்.

முன்னே வீற்றிருந்த வீரனுடைய சிங்க முகத்திலே ஒளி வீசிற்று. கண்கள் அறிவுப் பொருளை உமிழ்வன போலத் தோன்றின. உடல் முழுவதிலும் ஒரு புதிய திகழ்ச்சியும், பூரிப்பும் கண்டேன்.

பரவசமடைந்து குரு சொல்லும் வசனங்களை அநுபவ நிலையிலிருக்கும் சீடன் கேட்பதுபோல, அடங்காத தாகத்துடன் கேட்கலாயினேன்.

“மித்திரா, க்ஷத்திரியனுடைய கடமைகள் பலவற்றிற்கும் எது தாய் என்று கேட்டாய். க்ஷத்திரியனுடைய முயற்சிகளுக் கெல்லாம் அடியிலேயுள்ள ஊற்றெது வென்று வினவினாய். அதனைச் சொல்லுகிறேன் கேள். அது போர்!

போர் தான் க்ஷத்திரியனுடைய முதல் தர்மம். போர்தான் உண்மையான க்ஷத்திரியனுக்கு மூச்சு.

போரே அவனுடைய உயிர். எந்த க்ஷணத்திலே போரை நிறுத்து கின்றானோ, அந்தக் கணத்திலே க்ஷத்திரியன் பேடியாய் விடுகிறான். பின்பு அவன் மரம், அவன்பிரேதம், அவன் பொய், அவன் பேசுதற்கரிய இகழ்ச்சியாக முடிக்கின்றான். மித்திரா, நான் உனக்கு வேதாந்த சாஸ்திரம் சொல்லக் கூடியவனன்று. அதர்மம் ஆதியிலே எப்படி உண்டாயிற் றென்பதை நமது முனிவர் போன்ற ஞானிகளிடம் கேட்டுத் தெரிந்து கொள். ஆனால், ஒரு செய்தி மட்டும் நான் அறிவேன். அதர்மம் எப்போதும் நமது முன்னே நிற்கின்றது. எதன் பொருட்டு நிற்கின்றறது? உன் கையால் கொலையுண்டு சாகும் பொருட்டாக. என்ன சொல்லுகிறது? “அப்பா, உன் கையிலேயுள்ள கோடரியை என் தலையிலே அடித்து என் தலையை இரண்டு கூறாகப் பிளந்துவிடு” என்று சொல்லுகிறது.

அதர்மங்கள் ரக்த பீஜ முடையவை. கொல்லக்கொல்ல மேன்மேலும் பிறந்துகொண்டே யிருக்கும். க்ஷத்திரியனுடைய கடமை யாதென்றால் அவற்றை தன் உயிருள்ள வரைவெட்டித் தள்ளிக் கொண்டே யிருக்கவேண்டும். நாள்தோறும் ஸூரியன் இருளைச் சுற்றிச் சுற்றித் துரத்திக்கொலைசெய்து கொண்டு வருகிறான். சூரியனே முதலாவது க்ஷத்திரியன். எங்கள் குலத்துக்குப்பிதாமஹன்.

*

அதர்ம நாசத்திற்காகப் போர் செய்து கொண்டேயிருப்பது தான் க்ஷத்திரிய தர்மமென்று சொன்னேன்.

அத்தொழிலுக்குரிய பயிற்சியும் ஸாதனங்களும் கைக்கொள்ளுதல் அவசியமென்று கூறுதல் மிகையாம்" என்று முடித்தான்.

நித்தியமாக இருக்கும் அதர்மங்களை நாம் அடிக்கடி கொல்வதில் தான் என்ன பிரயோஜன மென்றெண்ணித் திகைக்கலானேன். அந்தக் கேள்வியை ஸத்திய ராமனிடம் கேட்டதற்கு அவன் சிறிதேனும் மயங்குதலின்றிப் பின் வருமாறு உத்தரமளித்தான்.

"தமோகுணம் கேட்கின்ற கேள்வி! மித்திரா, கர்மம் (தொழில்) செய்யாமல் மனிதன் அரைக்ஷணமேனும் இருக்க முடியாது. நீ விரும்பினாலும், விரும்பாவிட்டாலும் தொழில் செய்து கொண்டே யிருக்கவேண்டுமென்பது விதி. அந்தக் கர்மத்தைக் கடலலைப்பட்ட துரும்புபோலச் செய்யாமல், ஸூரியனைப் போலச் செய்வது பெருமையல்லவா? ஸாதாரண சரீர ஸுகங்களைப்பற்றிய காரியங்களிலே கூட மனிதன் இவ்வித யோசனை செய்வதில்லை. ஓயாமல் அழுக்காகும் உடலை நித்தியம் ஏன் தண்ணீரால் கழுவ வேண்டும்? கழுவக் கழுவ அது தான் மேன்மேலும் அசுத்தப் பட்டுக்கொண்டு வருகிறதே, என்று யோசித்து

எவனேனும் ஸ்நாநம் இல்லாமல் இருக்கிறானா? கணத்திலே தோன்றியழியும் உடலுக்குச் செய்யும் உபசாரம் நிரந்தரமாகிய தர்மத்துக்குச் செய்யலாகாதா?

மேலும், அதர்மம் தர்மத்திற்கு உணவு. ஆதலால் தர்மம் இருக்கும் வரை அதுவும் இருந்தே தீரும். இது நியாயமே. அதர்மம் முற்றிலும் இறந்து சூன்யமாய்ப் போய் விடுமானால், பின்பு தர்மம் உண்ண உணவில்லாமல் தானும் மடிந்து விடும்" என்றான்.

*

தர்ம லோகத்தில் எனக்கு நெடுங்காலம் வசிக்கும் பாக்கியமில்லை. க்ஷத்திரிய வீரனுடைய வீட்டை விட்டு வெளியேறிய பிறகு பலவிடங்களுக்கு என்னைத் தபோ முனிவர் கொண்டு சென்றார். அதன் பிறகு ஜீரணமாகாத ஓர் உணவு நெடு நேரத்திற் கப்பால் வயிற்று வலியுண்டாக்குவது போல, எனது புண்ணியத்தால் எரிக்கப்படாத ஓர் கர்மம் ஏதோ ஓர் மூலையினின்று வெளிப்பட்டு என் உள்ளத்திலே தர்மஸாதனைக்கு விரோதமாகிய ஓர் விருப்பத்தைக்கொண்டு நுழைத்தது.

தபோ முனிவர் எனக்குப் பல தார்மிகப் புதுமைகளைக் காட்டிக் கொண்டிருக்கும் போதே அவ்விருப்பம் மீட்டுமீட்டும் எனது ஹிருதயத்தில் கிளைத்துக்கொண்டிருந்தது.

சில தினங்களுக் கப்பால், ஒரு ஸமயம் என்னைத் தனியே விட்டுவிட்டுத் தபோமுனி ஏதோ வேலையாகப்

போயிருந்தார். பிராரப்த கர்மப்பயன்! நான் தனியேயிருக்கும்போது நீசமனம் இலேசாகப் பர்வத குமாரியின் உருவத்தைக் கொண்டு எதிரே நிறுத்தியது. “ஆ! என்ன இன்பமாயிருந்தது அந்தக் காலம்!” என்று நினைத்தேன். எதிரே நின்றே மோஹன விக்கிரஹம் இன்னும் சிறிது நெருங்கிற்று. நான் அதைத் தழுவும் பொருட்டாக எழுந்தேன். எனது கைகளுக்கிடையே மின் வெட்டு முன் பர்வத குமாரி வந்து நின்றாள். இதழ்களோடு இதழ் பொருத்தி ஒரு க்ஷணம் மோஹ பரவசத்திலே இருந்தேன். இரண்டு மூன்று பூமிகள் இடிந்து விழுந்தது போலப் “படேர்” என்று ஒரு சப்தம் கேட்டது. “கோ” என்றலறி மூர்ச்சை போட்டு விழுந்தேன். கண்ணை விழித்துப் பார்க்கும்போது பழைய திருவல்லிக் கேணியில் பழைய இடத்திலே என்னைச் சுற்றிச் சிலர் விசிறிக் கொண்டு நிற்பதைக் கண்டேன். “என்ன செய்கிறீர்கள்” என்று கேட்டதற்கு, “நீ பேய் கண்டவன் போல அலறினாய். நாங்கள் வந்து பார்க்கும்போது மூச்சில்லாமலிருந்தது. பலவிதமான சைத்யோப சாரங்கள் செய்த பிறகு இப்போது மூச்சு விடுகிறாய்” என்றார்கள். “ஐயோ, மூச்சுப் போயிருந்தாலும் பெரிய காரியமில்லையே, தர்மத்தைத் தவற விட்டேனே!” என்று கூறிக் கண்ணீர் சிந்தினேன்.

முற்றிற்று.

TAMIL HEROIC POETRY

K. KAILASAPATHY

Foreword by A.R. VENKATACHALAPATHY

An elegant and thorough examination of the riches of Sangam poetry

In this acclaimed comparative study, K. Kailasapathy, the celebrated Sri Lankan academic and critic, introduces and interprets ancient Tamil poems and analyses the stylistic heritage, themes and motifs pervading Sangam poetry while building the literary corpus's bridge to heroic poetry in other languages – most notably Greek. He identifies the formulaic expression, stock phrases and overarching sensibilities pervasive in the poems and, going much against the popular grain, expands on the notion that oral verse-making is central to Sangam poetry.

A nod to Milman Parry, this deeply necessary exploration of our neglected past is an engaging and accessible discourse on one of our most fertile literary ages and, with much agility, connects the dots in studying early Tamil poetry for a modern reader.

ALSO AVAILABLE IN EVERYMAN CLASSICS FROM
HACHETTE INDIA

PANCHALI'S PLEDGE

SUBRAMANIA BHARATI

SPECIAL BILINGUAL EDITION

Translated by USHA RAJAGOPALAN

Publicly honoured when he was a mere boy of eleven with the title 'Bharati' (one blessed by Saraswati, the Goddess of Learning), C. Subramania Bharati (1882–1921) is renowned as the herald of the renaissance in Tamil literature. The simplicity and lyricism that marked his poetry reflect a clear shift in sensibility and craft from the classical tradition, which had adhered to strictures of style, imagery and language for over 2000 years.

Panchali's Pledge is the English translation of Bharati's seminal work, *Panchali Sabadham*, which reimagines the pivotal Game of Dice incident in the Mahabharata, where coerced into playing a game of dice by Duryodhana and Sakuni, Yudhisthira, the eldest of the Pandavas, stakes and loses his kingdom, his wealth, his brothers and finally his wife, Draupadi. Enraged at the quiet indifference of those present in the assembly to her plight, Draupadi finally takes a pledge to avenge her ignominy with the blood of the Kauravas.

Bharati wrote and published the first of the two-part minor epic in 1912 while living in the French territory of Pondicherry to escape British persecution. It was intended as a political allegory of the ongoing freedom movement and as an affirmation of the latent power in women.

Usha Rajagopalan's translation seeks to complement what Bharati himself set out to do with the original text: to 'create an epic using simple phrases, a simple style, easily understood prosody and rhythm which the common man appreciates'.